MONARCH

MONARCH

A NICHOLAS AVERY THRILLER

M.D. ARGYLE

Monarch / Second Paperback Edition

Summary: "Almost-retired CIA officer, Nick Avery, runs to a former lover at the Monarch Inn in order to escape the CIA and terrorists out to get him for a murder he didn't commit."

This book is a work of fiction. Any resemblance to actual persons, living or dead, events, or locales, is entirely coincidental.

ISBN: 978-0-9899700-1-3

Edited by Kara Klotz

Cover Design by Melissa Williams Design

Author Photo by Meg Hall Photography at
http://meghallphotography.blogspot.com/

Visit author M.D. Argyle at http://mdabooks.com

To Adam

Chapter 1
West Virginia

The blood pooling on the floor under the assassin's back reminded Nick of butterfly wings. It spread from the twin wounds and sparkled in the sunlight filtering through the kitchen window.

The dying man's words came between gasps. "I'm not the only one, Avery. The others will get you. Both sides."

Nick raised his pistol and aimed between the assassin's widened eyes. A muffled pop from the silencer and it was over.

Killing was the worst part of Nick's job, but he'd never felt so emotional about it. Not like this, his finger trembling against the trigger. Nobody had ever targeted him before—in his own house, no less.

He wiped the sweat from his brow and glanced at the blood spreading across the white kitchen tiles. Blood meant death and death reminded him of Annabelle. The kitchen he was standing in reminded him of her. The entire house reminded him of her. The memories stung more than his wounds from the fight with the assassin.

Tucking the pistol into the back of his pants, he walked to a filing cabinet in the living room. His boots crunched on the remains of a vase knocked to the floor during the fight. Annabelle had bought the vase a year before she died. Stepping on the broken pieces was like crunching bones. Unbearable.

Slowing his breaths, Nick unlocked the top cabinet, flipping through the files until he found the papers for his other identity—a precaution he'd taken years ago. Illegal, but he didn't care. He pushed the papers into his pocket and started to close the drawer. He stopped.

His youngest daughter's wedding paperwork was at the front—paid bills for dresses, flowers, the cake.

The cake.

Red rose petals pressed into the best frosting he'd ever tasted.

He opened the file and saw the brochure—Cakes Made by Love. It had been so long since the wedding, since meeting Lilian. She didn't know how she'd opened his eyes. He'd thought about trying to see her again, but could he? Should he? She could offer him a safe place to hide. It was tempting.

He put the brochure in his pocket just as a shadow passed the kitchen window. Footsteps, barely audible. Someone must have seen movement through the partly-closed blinds in the kitchen. Damn.

He ran to his bedroom and shoved the rest of his things into a bag. Clothes, more weapons—one more pistol, a rifle, a box of ammunition. He had to get out, away from the dead body, from whoever was coming inside. Footsteps followed him down the hallway and he broke into a run out the back door. The yards in the West Virginia neighborhood had fences, mostly wood, some rotting and covered with dull green moss. Nothing Nick couldn't hop over.

He looked over his shoulder. Two men. They were catching up, a silent pursuit except for heavy breaths. It was the middle of the day. From what Nick could remember, everybody in the neighborhood worked. He hadn't lived here for two years, but even before then he was hardly home. Always working. Even now.

Except now he had been betrayed. The assassin proved it. Kyle must have sent him.

Slipping behind an old tool shed, Nick knew he could bring down the men. Easy. Maybe they were more of Kyle's men. Or maybe they were from the other side—the FBI or the CIA. Everybody was out to get him.

One of the men whispered an order to the other. Nick dropped his bag as they appeared from around both corners of the shed, angry growls erupting from their throats.

Nick brought the suited man down first, sending him to the dirt with a blow to the throat. He hadn't used a move like that for years. It sent pain through his wrist, which told him he'd done it wrong, but nothing he could do about that now. Damn, he was out of shape. He was used to working out in a hot, stuffy gym in São Paulo, punching his fists into dummies hanging from the wooden beams. Nothing like this.

As he watched the second man come at him, he reacted purely on instinct, just as he'd done with the Brazilian in his kitchen, and lifted his leg to kick the center of the man's chest. The man went flying into the fence. The wood slats cracked loudly. Splinters flew.

The man was taller than Nick. Broad shoulders, muscular, quick. Nick kept himself in control, adrenaline pumping through him, dulling any pain he'd felt earlier. He noticed the ring of sweat around the man's tight gray T-shirt. He had to be undercover, FBI, nothing to do with Kyle. His skin was pale, not tan from the Brazilian sun like Nick's. His fighting technique seemed stiff, straight from training.

Another blow. Nick blocked it, spinning around to kick the man's knees, but the man was faster and shoved Nick into the fence. Another slat broke. A splinter dug into his back. There was no time to catch his breath before the man jerked him up by his collar. The sharp scent of aftershave stung Nick's nose.

"You're under arrest. Come quietly or it's gonna get ugly."

Nick squinted in the mottled afternoon sunlight. He would never go quietly. Who had chosen these idiots?

Pinning one of Nick's arms against the fence, the man let go of Nick's collar and started to reach for the pistol in his shoulder holster. Nick inched the fingers of his free hand to his own gun. In less than a second, his trained assailant lay unconscious on the ground, a welt rising on his temple.

Nick tucked away his gun and pulled his bag from under the suited man's legs. Pain jabbed his spine, but he ignored it. He needed to retire. He had planned to, but he was the one who insisted on one last job, a last stretch to bury himself so deep he could ignore everything else.

He swung the bag over his shoulder just as his cell phone vibrated. He pulled it out from his pocket. It was Clara, his youngest daughter. Every week he talked to her from his office—except the past week when he'd been stuck in the Amazon with Kyle. How did she get this number? He had never given it to anybody outside of Langley and he'd ignored their calls for the past twenty-four hours.

He remembered his director's words. *We won't trace you unless you give us a reason to.* Now, looking at the two men on the ground, their faces in the dirt, Nick realized that he should have destroyed the phone before he'd left Brazil.

He imagined Clara waiting on the other end. She was eager to talk to him these days, her voice upbeat. He didn't want to ignore her, even if it was what he'd done most of her life. But he couldn't answer. Not now. He threw the phone onto the cement and crushed it to pieces with his heel.

He'd wasted enough time. He needed a safe place to figure things out and he knew just the spot. He stepped around the two unconscious men and pulled the brochure from his pocket. It had been three years. Lilian could help him, possibly in more ways than one.

He took a deep breath, anxious to see her again as he set out to find a car nobody would miss.

Chapter 2
West Virginia

Mr. Jackson and his wife smiled as they drank their coffee next to the crackling fire. Lilian had liked the couple the second they checked into her inn a week ago. Nothing seemed to upset them, even when they had found a spider in their shower and told her about it as they ate their croissants the next morning.

"This is the best vacation we've had since our honeymoon," Mr. Jackson said, smiling wider. "Everything's perfect. The food, our room, the forest, the lake. It's even better than you advertised." He lifted his cup toward the carafe in Lilian's hand.

"I'm so happy to hear that." Lilian's cheeks felt warm as she filled his cup. She loved guests who gushed about the inn. It made her feel like her hard work was paying off despite fewer bookings.

The pops of the burning wood almost drowned out the drumming rain. Mrs. Jackson snuggled closer to her husband, who looked up at the ceiling. "Strong rain, isn't it? Came out of nowhere."

Lilian straightened her shoulders. "Yes, it did. I'm sorry if it ruined your plans to hike the trails."

"Not at all!" Mrs. Jackson laughed. "I love summer rain. And it's even cool enough for us to enjoy a fire. Very soothing."

Lilian forced a smile. Last summer, a three-day rainstorm had flooded the inn. She did her best to hide it around the guests, but rain always put her on edge.

"The rain is nice, yes, but when it pours like this for too long, it's almost impossible to get up and down the road. We keep hoping the county will pave it, but they won't let the permits go through." She shrugged, hiding her annoyance. "They say there's not enough traffic."

"Then it's a good thing we're not leaving soon, eh?" Mr. Jackson laughed.

Lilian laughed, too. "That's true. Have a good night."

She left the room and headed for the kitchen. She had discovered the inn during an afternoon hike. She hadn't thought much of the old house the day she found it. She'd gone inside the second time she saw it. Her boots had crunched on the broken glass and dead leaves. Something half-buried beneath the decaying mess caught her attention—wings. Hundreds of them, faded orange and black, some obviously older than others—more decayed and brittle, almost translucent. They reminded her of intricately folded origami, beautiful yet flightless.

She stopped in the hallway, listening to the rain on the roof as the carafe weighed heavy in her hand. Maybe the journey had been more of an escape from her divorce than fulfilling a dream.

"Mom, there you are."

Turning, Lilian saw her son Devan rushing to her from down the hall. Drenched, he ran the back of his hand across his face and cleared away the water dripping from his short hair down his scruffy jaw. Lilian was constantly wishing he'd shave more often, but he was a man now and he seemed to like sporting the outdoorsman look now that he had finished college and lived at the inn.

"What's the matter?"

"The canoes are sinking. Again."

Lilian grumbled under her breath. She'd had to pay someone last summer to get the canoes off the bottom of the lake when they'd sunk during a rainstorm.

"Who left them untied?" she asked, trying not to sound annoyed with Devan or the guests. She was grateful for every moment Devan was around. Last summer, he'd been away visiting his father when the inn flooded; now he was here to help her with whatever she needed. The only downfall was that he was twenty-six and seemed to be getting antsy to leave for good. He wanted to join the Air Force and the thought made her feel sick.

"I don't know. One of the guests. I should have checked earlier."

They reached the front entryway. "How many?" She set the carafe on a shelf and took a pair of work gloves from a gardening tool basket.

"Four on the bank. Two tied to the dock and I think one sank already." Devan looked at the gloves in her hand. "You know, the canoes are really heavy, Mom. We can get them later when we've got more help."

Lilian cringed. If they waited, more canoes would sink. The more she had to get off the bottom of the lake, the more it would cost her. She shoved the gloves in her pocket and took a jacket from its hook. "We can try it together. I'll be fine."

Devan touched her arm, his expression softening. "Mom, it's just canoes. We can buy more later when business picks up. Are you worried about something else?"

Closing her eyes for a moment, she thought of the butterflies again. They wouldn't leave her mind lately. "I keep thinking about that article you showed me." There had been photos of clear-cut forests in Mexico, butterflies dropping to the ground when it got too cold, loggers claiming they had to make a living somehow. She didn't know how she could help except to raise more butterflies. At the moment, that seemed too small a thing to make any difference and it took time she didn't have.

"That was one scientist's prediction," Devan said. "They're not going to disappear."

Lilian bent down to pull on her boots. "I'm overreacting, I know."

"No you're not." When she finished tying her laces, Devan took her hand and helped her stand. "They're important to you, but even if they disappear, they're not the only thing that brings people here. We just need better advertising." He squeezed her hand. "I've never seen you so worried. I'm sorry I showed you the article."

Noticing the concern in his eyes, Lilian shook her head. "No, the rain's got me worried, too. It kills a lot of them." She imagined them dropping into puddles, beating their wings uselessly against the weight of the water.

Devan turned to the door. "Let's hurry before the bank overflows."

After she zipped up her jacket, Lilian followed him to the covered porch. On a dry night, bugs usually swarmed the lights hanging from the roof, but tonight was too wet. Deep pools had already formed across the grassy clearing that led down a hill to the lake. Lilian knew she'd be up to her ankles in mud by the time they finished.

"Maybe tomorrow I can try to get the canoes that already sank," Devan said, walking down the steps. "If I had somebody to help, I think I could do it."

The rain, hard as pebbles, soaked Lilian in a matter of seconds. She looked up to see Devan already disappearing down the hill. He was right. He could get the sunken canoes when the weather cleared, but he would need help from somebody strong. Maybe Mr. Jackson? He was in his early fifties, not much older than her, but could she ask that of a guest? Maybe she could get a volunteer from town because Mr. Barry, the man she'd hired last year, wouldn't do it for free.

"Look out!"

Lilian looked up, slamming into a dark figure as hands grabbed her waist. She looked into a man's handsome face.

"I'm sorry." He looked relieved to see her. "I called out your name, but you kept walking and turned right into me."

Lilian caught her breath. She hadn't seen him in three years, but she still recognized him—square jaw, steely eyes that were almost black in the dim light. She knew they would be soft and gray in the sunlight. He seemed to change like that, one moment dark and mysterious, the next as familiar as her own reflection.

She almost choked on her surprise, gasping for breath as she remembered him in the back room of her cake shop. She was already breaking out in a sweat. "Nick?"

Nick smiled, but his expression was uneasy. He tightened his hold. "Hello, Lilian. It's been a long time, hasn't it?"

Chapter 3

Nick didn't want to let Lilian go, even though her nervous smile showed she was uncomfortable. At the same time, he noticed her tight hold on him and it was getting tighter. Her touch sent the same excitement through him he'd felt the few times they'd met in her cake shop: meetings to discuss the cake—one for payment, another for last-minute details Clara was too busy to handle and then the long afternoon before the reception.

"What are you doing here?" Lilian asked, tensing beneath his hold.

She was more beautiful than Nick remembered, her dainty features accentuating the softness of her skin, her slender neck and long hair the same golden color of wheat fields in late summer. A thin crease between her eyes hinted at constant laughter—or worry. He squeezed her closer, but not too tightly. He didn't want to frighten her more. It was enough that he'd shown up unexpectedly, soaked to the bone, mud up to his knees.

"I need to talk to you," he said. "Can we go inside?"

She pulled away. "I have to help Devan with the canoes. They're sinking." She glanced at him before pointing to the lake. "Would you, I mean, could you help? Do you think you—"

"Of course." He touched her hand. "You go back inside. You look cold."

Her eyes widened. "What? No, I can help, too. I can't let—"

"I can handle this. I'm happy to."

Rubbing her arms, Lilian nodded. "Okay, thank you."

Nick waited until she'd gone inside and then turned toward the lake. It was strange to see and feel her. It felt wrong. Just like the cake shop. Wrong, but good.

Hurrying down the hill, he tried to keep his mind on more important things besides the way Lilian made him think of soft summer days and calm blue skies. Canoes. Devan. He didn't know Devan. In fact, he'd almost forgotten Lilian had a son.

Nick looked at the five old aluminum canoes scattered across the bank. Devan was already trying to pick up one on his own. "Need any help?"

The canoe slipped from Devan's hands and fell to the rocks with a bang. Devan turned around. "Who are you?"

"A friend of your mom's." Despite the growing suspicion in Devan's eyes, Nick grinned. "I just arrived. I came down to help you, if that's all right?"

"A friend?" Devan lowered his eyebrows. "Have we met before?"

"No." Nick shrugged and kept smiling as he looked Devan up and down. It was second nature for him to size up everyone he met. Part of the job. He could see Devan would hold up well in a fight—tall, strong, lean. He didn't look like Lilian. His skin was an olive tone, but instead of straight blond hair like Lilian's, his was brown and wavy.

Devan turned back to the canoe. "Sure, it's all right if you help. What did you do? Hike up here? The road's gotta be a mess."

"My car broke down on the highway." It was true. Sort of. The car he'd taken was just outside of town, in a spot nobody would notice for weeks.

Squinting, Devan shook his head. "Right. Let's get going."

They set to work. The rain kept coming. At one point it turned to hail, the pellets stinging the back of Nick's neck. He could handle the pain, but was glad he'd found the fedora in the car he'd stolen. He offered the hat to Devan when he noticed him flinching in the downpour of ice.

Devan shook his head. "No, we're almost done." He helped lift the last canoe above their heads. As they reached the top of the hill, Nick looked at the inn. His heart thudded, but it wasn't because of the climb. He noted how peaceful the inn seemed, even during a storm, and he worried about upsetting that peace by endangering Lilian and her guests. And Devan. He already liked Devan, how dedicated he was to get the canoes up the hill, hardly stopping to catch his breath. Nick guessed he was like that no matter what task he took on, just like his mother. Nick admired that kind of dedication—something he'd both excelled and failed at, always following through one hundred percent for his job, but hardly there for his family.

"Hey, thanks for the help." Devan smiled as they set down the canoe. The hail had stopped. The grassy clearing in front of the inn was dotted with white dime-sized balls that glowed from the lights of the porch. "I didn't ... catch your name."

Nick started walking. "It's Nick."

"Well, thanks." Devan caught up with him, keeping pace with his long stride. Nick kept his eyes on the inn. He was eager to see Lilian again, but his heart was still thudding. He wasn't sure how he would tell her why he had come, or even more importantly, why he hadn't shown up three years ago when they'd made plans to meet again.

"So how do you know my mom?" Devan's voice sounded on edge, obviously worried for Lilian.

As they reached the porch, Nick smiled warmly. "My daughter's wedding. She did the cake and desserts."

"Oh, right." Devan stared at him after they walked up the steps and saw each other in the light. Nick knew even his fedora couldn't hide the healing gash on his temple. He had already come up with a story, but he couldn't remember the last time he was so nervous to tell a lie.

"You all right?" Devan asked. "That didn't happen on the way up here, did it?"

"No, no. It's nothing. I need to talk to your mom."

Nick reached for the door, his heart racing as he stepped inside and noticed that Lilian had set his bag on the entryway bench. The zipper was open a fraction of an inch. Odd. Nick stared at it as he took off his boots.

"Nick?"

He looked up as Lilian emerged from a room down the hallway. She had changed her wet clothes and wore tight jeans and a green shirt that showed off her slender arms and collarbone. Nick swallowed and touched the brim of his hat. "Lilian."

She laughed, moving toward him. "No need for formalities. Thanks for helping." She reached for his hat and he put it in her hands, waiting for her reaction to his wounds.

Lilian looked at the gash, but didn't say anything as she led him down the hall to his room. It was furnished with antiques—classic, comfortable, genuine. Just like Lilian. Nick set his bag on the polished wood floor and Lilian handed him a key. He pushed it into his wet pocket. "Don't I need to check in?"

Her knuckles whitened around the door handle. "We can do that tomorrow."

For a moment, Nick thought she might turn and leave, but she stepped inside and closed the door, glancing at his forehead. She was going to ask. Damn.

Nick cleared his throat, waiting as she moved her eyes to his shirt and brushed past him. "I'll be right back." When he turned around, she came out of the bathroom with a white towel, smiling as she handed it to him. "I'm happy to see you, Nick."

He smiled and pressed the towel to his damp face. Lavender. It was her scent—how she had smelled when he'd first kissed her. Wiping the back of his neck, he fought the urge to pull her into an embrace. He wanted to feel her close again.

"I'm happy to see you, too." He hoped she heard the longing in his voice beneath the apprehension. He glanced at his bag. "But you need to know some things before you let me stay."

Lilian looked down at the bag and cleared her throat. "I was just about to ask why you're here. Why, after all this time?"

Before Nick could stop himself, he touched her shoulder. She stiffened. The rain pounded hard against the two windows on either side of the bed as the wind kicked up. Nick recalled the afternoon before Clara's reception, how Lilian had stopped preparing a batch of frosting just to listen to him. He'd already felt a connection to her from their previous meetings about the wedding—a connection he looked for in every woman he ended up sleeping with. But that afternoon, the connection with Lilian had been different. He'd been desperate to forget Annabelle's absence at the ceremony— an empty chair, the bitterness between Clara and Violet.

Lilian had made everything unpleasant melt into something sweet, like the frosting she'd let him taste from her slender finger.

He could do this. He could talk to her, tell her as much of the truth as she needed to hear. "I wanted to get in touch with you again," he said, "but too much got in the way."

"Too much? Like what? Why didn't you at least show up? All those plans we made to spend the weekend together. I wanted to show you the inn, the butterflies. I wanted things to work out between us, or least for us to try." Pink blossomed on her cheeks. "I know it was right after my divorce, but after our time together, I felt closer to you than I expected."

Nick pulled away his hand, unsure of how to interpret what she'd said. She hadn't been what he'd expected, either, but that had turned out to be a good thing. Did she feel the same way? "I don't know why I didn't show up," he said, eager to try and explain. "I'm sorry I didn't—"

He paused, realizing how bad he sounded. He studied the zipper on his bag. He had to know, but more than that he had to change the subject. This was too much awkwardness. He was sure when he told her more, she wouldn't be wishing things had worked out. "Did you look in my bag?" he asked as gently as he could.

Lilian's expression turned to surprise. "What? No. I would never look in your bag."

Of course she hadn't.

Nick silently cursed his training. He hated that no matter what situation he found himself in, his paranoia never left. Kneeling down, he set his towel on the floor and unzipped his bag, folding back the sides to reveal the disassembled rifle, his loaded pistol and boxes of ammunition.

Lilian crossed her arms and took a step back. "Why would you bring guns here?" She glanced at his wound again.

"I'm in trouble and you might be in danger with me here." The words came off his lips with a bitter taste, but no matter what he said from here on out, he was glad he was showing her the guns, letting her know what she was dealing with. Not like the cake shop where he'd skirted around every subject that could lead to questions about his career and lifestyle.

Lilian took another step back as she glanced at the door handle. "What do you mean by trouble?"

Nick thought of a thousand things he could say, but nothing sounded right. Finally, he said, "There are some men looking for me, but they shouldn't be able to find me here. I can camp in the woods. Or I can leave, if you want."

"In the middle of a rainstorm?" Her nervous laugh filled the room.

"I won't be offended if you ask me to leave." Nick leaned down and closed the bag, staring at it as he remembered the dead assassin on his kitchen floor and Anabelle's broken vase. Everything about his past seemed broken. It was probably best if he left right now, but his instincts told him he was safe. He'd taken precautions to get to the inn: a stolen car, switched plates, a call from a pay phone. He could spot a tail and there had been none.

"When I saw you outside I thought you'd come to see me again," Lilian said, uncrossing her arms as she headed for the bed. She straightened the throw pillows, smoothing out the wrinkles on the bedspread as she spoke. It was something Nick had noticed about her the first time they'd met—her constant fidgeting to get things done. "Then I noticed your dirty clothes and the wound on your forehead. And those." She turned around and pointed to Nick's wrists, her expression twisting with confusion.

Nick tugged his sleeves down over the red, swollen flesh.

"I couldn't get a hold of you the morning after you didn't show up," Lilian said, shifting the pillows again. "The number you gave me sent me to a woman who said you'd be back in a week. Then she'd transfer me to a busy signal. Three weeks of that and I gave up. So I called Clara. I still had her number from the wedding, but she wouldn't tell me anything about you. What was I supposed to think? You'd fallen off the face of the planet. I gave up. I moved on. But now—now you're here again, just as mysterious as you were before."

Nick walked to her and put his hands on her shoulders, gently helping her sit on the edge of the mattress. He tried to interpret the mixed emotions on her face. He always confused people, led them down roads they didn't want to go.

"Nick," she said, her voice filled with determination. "I should know better than to let you stay here, but I can't let you leave if you need my help. I'm not that heartless." She was quiet for a minute, her face perplexed. "Who's after you? How much danger are we talking, here? You can tell me the truth."

Nick's shoulders fell. It always came to that—the truth—with everybody he'd ever cared about. Why couldn't they understand there were layers to the truth? That he could be honest and lie at the same time?

He moved the desk chair in front of Lilian and sat down facing her. She clasped her hands in her lap.

"There are some people in South America trying to find me and I don't know for sure, but the CIA might be looking for me, too. They think I've done something I haven't really done. That's all I can tell you right now. I'm sorry."

"So you're here to hide from them?"

Nick almost reached for her hands, but kept himself still. "I'm here to hide, yes. Not for long. I just need to figure out some things and then I'll go. I don't want to end up hurting you again. I don't want you to think that's why I came."

Lilian grunted and squeezed her hands together until they turned white. "What could possibly hurt me? The divorce was the worst thing." Her voice lowered as she looked at her lap. "Everything Chris did to me. I told you all this before—about the affair. The only thing he left me was the cake shop. I use it for storage now." She looked up, her eyebrows knotted. "Chris is the reason I wanted to be with you."

Nick leaned away from her, surprised.

"I mean ..." She cursed under her breath and leaned forward. "I mean he's the reason I wanted ... you know, that afternoon, the reason I ... oh, never mind." Lifting a hand, she fiddled with the tortoiseshell clip holding up her wet hair. She smiled as if to wipe away her last words. "So you won't disappear tomorrow morning? It's okay that you did last time. I don't blame you." She dropped her hand from the clip. "At all."

That was when he knew for sure she hadn't guessed his secret. He thought it had been so obvious. "I won't leave in the morning," he said, "if you don't want me to."

She stood and ran her trembling hands over her arms. "I think I should go. We can talk tomorrow."

"Maybe that's best." Nick stood and walked her to the door. He didn't want her to leave. He didn't want to lie in bed alone listening to the rain. "Lilian ..."

She turned to face him, her eyes damp. "Nick, I was upset when you didn't show up and that must mean something." Her breaths slowed as she lowered her hand. "I think I should go."

"Yes." He moved closer, wanting to embrace her, but finally opened the door. "Good night, Lilian."

Her eyes connected with his until he shut the door and turned to face the empty bed.

Chapter 4

The rain drummed on the roof for hours. Shifting across the mattress, Nick tried to find the perfect spot that would lull him to sleep, but it wasn't there. He couldn't get warm and his mind moved too quickly over the past five days, past the long, lonely trek out of the jungle back into São Paulo. He'd worried Kyle was on his tail, but now that he felt safe, all he could think about was how it had started in that hot jungle, a small campfire at the base of a tree, mud caked on his hands and face, the stench of sweaty men as they smoked pot and ate cold meals out of tins. Nothing could mask how bad they all smelled. Nick could still smell it in his memory and the scent of lavender on his pillow faded away.

He remembered leaning against a tree trunk as he lit a cigarette, the flame bright in the jungle darkness.

"You think we'll get there tomorrow?" he asked Kyle across the fire.

Smoking his own cigarette, Kyle inhaled and closed his eyes. The mud on his face was as dark as his skin. Nick could hardly see him. "We'd better. These guys are losing it fast. Two weeks in this hellhole is enough to send anyone over the edge."

They both spoke English, a language the native Portuguese-speaking men traveling with them didn't understand. They all blended into the darkness, their camouflage hiding them well. Most of them were lying down to go to sleep now, some of them already snoring.

"My GPS showed me we're close, but Ferreira made a guess about the exact location, so who knows." Kyle cleared his throat and spat on the ground. "Catarina better be there."

Nick stayed silent. Kyle was right. Catarina seemed to be their last shot at finding Ferreira—the drug lord they worked for undercover, but had never met—because nobody knew how to find Ferreira. The CIA wanted to stop him so badly they'd left Nick in Brazil for two years trying to get a good lead. Everyone before him had failed.

"It's hard to believe one of Ferreira's own cartels kidnapped his wife," Nick said, thinking out loud. "How'd they find her? She's as untraceable as Ferreira. And it seems too convenient that he asked you to get her back. I thought he would've asked someone higher up—someone he actually sees in person."

"I'm closer to him than you think. I keep telling you that." Kyle took a long drag on the cigarette, the end of it glowing bright orange. "Isn't this how we planned it? I get his trust, you follow? She'll cave. It'll just take the right bribe and you're the best at that."

"Twelve solid assets in two years," Nick chuckled. What made him most proud was the number of men he'd recruited to spy for the U.S. government. Hundreds throughout his career. Granted, none of them here in Brazil had led him to Ferreira so far, but they were loyal and they'd given secrets that had helped him get closer. Like the fact that Ferreira's marriage with Catarina was in major turmoil, mostly on her end. A wrong move on her part would likely put her on Ferreira's hit list, so it wouldn't take much to convince her that the U.S. could fix everything for her in return for her husband.

Nick finished his cigarette and tossed it into the dying fire. He rarely smoked, but the jungle made him nervous. "I'm done after this. I thought I needed this assignment, but I didn't realize it would last two years and land me here in this damn jungle. I guess it's getting my mind off things."

"Your wife?"

"Yeah."

"Sorry, Nick. You need to get over that."

"I know." He knew it all too well, throwing himself at any woman he thought might drown his pain. For seven years he'd thought that would fix his problems, but nothing was fixed yet.

Kyle kept smoking and in the dim light from the fire, Nick saw him staring at the ground, digging his steel-toed boot into the spongy soil. "I lost my son to drugs."

Nick looked up, surprised to hear Kyle talk about something personal. He rarely mentioned anything about his life outside of his cover for their assignment. "When did that happen?"

"Few years ago. An overdose."

"I didn't know." Annabelle had overdosed. He knew what that loss felt like. "You told me you were never married."

"I wasn't."

"So is that what got you in the DEA?"

"You mean trying to fix drug problems? Nah. I'm just here for the money." Kyle's laughter filled the small jungle clearing. Nick joined in, knowing Kyle's sense of humor. Money was the last reason either of them did their jobs. Nick had always felt that Kyle wanted to make a difference. His loyalty to the U.S. had carried them through a year of hard work together.

"You're lucky the agency's leaving you alone," Nick said. "I've never seen them keep an agent in one location so long." He chuckled. "And with a lousy CIA officer, too. Practically unheard of."

Kyle's white teeth gleamed through the darkness. "CIA's kept you here, too. We're in too deep, too close.

And your reports back to Langley are stellar. I don't deserve that kind of praise."

Nick stayed quiet, unsure of what to say. He didn't usually get along with men he had to team up with. He worked best solo. But he liked Kyle's efficient methods.

Kyle tossed his cigarette into the fire and laid down on his bedroll. Nick stretched himself out on his own bedroll and put his hands behind his head to stare at the dark canopy above. Layers of broad, flat leaves and boughs dripped with moisture. They were coated with moss, the scent of it heavy in the air. It was a sweet smell, in its own way, but Nick hated the utter darkness of the jungle. No sky, no stars. He broke the silence. "Sorry about your son."

Kyle rolled his back to Nick, his voice muffled. "It's okay, man. That's why I'm here." He paused, his breaths deep and loud. "You know, you should do something about your wife. It seems like you're ... running."

Shifting across his bedroll, Nick tried to ignore the stench from his own body. The mud on his face smelled like rot and mold. "I think I was running long before she died." He clutched his rifle close and moved his backpack beneath his head. The darkness above him shifted into different shades of black. When Nick closed his eyes, he heard wings whizzing around him, soft and delicate. He pretended they were butterflies instead of mosquitoes and flesh-eating gnats. A chorus of frogs started up and he fell asleep until he felt small bits of sun warm his face. The group packed up and left camp as fast as they could.

"Should be soon," Kyle said five hours later as they were still making their way through the dense vegetation. With his machete, Nick cut at vines and ferns blocking their way and ignored the mosquitoes buzzing in his ears.

He crept as lightly as he could, sure they'd reach a clearing any minute. They were supposed to find a bunker of some sort—one of many that Ferreira's cartels kept in the middle of nowhere. Drug stashes, trades and hideouts. The cartel that had kidnapped Catarina had supposedly brought her to an old bunker they thought Ferreira had forgotten. They wanted to use her as leverage to raise their rates from Ferreira, but they were beyond stupid if they thought it would work. Ferreira didn't respond to threats; he simply killed people who made them. Which was Kyle and Nick's job today—with help from the men they'd brought along.

"I'm not in the mood to get shot, so this better work," Nick said. He wiped away a layer of sweat from his neck. Mud coated his hand. It smelled like rot. They'd mixed it with live termites ground between their palms—a natural bug repellent. If Nick ever got out of here, he was going to take the longest, hottest shower of his life. He'd been in some bad spots during his career, but this was topping them all.

"You won't get shot," Kyle said and chuckled. His rifle, always aimed at the ready, gleamed in a sudden patch of sun shining through the canopy. "They've probably got bulletproof vests, but we have AKs and at close range they don't stand a chance. Just blow the hinges on the door like we planned and let them do the rest." He jerked his head back at the five men behind them. Most of them looked like they could barge through a wall. That's why Kyle had chosen them.

Nick's arms began to ache and he wondered why he'd agreed to do the hacking and slashing with the machete today. Sweat poured down his brow. His rifle slung across his shoulder felt like it weighed twenty pounds more with each passing minute.

"Ferreira asked me to do this for a reason," Kyle said right behind Nick. He straightened with pride and grunted. "I have more experience in stealth combat than most of his men and I've played to his terrorist movements instead of just the drugs. You know that's a side job. It's nothing. These bastards who took his wife are gonna get what they deserve."

As long as Nick had known Kyle, he'd been impressed by how convincing he was, even when he didn't have to be. It was a method that worked. Still, he didn't like how Kyle talked lately, as if he really was on Ferreira's side and not just trying to get to him.

"Whatever reason he picked you," Nick said with heavy breaths from the heat, "it's a good thing he let you choose your own men so we could do this assignment together. That's the only way this would work to get to Catarina." He peered through the steamy vegetation and noticed more light shining down into a clearing up ahead. He caught a glimpse of the bunker and lowered his machete. "Show time," he whispered.

Kyle grinned. "You know you like this."

"No, not really." Nick put away his machete and pulled his rifle into position. The cap on his head felt tight, smothering. "I haven't been in conditions this uncomfortable since the Farm at Langley. And I quit the Army for a reason."

"You and your cushy desk job."

"I don't always have a desk job."

"Most of your recruits happen at business parties with a Drambuie in your hand."

"No they don't." Although Nick had to admit that he drank scotch much too often. He turned to see the five men waiting for them to give orders. "We'll pick this up later," he said, smiling at how Kyle tried to annoy him. "You circle the bunker, look for guards and I'll get ready to blow the door."

Kyle nodded and Nick moved north to find a waiting place. When he found a spot with a good view of the door, he crouched down and stared ahead. In the center of the clearing stood a small concrete bunker overgrown with tangled vines and moss. He imagined Catarina inside, bound and gagged, probably beaten and other things he didn't want to imagine. He didn't even know her, but he'd heard she was breathtaking in looks and personality. Of course, no lesser woman would belong to Ferreira.

Searching the perimeter of the clearing, Nick spotted a guard rounding the corner of the bunker. He was dressed in black, wore a bulletproof vest and his boots were laced tightly up his calves. He held a rifle, but seemed relaxed.

He hadn't spotted Nick or the other men. Dragging his feet, he looked around, yellow sun-patches brightening his dark skin.

Ready to take out the guard as soon as he had a good shot, Nick aimed his silenced AK-47. He didn't want to kill the man, but he'd have to in order to keep him quiet. One, two, three—head turning toward him, aim right between the eyes, pull the trigger.

The guard collapsed and Nick looked for Kyle. He spotted his hand giving the signal to move forward. Slowing his breaths, Nick counted to ten. He would never get used to killing someone, no matter how many times he had to do it, but he had to get over it. It was time to blow the door.

He made his way into the clearing, past the dead guard and to the door. The bolts looked strong, but not strong enough for C-4. He dropped to one knee, slid his backpack to the ground and dug out what he needed to set up the explosive. He had only done this once before in his life, but Kyle had asked him to do it and he was at least comfortable with it. All he really wanted to do was get to Catarina and talk to her. He was sure he could get what he needed from her and end this nightmare.

With the small amount of explosives in place—just enough to blow the hinges and hopefully not hurt anyone inside—Nick rushed back to the trees, remote detonator in hand. He pushed the button.

A quick, fiery blast. The ground shook and the door burst free. Within seconds, Kyle and four other men rushed into the clearing. They tossed a stun grenade inside the doorway and a loud bang and quick burst of light rippled through the air. Nick aimed his rifle at the door, waiting for an onslaught of gunfire. Kyle and his men rushed inside the bunker. Rapid shots. A woman's scream.

Catarina.

They had orders not to hurt her. Nick ran forward, then stopped.

Kyle stood in the doorway, his rifle aimed at Nick's head. "Drop your gun," he ordered.

"What?" A chill ran up Nick's spine. He laughed. "Real funny. Is she in there?"

"I said drop it."

Another chill. Nick raised his rifle higher. "Who says I won't shoot you first?" He froze when a gun barrel touched the back of his neck. He hadn't heard anyone behind him. Not over the explosion.

"Me."

Nick recognized the man's voice as one of the five men they'd brought along. Shit. What was going on? He lowered his rifle and glared at Kyle. "Are you kidding me?"

"No." Kyle's face was completely blank. Nick had never seen him so serious before. He looked like a machine—muscles tense, jaw grinding back and forth as he waited for Nick to comply. Nick dropped his rifle and put his hands in the air. Birds sang loudly through the trees, a chorus that echoed in Nick's ears long after he entered the bunker.

Chapter 5

Devan stared at an F-15 Eagle looming over him. It seemed larger than it should in the poster taped to the ceiling. Devan never tired of looking at it, imagining what it would be like to know that kind of power beneath his fingertips. He'd rather be flying planes than anything and sometimes that was what he planned to do—leave his mom just like his dad was always telling him to. He groaned. No matter what he gave up or how hard he worked, nothing seemed like it would save the inn or make his mom happy. Maybe it wouldn't matter if he left.

He pulled his blanket up to his chin, reveling in the quiet of his room before he threw back the covers and pulled on a T-shirt and jeans. It would be a long day and with the cut in staff members, he had twice as much work to do. A family was supposed to arrive that morning: three children and two dogs for a solid week. That meant rowing the kids around the lake fifty times and worrying about them breaking things around the inn. And Rachel, the live-in cook, would need help in the kitchen with meals.

At least Nick was helping with all the maintenance. For the past two days he had followed Devan around, assisting him with whatever came up: a broken step, yard work, painting. There wasn't time for much conversation. Nick would either set himself to work or talk to Lilian, once in a hushed whisper that made her giggle. Devan couldn't remember the last time he'd heard his mom giggle like that. He wasn't sure how he felt about her and Nick. It seemed so fast.

Rachel knocked and cracked the door open. "Devan, the new guests are here. What'd you do? Sleep in?"

"Yeah." He gave her an apologetic shrug. She was the same age as him and worked just as hard as he did. She cooked and cleaned rooms on the days other staff members were away. She always looked tired.

"It's okay," she said, her voice dragging. "It's been hard since Lil let the others go. But she was asking for you. I think that Nick guy wants to get the canoes off the bottom of the lake." She squinted. "You think you can do that? Didn't Lil hire somebody last time?"

"Yeah, it cost a lot. I told Mom we should buy better canoes, the ones with Styrofoam so they won't sink because the ones we have now are ancient—I think they were in the boathouse when Mom bought the inn." He shrugged. "I'll do what I can, Rachel."

Her mouth dropped open. "I didn't mean to say you can't do it." She gripped the door and leaned in farther, a twinkle in her eye. "I'll bet you could do it even without Nick's help."

Devan laughed. "Maybe."

"You could." Rachel reached up to adjust her hairnet, failing miserably as half her chocolate-brown hair fell to her shoulders, uncombed and frizzy. She never looked put-together no matter how hard she tried. She'd been that way since he'd first worked with her in his mom's cake shop, her face covered with flour as she tripped over her laces around every corner. Devan liked the way she scrunched her tiny nose whenever she had to cook cabbage. Her mother was Greek and it showed in her olive skin and almond eyes.

He followed her out the door and down the hall and laughed when her hair fell out again. "Maybe you should try some clips or something."

"Oh, go help your mom." She flicked her hand at him, grinning as she disappeared into the kitchen.

Devan hurried through the inn to the porch, where he looked past the kids playing in the clearing. The turquoise lake was a smooth mirror reflecting the endless rolling hills blanketed in forest. So calm, as if begging for a stone to send ripples across its glassy surface.

Devan spotted his mom and Nick on the dock and started jogging down the hill. They were in deep conversation; Nick had his hands in his pockets and Lilian had her arms folded. She started in Devan's direction when he reached the dock.

She looked flustered and out of breath when she reached him. Taking his arm, she turned him away from Nick. "I got a call this morning." She motioned for him to walk with her up the hill. It was still muddy in places, but the stone steps were dry. "A couple wants to do a wedding up here next weekend."

"Next weekend!" Devan stopped in his tracks, but his mom kept walking.

"Yes, so we're going to have to hire some temporary help. I need supplies from the cake shop. They want me to do the cake." She looked over her shoulder, her expression urging him to catch up with her.

He reached her, thinking how much work it would take to get a wedding ready in a week. Normally they had months to plan and prepare. "Are you sure you can pull it off in a week?"

"They have a planner who's doing most of the work." She squinted from the sun. "They're paying well, Devan. We need the money."

Money, yes, but it wouldn't be enough to hire more staff permanently. "You haven't made a cake in years."

She laughed. "I know. I'll need you to go into town to get my stuff and ..."

Devan stopped walking when her voice trailed off. She was looking behind her shoulder at Nick still on the dock. "What?"

"That's how I met Nick," she said with a soft smile. "The wedding. I haven't told you much about him because he's ... I don't ..."

Devan waited for her to continue, but she didn't. "Yeah, he told me you did the wedding cake for his daughter."

"You were just finishing college. Her name's Clara—about your age, actually. She wanted a cake covered in rose petals." She let out a dramatic sigh. "I still remember that cake. It was exquisite."

Devan noticed her softened expression and distant gaze as she slowed down to look at Nick again. "Anything else you want to tell me?"

Lilian started up the hill again and Devan followed, wondering what was going on with her and Nick. She had woken earlier every morning since Nick's arrival, walking with an extra bounce in her step, smiling more than usual. But the next second she would be on edge, as if the smallest "boo" might make her jump. Devan didn't want to pry into her love life, but something was obviously wrong—and it had to do with Nick.

"Mom?"

She stopped before reaching the clearing. "What?"

Devan made sure she was looking at him before he spoke. "I need to know you're okay."

A chocolate Labrador barreled between them and they both jumped back. Lilian waved her hand, apparently done with the conversation. "I'm fine. You'll pick up some cake supplies for me?" She stepped closer, lowering her voice. "And will you take Nick with you? He's got some business he needs to take care of."

Devan leaned forward and kissed her cheek. "Sure, Mom."

Devan parked his truck in front of Cakes Made by Love, a brick building with a plate-glass window overlooking a maple-lined street.

Devan loved his hometown. He loved the small high school and the friends he'd made growing up. Since his mom had started the inn, though, he'd been separated from everything, spending most of his time in the mountains while everyone else moved on. He missed his old house that his dad had sold to buy a home in Charleston with his new wife. He missed the fenced yard, the clean-cut landscaping he and his dad had spent years perfecting, the neighbors who'd wave to him as he mowed the lawn every Saturday morning. That familiarity was gone.

He looked around. At least the town hadn't changed. It sat at the base of the mountain—one grocery store, one gas station and a post office run out of a house next to the city hall. On the way down the mountain, Nick had explained that his parents were from here, which was why Clara had wanted her wedding in the same church as her grandparent's ceremony.

"It's too bad your mom closed the shop," Nick said, unbuckling his seatbelt. He chuckled. "I've been wanting a good piece of cake."

Despite his chuckle, Devan thought Nick seemed annoyed by the drive down the mountain. His jaw had been clenched most of the time. Devan figured it was from how fast he'd driven on the dirt road. But he liked to drive fast—if he tried hard enough, it almost felt like flying.

Nick glanced at the scrawled title above the window. "She made beautiful cakes."

"Yeah." Devan twisted his key in the lock. "I have to find a few things. I'll be right back." He went to one of the storage rooms in the back.

Though the scent had faded long ago, he remembered the air thick with the aroma of sugar. Switching on a light, he faced a wall lined with labeled cardboard boxes and bins. His mom would need spatulas, tips, sifters and Tylose powder for the gumpaste. Baking cakes had become a nostalgic connection to his mom, something he never wanted to forget.

He gathered the supplies into a box and left the room to find Nick leaning against a counter. He'd found a dusty binder of Lilian's and was flipping through the photos of cascading tiers.

Devan had forgotten about the binder. His mom had never taken it to the inn with her. She'd left behind most everything related to the cake shop—everything connected to his dad. At the same time, she refused to sell the shop, refused to let it go even though the lease cost them extra money every month.

Devan moved closer. "Are you ready?"

Nick straightened his shoulders and turned with a half-smile. "Just another minute. Your mom asked me to find a picture for her, a cake covered with rose petals. It's the one she made for my daughter, Clara. Here it is." He straightened and proudly tapped a finger on the photo.

Devan leaned forward to look at the intricate tower of red tiers separated with bands of white ribbon. He had to admit it was exquisite.

"Your mother wants to use butterflies instead of roses," Nick said. "With wings made out of frosting."

"I've been meaning to ask you," Devan said slowly. He didn't want to overstep his bounds, but he couldn't keep it in any longer. "How do you know my mom? I mean, there was the wedding, but she's never mentioned you before." He cleared his throat, remembering his mom's giggles and blushes. "You're very close."

Nick stared past Devan, his eyes distant. "A little bit. I hope that doesn't bother you."

"I'm not in charge of my mom or anything, but she's been acting weird since you got here." Devan waited a moment to see if Nick would react, then deepened his voice, trying to sound as stern as he could. It was difficult. Nick was half a foot taller and his muscles were intimidating. "I don't like it. I don't want her hurt again."

Nick looked Devan in the eyes. "You mean like your dad hurt her?"

"Something like that." Devan almost stepped back, but kept his ground. He was glad when Nick softened his expression and leaned against the counter.

"I know I seem secretive, but it has nothing to do with you or your mother. I will never hurt her or you."

Nodding slowly, Devan thought he might be able to trust Nick. There was kindness in his expression. Honesty. "So why are you here?"

Nick straightened his shoulders. "I need to—"

A knock on the door interrupted him. A policeman peered through the glass. Officer Harris. "Hey, Devan?"

"Hi there." Devan headed for the door, smiling. He'd known Officer Harris, or James, as most people in town called him, since he was five.

"Everything okay?" James asked as Devan opened the door. "I haven't seen anybody here for months, not since the flood happened next door."

"Yeah, everything's fine." Devan glanced at Nick, who turned his back to them. He opened the binder and started flipping through the pages again.

"Alright, just checking. How's your mom?"

"Pretty good." Devan followed James' gaze to Nick.

"Friend of yours?"

Devan opened his mouth, but shut it again. For some reason he felt an urge to keep Nick's name a secret. Maybe it was because he'd noticed that his mom hadn't checked Nick into the computer system, or the way he avoided the guests and ate all his meals in his room. Devan felt sorry for him. "Yeah, he's a friend."

James' green eyes twinkled, annoying Devan. That was one of the bad things about a small town—nosy people. He liked James, but did he really have to pry?

"So that's why she's doing 'pretty good.'" James gripped the edge of the door and leaned in farther. "Who is he?"

Devan shrugged. "She doesn't want me to say much, you know?"

Nodding, James let go of the door. "I understand. Have a great day, Devan."

"You, too." Devan shut the door and turned to face Nick who closed the binder and spun around.

"Thank you, Devan, for not saying anything to him."

"Uh, sure. Is there a reason why?"

"I'll tell you in the truck. I need a ride to Charleston."

Chapter 6

As soon as Nick climbed into Devan's truck, he fastened his seatbelt and prepared for a wild ride. The way Devan had driven down the mountain earlier, Nick would consider himself lucky if they made it into Charleston without getting pulled over.

"There's a speed limit, you know," he said as Devan rammed his foot on the gas.

The truck sped up even more. "Nobody drives the speed limit here. They drive too fast or too slow. I always drive like this. Nobody cares."

Nick kept his expression calm even though his irritation was getting stronger. Devan's speeding would get them pulled over by a cop and there would be no way to avoid face-to-face interaction like he had in the cake shop. He was still glad, surprised even, that Devan had glossed over details to the officer. He lowered his voice. "I'm sure people drive fast around here, but once we're in Charleston—"

"Don't worry. Is there a reason you're so paranoid? Why didn't you want me to tell James about you?" The speedometer inched higher as they entered the highway. Devan seemed to have more confidence behind the wheel of his truck, probably because he felt in control. There was a lot about Devan that seemed familiar.

"I'm paranoid for certain reasons," Nick said. "Though it's probably better to say careful."

Devan's voice was softer as he asked, "Okay, so why are you careful?"

Nick crossed his hands in his lap, staring straight ahead. He had rehearsed what he would say to Devan, but for now he wanted to ease into the conversation, and remembering that Devan had mentioned the Air Force when they were repairing a broken stair, he decided to start there.

"So," he said with a smile. "When do you think you'll join?"

Devan was silent as he wove his way around slow cars. "The Air Force?" he finally asked.

"You were talking about it before. I started out in the Army, you know."

"I thought you looked military. Is that what you're doing now?"

Shaking his head, Nick remembered his headstrong days in training, how sure he had been of what he wanted out of life. He'd wanted respect and a thrilling career, but like Devan, he'd hesitated for several reasons, one of them being a girlfriend who'd begged him not to do something that would send him overseas—or get him shot. Lots of drama and tears. "Not exactly. Is it a girl you're wanting to stay for, maybe?"

"No, not a girl. I haven't joined because my mom, the divorce, I mean ... What do you mean, 'not exactly'?"

Nick squeezed his eyes shut. "I'll tell you in a minute. For now I need you to drive to a phone store. I'll give you directions when we get closer."

"Don't you have a phone?"

"No." Nick felt his empty pocket, his mind wandering over the phone call from Clara that he hadn't answered. The number hadn't been from her downtown office. She worked long hours as an executive assistant, and it seemed odd to him that she had called from her cell phone number at a time she normally would have called from her office phone. Had she been in danger? Was she now? For two days he'd wanted to contact her, but kept himself from doing it until now. He wanted to make sure nobody could trace the call back to him.

Devan glanced in the rearview mirror. "There are stores back in town. Why do we need to go all the way—"

"Just drive." Nick looked back at the road. "I'm going to give you cash for the phone. We'll need to park a few blocks away. I can't go inside with you."

The truck slowed down. "Why?"

"I'll need you to ask for a specific kind of phone. Some people would call it untraceable, but that's not exactly right. They can be traced with cell phone tower triangulation, but if I'm on for only a few minutes, the trail runs cold."

"So your name isn't attached to the phone? That kind of thing?"

"Sort of."

Devan nodded. "That's like a pre-paid phone."

"Kind of. A name and address aren't assigned to the phone, just like a pre-paid phone, but the guy who owns the store we're going to ... I trust his merchandise." Nick leaned his head back on the seat. He wanted to explain that Larry, the store owner, got his phones from the black market, and that he had been the one to show Nick how to get his false ID all those years ago.

Larry was one of those men that if you wanted your ass covered, he could help. All sorts of government officers used him when they thought things might go sour with their jobs. A well-kept secret from the government so far— the last Nick had checked. The only problem was that although Larry could usually be trusted with who he dealt with, Nick didn't want him slipping his name to anyone with the right amount of cash. He was sure Kyle might come asking, so Devan would be a good go-between.

The truck slowed even more. Nick breathed easier, but only for a second. He stared straight ahead, trying to concentrate on the details. "Don't tell the sales guy about me, whatever you do. He'll ask why you're purchasing the phone. Tell him it's for the L Project."

"The L Project?" Devan's knuckles turned white around the steering wheel.

"Yes. Newbies always use that term. He shouldn't give you a hard time if you use it." As he had done since they got into the truck, Nick checked the road around them, including the rearview mirror. He memorized the license plate of the car in front of them. And behind them. Damn, he was paranoid. He had never noticed how bad it had become. Knowing that people were looking for him made it different. Personal.

Knuckles loosening on the wheel, Devan grinned. "So what is this? Like spy stuff?"

"No." That was always the easiest lie to tell.

"Oh, well that would be cool if it was."

Devan's laugh sounded nervous, and Nick scowled at the road, annoyed Devan was laughing at all. "I'm trusting you," he said softly. "Don't take anything I say lightly."

Slowing the truck even more, Devan coughed. "I'm sorry. Are you in some sort of trouble?"

"Yes. You can't tell anybody about me. Especially cops. But I think I can already trust you with that."

Devan rubbed his thumb on the steering wheel, and once again, Nick tried to relax, but only tensed more in response to the effort. He watched the speedometer inch lower until they were finally at the speed limit.

"Does my mom know you're asking me to do this?" Devan asked.

"She knows I'm in danger and that's all."

"What?" Devan turned in his seat, glaring. "She trusts you. Why wouldn't you tell her?"

"I have my reasons. I'll tell her when the time's right." Nick nodded at the windshield, indicating Devan should keep his eyes on the road.

"Why's this phone so important?"

"I need to get in touch with my daughters. I need to make sure they're safe."

For the rest of the drive, Nick drilled Devan on what to say and how to act. He made sure he knew how to handle the money so he didn't seem nervous, and told him to look the clerk in the eyes, never at the floor. "You have to act natural but tough. It's an art," Nick told him over and over. "Now practice what you'll say."

Devan rehearsed everything; Nick was surprised how naturally it came to him—like when he had spoken with the officer. It was a good thing the kid could lie his pants off.

Devan parked the truck and took the cash. "Don't worry," he told Nick with a bright smile before shutting the door. "I'll get what you need."

Nick watched him disappear around the corner, hoping he was right, but it wasn't getting the phone that worried him the most. It was what could happen afterward.

He studied the quiet street, looking for cameras, memorizing the few cars parked along the curb. Something felt wrong. He undid his seatbelt and leaned forward, his muscles tensed.

Nothing.

He was just being paranoid, as usual. Larry, the sales clerk, would look Devan up and down. He would wonder who the hell he was. He would make sure Devan was serious, count the money twice, give him the wrong phone at first.

Devan came around the corner, his face grim. He walked with an even stride, looking side to side as if he expected someone to jump out and attack him, and he would have no problem taking them down if they did. Nick couldn't help but smile.

"Got it," Devan said when he climbed back in the truck. He handed Nick a small black phone. "Did I do okay?"

"Do you think you did?" Nick turned the phone over in his hands, relieved to see it was the right one. He'd used one before for some job in the past. For now, he'd find out if his daughters were safe, then use it to find Catarina. She was the key to getting him out of this mess.

"I think so. I've never done anything like that before."

"I hope you don't have to again," Nick said as he fastened his seatbelt and Devan started the engine. "Thank you for doing this. It means a lot to me."

"No problem. I hope your daughters are okay."

Nick opened the phone and stared at the numbers. His fingers itched to dial Clara's number. Violet's, not so much. Talking with her was painful.

Chapter 7

On the day of the wedding, Lilian busied herself with making the cake, not noticing her face was dusted with flour until she sneezed and a cloud drifted in front of her eyes.

"Here," Rachel said, handing her a wet washcloth. "Nick's on his way. He was looking for you just before I got here."

"Oh." Lilian dabbed her face with the cloth as she broke into a sweat. She'd been so busy preparing for the wedding she hadn't had time to acknowledge Nick, let alone spend time with him. If he wasn't helping Devan, he was in his room using her laptop. Sometimes late at night she passed by his room and leaned close to the door. She always heard keystrokes, a low voice. She ached to knock, but never did.

"So," Rachel said, a smile playing on her lips as she started washing a plate, "what's going on between you two, anyway? You've hardly said a word about him."

Glancing at the closed kitchen door, Lilian dropped the cloth on the counter. "Nothing's going on. We met a few years ago, but it was ... nothing." She stared at the door, expecting Nick to walk in any second.

"It was something," Rachel said, snickering. Steam from the hot water rose around her face. "You've avoided telling me about him all week. Spit it out."

Lilian's cheeks grew hot. Fantastic. Now she was blushing. She looked at the door again, remembering Nick's smiles and laughter as they'd become more comfortable with each other on the floor of her cake shop, talking about nothing and everything at the same time. She could still taste the frosting on her fingers as she licked it off, Nick watching her until she let him lick some off, too. How could she have done that? She'd known she was using him to make herself feel better about Chris' affair.

"I can't tell you about this, Rachel," she said quietly, staring at the six-tiered cake in front of her. All she needed to do now was attach the butterflies.

"Why not?" Rachel shut off the water and put her hands on her hips. "We're always sharing stuff. How is this different?"

"He's different. It's complicated."

A group of temps rushed into the kitchen from the back door. They were all young, dressed neatly in black and white, their aprons as crisp as their happy faces. A few stopped to admire the cake, and Lilian stepped aside. She said something to them, nodding and smiling, but her thoughts were a thousand miles away. When they left, she picked up one of the butterflies. They had taken three days to create out of black and orange gumpaste, candy, and tiny pearls of white sugar. She'd forgotten how much she loved creating things with her hands.

"Alright," Rachel said with a heavy sigh. "Whatever kind of 'different' he is, it must be good. You've been all twittery since he got here."

"Twittery?" Lilian tried not to laugh, but couldn't stop herself. Rachel liked to make up words.

Rachel giggled. "Yeah, you know—jumpy, gazing, sighing."

"Hmmm." Lilian let her smile fade. She'd been twittery, as Rachel called it, but she'd also been so distressed she couldn't think straight.

As much as she could, she focused on the butterflies and attached them into a cluster on the bottom tier, then spread them into flight up the cake until they reached the wedding couple. Her eyes filled with tears. She had avoided the memories until that moment, but couldn't shove them away now. Her own wedding. Chris. Vintage satin buttons all the way up her arms, Chris' fingers fumbling with the scratchy tulle of her blusher veil.

A hand touched her shoulder and the memory of Chris vanished. She turned to look up at Nick, her heart skipping beats. She was never sure what to say when she saw him—if she should tell him she was sorry for what had happened or if she should pretend it had never happened. So she hung out somewhere in the middle, feeling like she might fall flat on her face any second.

"May I interrupt?" he asked with a smile.

Rachel, now filling a plate with cookies, cleared her throat and spun on her heel. "I'll be back in a sec."

Lilian blinked away her tears as Rachel left the room. "There's nothing to interrupt. I'm finished." She gestured to the cake and smiled proudly.

"It's beautiful." Nick leaned forward and studied the butterflies. "These are incredible, Lilian. So many things you do are incredible." He stepped closer. "I want to talk to you tonight. In my room."

Lilian turned to the cake. "Are you going to tell me what you promised? Or ..." She couldn't finish, and picked up an extra butterfly.

"We can talk somewhere else. It's up to you."

Lilian saw the hope in his eyes, almost desperate. How was she supposed to react to him? Part of her was hopeful, but another part was frightened, and everything in between made her head swim. She took a deep breath. She could do this, one step at a time. "Your room's fine." Her fingers tensed around the butterfly in her hand, making her jump when it broke in two.

"Tonight, then. I'll be awake whenever you're ready. I'll go help Devan and the others set up."

"Thanks, Nick." Lilian slowed her breaths as he left the kitchen.

She was surprised how clean Nick kept his room. He had been eating most of his meals away from the other guests, and a small stack of dirty plates sat on the oak dresser next to the bed. Other than that, nothing looked out of place.

Maybe he had straightened the room up just for her, but he struck her as always neat and methodical—the precise ticking of a clock, never wavering.

Except now.

Lilian noticed the sweat on his brow when he closed the door and turned to face her. "Sit where you like." He walked to the desk next to the bed.

Exhausted from the busy day, Lilian sat on the edge of the mattress and crossed her arms, suddenly cold as Nick stood behind the desk chair and gripped the back with both hands. "I told you Annabelle died," he said with a tremor in his voice. "I didn't tell you how."

"Oh." Lilian squeezed her waist tighter. Annabelle. She blinked, trying to remember if she'd heard the name before. It was close to midnight, and her mind was fuzzy. She remembered Nick's tuxedo, the pain in his eyes when he'd talked about Clara's wedding, the empty chair next to his—in memory of his wife.

"I loved her," Nick said, clenching the back of the chair. "She loved me for a long time, but my job got in the way." He shifted his feet and pressed his lips shut. Lilian thought he might stop for good, but he finally continued, his voice more nervous than before.

"I was always gone doing things I couldn't tell her about, spending time with people she didn't know. It affected her more than I thought it would. She knew what she was getting into when we married. I told her as much as I could. But it wasn't enough." He let go of the chair.

Lilian unfolded her arms, afraid she might look like she was being judgmental. She didn't think any less of him for doing his job or loving his wife. In fact, the more she saw how much he'd cared for Annabelle, the softer her feelings were. She leaned forward, hoping he saw the understanding in her eyes. It wasn't like she didn't have things to confess.

He looked at his feet. "She stopped trusting me. She wanted a divorce."

Lilian lowered her voice, trying to hide her discomfort. "I'm sorry, Nick."

He shook his head. "No, no. Don't be sorry. She had every right to feel that way, and I consented. I was heartbroken, but nothing I said or did changed her mind. I don't think she was angry; she seemed disappointed." He stepped around the chair. "The hardest thing was that I couldn't get through to her. She shut me out—built a wall."

Lilian looked at the floor. She had done the wall thing to Chris, blamed him for everything, insisted on a divorce. She remembered Chris' pleading at first, how bad he'd said he felt for cheating on her. Then he'd blamed her, and that was the last straw. She looked up at Nick, wondering what he did for his job and what could have pushed his wife into such a state.

"How did she die?" she asked.

"It was an accident. She ..." Nick pushed his hands into his pockets. "She had to take sleeping pills—she was like that our entire marriage. Nothing serious. She worried a lot and overdosed one night when I was away. Too much alcohol combined with the pills, and she never woke up."

Lilian sat still, her fingers numb. She noticed that Nick had arranged the pillows the same as she had. She wanted to be closer to him more than ever. She wanted to tell him he could trust her, that she could be better than Annabelle. But the words were difficult to find. "I'm not sure what to say."

Nick narrowed his eyes. "I'm not finished."

"Oh."

"I changed after she died. Started drinking, convinced work to give me back-to-back assignments. I was never in the country. For a few years, I lost contact with my daughters."

"That would be hard to deal with. I can understand—"

Nick leaned down to look her in the eyes, appearing almost frightened. "I used women to try and forget my pain. I became what Annabelle thought I was."

Lilian shook her head, not quite understanding. Something was sounding awfully familiar. "You mean you—"

"I met you seven years after Annabelle died. I'd been with a lot of women by then. Not relationships, just ... used them."

Leaning away, Lilian let his words sink in. Mostly, she felt numb underneath the shock. Used them? She opened her mouth to say something, but nothing came. He couldn't be confessing what she herself had done, if it was even the same thing.

Nick squeezed his eyes shut. "I know how bad all of this sounds. I'm sorry."

"So when you met me, I mean, are you saying you used me?"

He opened his eyes. "When we met, I realized for the first time what I'd become. Yes, I used you. I felt alone after marrying off Clara that day. Alone and desperate for something, someone."

Lilian put a hand to her forehead. She couldn't believe what had happened. They'd ended up in each other's arms for entirely selfish reasons on both their parts. Suddenly, she didn't feel as guilty.

"Nick, it wasn't just you," she said quietly. "I was going to sign the divorce papers the next day. I was a wreck. Angry. I wanted something I could throw back in his face. I used you, too."

He nodded. His eyes searched her face. "Thank you for telling me that, Lilian. This has been difficult for both of us." He knelt down in front of her and put his hands on her knees. "I'm sorry for what I did, if I hurt you."

She sniffed as she remembered opening the buttons of his tuxedo shirt. The only thing she hadn't expected was to like him as much as she had. When he hadn't shown up the next morning she was more disappointed than she thought she'd be, and three years later, there was still something about him she didn't expect. She wanted him to move his hands farther up her legs even though she was telling herself to push him away, to stand up and leave the room. But she couldn't move.

"You said I made you realize what you'd become," she said, carefully choosing her words. "When did that happen? I never thought for a second you were lying to me—or using me."

"That's because I know how to lie. It's part of my job." Nick took his hands off her knees and stood up. "But I'll never lie to you again, Lilian. The first time we kissed, I knew you were different. You needed me. Nobody had needed me for such a long time. Not like that." He shook his head. "And I don't mean you needing me to get back at your husband. It was something else. You really wanted to be with me."

She blushed, almost annoyed how much he was affecting her. Maybe it was his honesty, the plea in his eyes for her to understand. She did understand, but then she thought about him using other women besides herself. He said she was different, but she wasn't sure she could trust that claim. "Maybe you should go," she said, struggling with how she should feel.

He backed away. "I understand. You're right. Lilian, I'm sorry. I'm sorry for everything, especially this." He looked around the room.

"Especially what?"

"Coming here, confusing you. Everything. I'm sorry." He shoved his hands in his pockets. "I have to be honest with you," he said slowly. "Before I let this go any further, before I mess things up again. I'm not finding anything to get me out of the mess I'm in, and I have to fly out of the country. There's a woman who might be able to help me, and I need to find her."

"Oh." She looked away and focused on his stack of dirty dishes on the dresser, brownie crumbs sprinkled across the top plate. He loved Rachel's brownies; he'd even helped her make them one afternoon. He'd helped Devan, too. They'd retrieved the canoes off the bottom of the lake, repainted lines in the parking lot, fixed the boathouse roof—so many things she'd put off. She didn't want Nick to leave, not just because he helped her with the inn, but because she knew she'd miss everything about him when he was gone.

Chapter 8

"It's almost midnight," Devan chuckled to Rachel, who was sitting next to him on the porch. "Where are they going?" He watched the newlyweds tiptoe across the clearing, their silhouettes merging as they stopped to kiss.

Rachel sipped from her glass of iced tea and suppressed a giggle. "Skinny dipping," she whispered. "I'll bet you anything."

So far, the couple seemed oblivious to him and Rachel. Devan watched them out of the corner of his eye. Their kissing reminded him of the wedding earlier that day, of flowers, cake, girls in frilly dresses talking about boys and love and marriage. It was all so superficial. Marriages never lasted.

"You're probably right," he said as the couple stopped kissing and headed down the hill toward the lake. "Skinny dipping."

He picked up a fork from the plate in his lap. His mom had saved him a piece of cake, but this was the first chance he'd had to sit down and eat it. He took a bite, savoring the butter crème frosting as he watched the wedding couple. If they stayed near the front of the lake where it met the bottom of the hill, he and Rachel wouldn't see a thing.

He swallowed and sighed with relief that he wouldn't have to go inside to give the couple their privacy. He was comfortable out in the cool air, finally able to relax after a long day of work.

Rubbing her arms, Rachel shuddered. "I wouldn't go swimming. The lake's got to be cold."

Devan leaned sideways and bumped her shoulder. "Nah, they have each other to keep warm. Don't you think it would be fun to go swimming at night?"

"Well, yes, but in a swimsuit. And alone." She gave him a disgusted scowl. "I wouldn't go with you. We're too … I don't know."

"It would be weird." Devan looked away. He had always been comfortable with Rachel, but imagining her naked suddenly made him fidget. He tried to hide it by taking another bite of cake.

"Totally weird!" Rachel giggled. "The last thing I want to see is you jumping into a lake with nothing on."

Still looking away, Devan swallowed. "Same goes for you, Rach."

He was glad she'd dismissed the thought as silly. He cleared his throat and stared at the roses and honeysuckles planted near the porch. The flowers reminded him of the cake shop, of seeing his mom surrounded by sugar and petals. These days she was more concerned with repairing things than creating them, a part of her that had died with the divorce—a happy, carefree part Devan tasted in his mouth. He looked at the cake. "Have you noticed a difference in my mom?" he asked. "Has she said anything to you about Nick?"

Rachel grinned. "Oh, Lil's in love with him. The way they look at each other. How could you miss that?"

"I haven't missed it. Just wondering what you thought."

"I think it's wonderful. I've never seen her so excited about someone. She seems nervous, but I think it's because Nick's handsome and sweet and helpful. She got so used to ..." She coughed. "Your dad."

Looking back at the cake, Devan picked at a butterfly. When it snapped off, he closed his fingers around it. "My dad isn't a bad person."

"I know, but he had an affair. I think deep down Lil's expecting every man she meets to stab her in the back. She deserves someone faithful."

"And you think that might be Nick?" Devan looked up from his fingers caged around the butterfly. It felt heavy.

Arching her eyebrows, Rachel leaned forward and rested her chin in her hands. "It's only been a week, but Lil said they met years ago. Did you know Nick, then, too? You two are pretty close."

"No, I was at school." Devan turned his attention to the lake where ripples broke the calm surface. He hadn't thought of himself as close to Nick. "I don't know a lot about him, either," he said, looking down at the butterfly showing through the breaks in his fingers. He remembered Nick's promise never to hurt him or his mom, the way he'd carefully explained to Devan how to buy the cell phone, the urgency in his eyes when he spoke of his daughters. "But I know he would never hurt my mom. If she had somebody like him around, I'd feel better about leaving."

"To join the Air Force?"

Devan tightened his fingers, almost forming a fist. "Yeah, but I can't. Not yet. Not until I know she'll be okay."

"You know she'd be fine without you," Rachel said, lifting her chin from her hands. "She was fine when you were finishing college. What makes you think—"

"You don't know her like I do." Devan grabbed the plate in his lap and stood up. He could see the newlyweds swimming away from the bank. They left a knife-like slice through the water, cold and black.

"You're right that your mom needs you," Rachel said, touching his hand at his side. He was still holding the butterfly. Because it was made of gum paste, it looked and felt like plastic, but he knew it was brittle. "And I think it's great you're here with her. Just don't forget about you, okay?"

Before he could answer, the door behind them opened and Nick and Lilian stepped onto the porch. Carrying his bag, Nick was dressed in jeans and the long-sleeved shirt he had worn when he'd arrived. He gave Devan a lopsided smile. "You two are still up, huh?"

Devan narrowed his eyes. "What's going on?" His mom looked like she might burst into tears.

"Nothing," she said, looking away. "I need to give Nick a ride. I'll be back in a few hours." Her words sounded mechanical. Devan noticed her hand reaching for Nick's, but she pulled away as they walked forward.

Devan stepped back for them to head down the steps. Something felt wrong. The fear in Nick's face, the coldness in his mom's voice. He shoved his plate at Rachel and rushed down to touch his mom's shoulder. She and Nick turned to him.

"Mom, do you need me to go with you? You look tired. If Nick's not coming back with you, I don't think you should be driving by yourself." He reached for her arm, but she stepped back, colliding with Nick.

"No, Nick doesn't want—" She stopped when Nick grabbed her hand.

"It's okay. Devan's right. I'd rather you not drive alone after you drop me off. Thank you, Devan." He smiled warmly. "You okay to drive?"

When Devan climbed behind the wheel of his mom's Jeep he realized he was still holding the butterfly. He set it in his lap, hoping to keep it hidden in the darkness. He started the engine after his mom buckled her seat belt next to him and Nick settled in the seat behind her. An awkward silence ensued.

Nick cleared his throat. "There's something I need to ask you two."

Devan maneuvered the Jeep around the familiar ruts in the road. His stomach tightened. He suddenly wished he hadn't eaten any cake. He didn't like that his mom's hands were clenched into fists in her lap, or the trembling in Nick's voice. Everything felt bumpy, like the road.

"My family's in danger," Nick said, leaning forward between the seats. "As your mother already knows, Devan, I'm leaving tonight because my daughter's husband has gone missing. I got the call from her ten minutes ago. I've got to take care of things and make sure she's all right."

Devan glanced at his mom. What was going through her mind? Had Nick told her about the phone and long drive to Charleston? Her eyes were wide, staring straight ahead. Devan wanted to comfort her, but it would have to wait.

"Which daughter? How long has her husband been missing?"

"Clara. She's in California."

Devan drove through a puddle in the road. Mud splattered across the windshield, encasing them in darkness until the wipers brushed it away. Devan imagined

72

Nick's daughter alone and frightened. He didn't know what he'd do if his mom went missing, if anybody he loved disappeared.

Nick reached between the seats and touched Lilian's shoulder. She seemed to relax. "But I have to go get her. I want her safe. Her sister Violet is in England, but I'm going to book her a flight and bring her and Clara to the inn, if that's all right with you two."

Lilian turned around. "Of course."

Devan watched the shadows on the road, sharp and jagged from the headlights. He didn't know how old Nick's daughters were, but he guessed around his own age. Surprised by how worried he was for two girls he didn't even know, he glanced at Nick in the rearview mirror. "How much danger are they in?"

Nick stared straight ahead, his lips pinched into a thin line.

Chapter 9
San Diego, California

Nick stepped into Clara's apartment, his heart beating fast as he glanced at a smashed mirror on the entryway tile. In the living room, sunlight shimmered through the bent Venetian blinds. It looked like there had been a fight, but Nick knew better. He slipped his key into his pocket and relaxed. Whoever had left the mess was gone. They'd done it out of anger. Or maybe they wanted to send a message.

He listened for any signs of life, but the apartment was silent. Heading into the living room, he noticed the white couch pulled away from the wall. Blood was smeared across the arm. Nick's stomach turned. Not Clara's. It couldn't be Clara's. She'd told him nobody had hurt her. Jeffrey's, then?

Nick stopped in his tracks. He felt trapped, as if the walls might close in any moment. He escaped into the kitchen, stepping around a broken dish on the tiles. A warm breeze blew in when he opened the French doors. It was tinged with the scent of Clara's potted camellias. She'd been planting camellias since she was a child. They were her flower, like Violet's were violets.

In the distance, the San Diego coastline stretched as far as Nick could see. Any other day he would think it was beautiful. Today, he didn't care.

Since the deck seemed untouched, Nick closed the doors and headed down the hall to Clara and Jeffrey's bedroom, scanning everything in sight. A comforter thrown on the floor, rumpled around scattered jewelry and a black lacy bra. A glass of wine spilled on the bed sheets. Red.

Nick froze, staring at the wine stain. It was wing-like. It reminded him of the blood on his kitchen floor.

"Clara?" he called out.

A whimper came from the closet, and he tore across the room and yanked open the oak doors. It was a walk-in closet. He stepped inside, looking along the floor as he brushed past Clara's dresses hanging on one side and Jeffrey's tailored suits on the other.

"Daddy?" The voice grew louder. "Is that you?"

Nick's heart jumped at the sound of her voice. He was so glad to hear her, to know she was close. He took another step forward, almost tripping on a pair of dark high heels. That didn't surprise him; Clara usually wore heels unless she was swimming. He was sure Violet, a good four inches taller, had given her some sort of a complex. "Are you alone? Clara?"

"Y-yes." Another sob.

Nick spotted her bare feet and shoved aside Jeffrey's suits. She had pushed aside a rack of Jeffrey's shoes and was sitting with her back against the wall, her knees up to her chin. She looked up and sighed. "I knew you'd come."

Crouching, Nick took hold of her trembling shoulders and tried to lift her, but she wouldn't budge. "Clara, honey, help me out here. What happened?"

She broke into a stream of sobs. "Jeff left," she whimpered. "Two men came, and he hid me in the closet. That was last night."

Slow. He would have to take this slow, no matter how badly he needed to know where Jeffrey was. Once his eyes adjusted to the darkness, he studied the floor around Clara. "Is that loaded?" he asked with a raised eyebrow at the nine-millimeter pistol on the floor.

"Yes."

He picked up the weapon and checked the safety, remembering how many times he'd taken Clara and Violet to the shooting range when they were young. It had been one of the only things they'd done together consistently. He held up the gun. "Did Jeffrey give this to you?

"No, I got it out of the safe when he didn't come back."

"You still only have the two, right? The Glock and the Beretta?" He'd bought the Beretta for her, and although she could defend herself, Jeffrey was the one most prepared to take on intruders. He'd been trained in the Air Force and the DEA. Where was he?

"Yeah, the Glock and the Beretta. Jeff took the Glock with him—wherever he went."

"You really don't know? Clara, you've got to tell me exactly what happened so I can figure out where he might be."

Her voice trembled, growing higher. "I know, I know. We were getting undressed from a party when it happened. We heard someone banging on the door, then they came inside. Jeff grabbed his knife and told me to hide in here and they were all yelling in Portuguese, but I couldn't understand it. I didn't even know Jeff could speak Portuguese, but he was. Then they said your name." She whimpered with a shudder, and then stiffened. "I would've called the DEA office to see if they know what's going on, but since I know what you do, I thought I would wait and tell you first."

Nick froze and he gave her a stern look. "What do you think I do?"

"You're a spy, Daddy." She straightened her shoulders and wiped away the last of her tears. "I guessed that forever ago. And Jeff told me when we got married."

Nick stared at the gun in his lap. He'd known for a long time that Clara had guessed what he was, but he'd never once heard her say it. The word "spy" never sounded right, no matter whose lips it was coming from. He wasn't James Bond. He didn't actually spy for anyone; he recruited people to spy on their own governments in other countries. Assets. But even that could get complicated.

He touched Clara's damp cheek. She looked like Annabelle, soft blue eyes and silky, flawless skin. Not like Violet, a spitting image of himself—darker complexion and squinty, grayish eyes. "So you called me because these men said my name?"

"Yes, and because Jeff didn't come back. He didn't answer his phone." She lowered her head. "I hope it wasn't too dangerous for you to come get me. I feel like I shouldn't have called you. "

Nick touched her hand, gently working it away from her knee. Her fingers were so cold and stiff they felt like they might snap in half. "Don't feel bad for calling me. I would be angry if you hadn't." He almost added that he at least had a few more days, maybe weeks, before the CIA caught on to his false identity, but stopped himself. He didn't want to worry her more than he had to. Still, she needed to know some of the facts. "There are people after me, honey."

"Jeff said your job isn't very dangerous. Who's after you?"

Taking a deep breath, Nick said, "The CIA and some men down in Brazil."

"Brazil?" Fear crept into her eyes.

"Yes, why?"

"They kept saying Brazil over and over." Her eyes widened. "Maybe that's where Jeff went."

"That's just great." Nick's mind raced through a million possibilities. Was Jeffrey in with Kyle? That would explain the connection to Brazil and why they'd said his name. Whatever Jeffrey was up to, Nick guessed it wasn't good.

He rubbed his thumb over Clara's fingers. They were beginning to warm up and relax. Clearing his throat, he tightened his hold. "Has Jeffrey ever mentioned a man named Kyle Mendez? He works in the same DEA office as Jeffrey."

She shook her head. "No, but there's been other things that have ... never mind."

"What other things?"

"Nothing." Her voice tightened, and she struggled to sit up. "I need some tea or something."

Nick helped her up and followed her down the hall. She looked like she might fall over any second. He understood she was frightened, but he'd never seen her like this. Violet might fall apart, but not Clara. Clara was his fighter.

"You sit on the couch," he ordered. "I'll get the tea." He walked past the broken dish and filled the tea kettle. Stealing a glance at Clara in the living room, he saw that she had settled into the sofa with a small pillow in her lap. No tears. That was good.

"You're sure there were two men?" he asked when the tea was ready. He handed her a cup and sat down next to her.

She put the cup to her lips, steam drifting across her face as she closed her eyes. "Yes, there were two different voices."

"And you couldn't understand anything they said except for my name and Brazil?"

"I only speak Spanish, Daddy, you know that. Jeff kept going back and forth between Spanish and Portuguese. He told them to stop breaking things and asked them what they wanted. They talked for a long time, and then they came in the bedroom and smashed more things."

"They didn't check the closet?"

"They looked inside, but I guess they didn't see me."

"And that was it? They left after that? Where did the blood come from?"

Clara turned to look at the arm of the couch. "I don't know." She leaned into him, almost spilling her tea. "It might be Jeff's. What if he's dead, Daddy? I could have done something. I could have grabbed my gun out of the safe when they were talking. I could have tried to climb out the window to get help. I could have—"

"Shhh." He put an arm around her and squeezed. "Let's just focus on what happened. Did Jeffrey seem upset or frightened when he left? Did it sound like they were forcing him to go with them?"

Clara set her tea on the coffee table and buried her face in her hands. "Kind of. They seemed upset the bedroom was empty, that they couldn't find me."

"What?" Nick pulled away. "They only wanted you?"

"I don't know." Her breaths came faster against her hands. "Jeff was acting so weird. I've only heard him like that when ... I don't know. It's like he expected this to happen."

Chapter 10
West Virginia

Devan took a deep breath of sweet mint and cedar as he brushed his hands over the ferns that lined the trail. He hiked by the lake whenever he had the chance, but even in the silence he could never decide what he wanted most. Sometimes he wanted to go live with his dad who seemed to always know what he wanted, even through the divorce. It confused Devan. It made him feel like he was missing something, and no matter where he looked he couldn't find it.

Lost in his thoughts, he hiked farther than normal. When he turned around, the inn looked like a miniature doll house on top of the hill, undisturbed and pristine. It was early enough that nobody was awake, not even his mom. That didn't surprise him. She had been quiet for the past four days since Nick had left, sleeping through her alarm, working through the hours with distant eyes.

She had insisted Devan take a morning off, so he was going to make the best of it. When the sun crept higher into the sky, he wiped a film of sweat from his brow and headed down to the lake.

The water was cool when he stripped to his underwear and jumped in. Breathing hard after several laps, he finally stopped and floated on his back, smiling at the clear sky as he remembered his conversation with Rachel on the porch. Skinny dipping. For some reason it sounded fun and exciting, especially if he could try it with Rachel. But it wasn't likely she would consider it any time soon.

After another few laps he stopped again. A figure with dark hair was swimming toward him. His heart pounded.

"Rachel?" he called out, but she didn't stop. She was several yards away, swimming crawl stroke, so her face appeared and disappeared on every third stroke. As she neared him, he saw that it wasn't Rachel. The woman slowed and drifted toward him, smoothing back some stray hair with a delicate hand.

"Hi." She swept her gaze down the bank where Devan had left his clothes and backpack. "I didn't know anybody else would be swimming here."

Devan cleared his throat, shocked by how pretty she was. "Me neither."

She swam closer and stopped right in front him. "I need a break." She smiled. "You must be Devan Love, right?" Her eyes were the same color as the sky. Devan couldn't stop staring at them. She was close enough he felt her warmth through the water. Her toes brushed against his, and his heart rate doubled.

"I'm Devan, yeah." He was suddenly aware he was mostly naked. He almost reached his hand out of the water to shake hers, but pulled it back at the last second. He felt like an idiot. "How'd you know who I—"

"My dad told me all about you. Didn't he tell you I was coming to stay?"

Devan almost stopped treading the water. She was one of Nick's daughters—Clara or Violet. He hoped she wasn't Clara. Clara was married.

He looked away from her tan shoulders. "So Nick's your dad?" He stared at the ripples his hands made as they treaded the water.

"Yes, I'm Clara."

Crap. Why did she have to be so unbelievably gorgeous?

The ripples in the water grew larger. Devan forced a smile and looked up. "It's nice to meet you." Then he remembered Nick's silence in the Jeep. "So is everything all right? Is your dad still here?" He looked past her, scanning the other end of the lake. But the inn was too far away for him to see if new cars were in the parking lot.

Clara shrugged. "Everything's fine. Dad just dropped me off a few hours ago. We've been in the car for four days, so a swim sounded nice." She laughed. "Your mom thought I was crazy."

Devan chuckled, thinking of his mom's reaction to Clara jumping in the lake right after arriving. She'd probably try and convince her she needed to take a nap or something. "No more crazy than me. But your dad was worried about you when he left. He said your husband was missing."

A breeze swept across the lake, raising goose bumps on Devan's skin. A shadow fell across Clara's face and her smile faded. "I should go."

She dove under the water and glided past him, emerging several yards away. Her arms cut through the water, each stroke strong and efficient until only small waves rippled in the distance.

Nick was gone when Devan hiked back to the inn. He found his mom in the library, sitting alone with an open magazine on her lap.

"Are you reading that article again?" He reached for the magazine, but she pressed her hand on top of it.

"No, it's a different one." She looked up with a stern face. "Did you know they thought the monarchs were going extinct ten years ago? They were wrong." She tapped her finger on the glossy article photo at what looked like a pile of orange and brown leaves under a cloudless blue sky.

Devan leaned down to get a better look. His mom smelled different, a musky scent probably left over from Nick's short visit. Devan didn't understand why she was worrying about butterflies when the man she obviously cared about had taken off again.

"It's dead monarchs," she said when he crouched down in front of her. "Millions of them. They got too cold. See?" She pushed the magazine forward and he slid it from her lap.

"Maybe we should look into raising them again." He ran his fingers over the picture of the butterflies, remembering when he'd finished college and moved in to help with the inn. Cages. Caterpillars. The pungent scent of milkweed. "The guests liked to watch them," he said, his voice distant. "Remember? Now's the time to raise them again if you want them to migrate."

His mom sighed and looked at the ceiling. "I know, but it takes a lot of time, and there have been enough around we don't have to do that. The guests like to try and find them during their hikes, anyway."

Her excuses sounded empty. Devan hadn't thought much about it until now, but she hadn't bothered getting out the cages for the last several springs, insisting that raising the butterflies wouldn't make any difference.

"There used to be enough around here," he said, looking into her glazed eyes. "Are you okay?" Taking her hand, he squeezed until she looked him in the face.

She shrugged. "I'm fine, sweetie. Why?"

"Aren't you upset about Nick leaving again? I just met Clara swimming in the lake. She said he was here." At the thought of Clara he looked away.

"He was, but he left to go get Violet. She's landing in New York this evening."

"He's driving?" It wasn't too far to drive, but flying would certainly be faster.

"Yes, that's the safest way for him, I think. But then he's flying out of the country." Her hand tensed in Devan's, and she leaned forward. "Honey, you know how serious this is, right? That you can't tell anybody about Nick? That his daughters need to be safe here?"

"Yes, Mom, I know." He let out a short laugh. "Who would I tell? The family who wants me to row their kids around the lake every day? And how is he flying out of the country when people are looking for him?" He thought of the precautions Nick had taken just to buy a cell phone.

Lilian shrugged. "He flew to California just fine. He knows what he's doing." Leaning down, she took the magazine from Devan and smoothed her hands over the open page. "He saw this on the plane and brought it back for me. He said there's something about the butterflies he's trying to figure out."

"About our butterflies?"

"Something connected with them, yes." She closed her eyes. "And from the way he talked about it, I don't think it's a good thing."

"It'll all work out." Devan patted her hand on top of the magazine. "I trust Nick, and I trust this inn. Dad left you with the cake shop, but I'll never leave you with all of this. I don't think Nick'll leave you eith—"

He stopped short. He was already comparing Nick with his dad, and as far as he knew, Nick hadn't committed to anything. He pulled his hand away and stood up. "Sorry, Mom. I didn't mean—"

"No, you're right." She stared at her lap, seeming to focus on her bare ring finger. "I know you still love your father, Devan. A part of me does, too." She looked up and sighed. "So, you met Clara."

"Yep." He looked away before the flutters in his stomach affected his expression. "She seems very nice. Good swimmer."

Devan helped guests for the rest of the day, keeping his eye out for Clara, but by the time early evening arrived, he still hadn't seen her. In fact, nobody had seen her since her swim that morning.

"She needs time away," his mom said with a curious look. "Why are you so worried?"

"No reason."

Which was a complete lie. Devan couldn't get her off his mind. He kept wandering out onto the porch to see if she was still swimming or walking along the bank. What if she was hurt?

Trying to distract himself, he went to the kitchen around dinnertime to talk to Rachel. She always made him feel better, and she'd probably want help serving dinner.

He washed his hands at the sink, breathing in the warm scent of hot bread and oregano.

"Yeah, it was weird," Rachel said as she pulled a batch of rolls out of an oven and set them on the counter. "Nick showed up with her early this morning and she went straight to her room. The next thing I knew, she was walking down to the dock in her swimsuit. Nick said it was normal. I think it's quirkish."

Devan laughed and grabbed a pastry brush. He began brushing butter over the golden mounds of bread. "So you think it's weird she wants to swim?"

"Maybe it's more sad than weird. Nick said she's having a hard time."

That was putting it lightly. Or maybe it wasn't. Clara had seemed relaxed in the water until he'd mentioned her husband. "I think she's stressed out," he said, remembering the anxious look in her eyes before she swam away. "Her husband's missing and her dad's in some sort of trouble. I guess she wants to be alone."

Rachel's mouth twisted into a smirk. She put her hands on her hips. "You met her out on the lake, didn't you? You swam together."

"How do you know that?" He looked away. He kept forgetting how well Rachel could read him.

"Because your hair was damp when you got back and you smell like a fish." She scrunched her nose and snatched the platter of rolls from the counter. "No way I'm letting you help me serve dinner. You should go shower."

Devan fought the urge to kick her in the shin—lovingly, of course. He grabbed two rolls before she slipped past him through the swinging door.

He wasn't about to go shower. He needed to find Clara and see if she was okay. He needed to see her blue eyes again, the sun on her shoulders, the soft smile on her lips. He'd never been so immediately attracted to anybody in his life. It made him think of his dad and the affair, his mom's complaints that too many men had no control when it came to a beautiful woman. Maybe she was right. Or maybe he needed to go on more dates. He laughed at himself as he searched the grounds around the inn. He'd been helping his mom so long that his trips into the city for a date or drink with friends had become infrequent.

Finally, he found Clara at the boathouse next to the inn, still wearing her swimsuit. With her back to him, she sat on the wood steps, the sunny backyard of the inn silhouetting the slim curves of her waist. She had her knees pulled to her chest as she picked at a loose nail surrounded by white peeling paint.

"Clara?"

She whipped around, her eyes wide. "Oh, Devan, it's you." Turning, she relaxed her shoulders and picked at the nail again. "I've worried everybody, huh?"

"A little." Devan sat next to her, but kept his distance. "I think everybody understands you need to be alone." He dug his toe into the dirt. "Do you want me to leave?"

She met his eyes. "No, please stay." She smiled. "I'd like somebody to talk to. I guess I'm just, I'm not sure what I should be doing. I feel strange here." Her eyes glistened with tears, and she glanced at the roll in Devan's hands. He'd already eaten the first one. He handed it to her. She had to be hungry.

"Rachel made them," he said as she took a bite. "She's a great cook."

"Yeah, she is." Clara took another bite and chewed quickly. "I'm starving, sorry."

"Don't be sorry." He liked the softness in her voice, the way she held the roll close to her lips as she chewed, as if it might disappear. He cleared his throat. "Dinner's ready inside. The other guests are eating if you want to go change. Or you can eat in your room if you want. Your dad did that almost every meal."

"That sounds like him." She finished the roll and licked her fingertips, her wedding ring glinting in the sunlight. Devan wondered how much she loved her husband. Was she thinking about him that second, wishing she could be alone with her thoughts? Maybe he shouldn't have interrupted her. He leaned away.

"Dad never ate with us when we were growing up," she said, staring at her ring. "But he always had dessert with me and Violet. That was our thing, I guess. Until..."

Devan followed her gaze to the forest surrounding the inn. The evergreens were dark and cool compared to the sunny clearing. Secluded, almost inviting. The distant chattering birds echoed from the heavy forest canopy. When Clara buried her face in her hands, Devan moved an inch closer. He wasn't sure what to do.

"I don't even know what I'm doing here," she said into her hands. "I should be at work. My boss had a million things going on this week, and he'll have a hard time without me there. Or I should be with Dad, or trying to find Jeff. But I ... he ... he won't come back." Tears seeped through her fingers and slid down her knuckles.

Devan couldn't stand it any longer. He inched closer and wrapped his arm around her shoulders, pulling her to him. She relaxed in his hold, her sobs stopping. "Thank you," she whispered, resting her head on his chest. She wiped the tears from her cheeks. "I'm sorry. I've needed to cry for four days, but my dad wants me to be strong like him."

Squeezing her shoulders, Devan took a deep breath and caught the scent of her hair. Rachel was wrong. The lake water didn't smell like fish. It smelled like wet stones and sweet grass. He squeezed her tighter and gathered his courage to speak. "You hardly know me, but how can I help? Anything?"

She pulled away. "I don't know. I'm too old for this crap, dumped here like a child, like I can't take care of myself." Looking down at the cracked paint on the stair, she started peeling it back with her manicured nails. "But he's right. He's always right."

"I doubt he thinks of you like that, like a child."

"He shouldn't; I'm twenty-five."

"My mom does the same thing." Devan laughed, thinking of his mom's little worried glances if he complained about feeling unwell or seemed upset about something. He was sure she'd catch on to his feelings about Clara. He had to get a grip. "We are their children." He hoped Clara would smile, but her mouth dropped into a frown instead.

She shrugged. "Jeff treats me the same. It must come with the job."

"So your husband does the same thing as your dad?"

She straightened. "Oh! No, no. Well, he used to. Kind of. When he worked in the Air Force. He was an SIO."

Devan's heart skipped a beat. "An SIO? That's a Special Investigations Officer. Nothing to do with the planes."

"Yeah. That's how he met my dad." She wrinkled her brow. "How much has he told you, anyway?"

"Not much about his job. It's obviously a secret." He emphasized the word obviously, wondering how much Clara knew about her dad.

"Obviously," she said, rolling her eyes. "It makes me so mad. Jeff works behind a desk now, and he still keeps stuff from me." She squeezed her eyes shut, digging at the paint again. "Lots of stuff."

"Oh?"

She kept her eyes shut. "I hope my dad doesn't find him."

Chapter 11

Lilian tried to forget about Nick as she waited for him to return with Violet. She tried to forget about him at dinner, but they ate brownies for dessert and she couldn't stop staring at the crumbs on her plate. She tried to forget about him when she got in the shower before bed, but the water shimmering on the gray tiles reminded her of the color of his eyes. She loved that color, like the lake right before the sun rose.

When she turned off the water the mirror was fogged up. Her reflection looked smudged. Wrapping a towel around herself, she reached out to touch the mirror. Her finger squeaked along the glass as she drew a stem, petals and leaves of a slender lily, then stood back to admire her work. Nobody called her Lily anymore.

Sighing, she reached her hand out again and drew wings, dots, a bumpy thorax and two antennas. She drew the butterfly's legs resting on the lily. Another step back. She wasn't thinking about Nick now. Oh, wait, she was.

With a sigh she stared at the mirror and focused on the pieces of herself showing through the lines she'd drawn. Skin and a white towel. She wondered if that was all Nick saw of her. Pieces.

She changed into her clothes and wandered into the kitchenette at the back of her room, putting on a kettle for tea before she checked her cell phone. He hadn't called. She looked at the clock. Twelve-thirty.

A knock on her back door made her jump. It was Devan peeking in through the small oval window, probably out for a short walk to make sure the boathouse was locked.

"Why are you still up?" he asked when she unlocked the door to let him in. He looked tired, his shoulders drooping.

"I'm waiting for Nick to get back with Violet." She left the door open after he entered, and the cool evening breeze drifted across the room. It smelled like the lavender she kept growing beneath her windows.

Devan took a tea cup from the cupboard. "I told you I'd stay up and get them settled. What's the matter?" He turned to her as he poured some tea and heaped two spoonfuls of sugar into the steaming liquid. They drank tea together at least three times a week, always in the evening after the guests were quiet. Lilian loved these moments, stretching her legs out on a chair at the table as she listened to Devan's voice—so much like Chris' when her marriage was happy. Devan liked to talk just to talk: things he'd seen during the day, guests that annoyed him, new plans he'd made to upgrade his truck, or sometimes he'd even talk about a girl if he'd been on a date. That hadn't happened for a long time.

In a way, Lilian was relieved, but as she sat down at the table, she remembered Devan's obvious interest in Clara—his long, dreamy look at her the first moment she'd seen them together after dinner. She shifted in her seat. "Nothing's the matter." She traced the wood grain pattern on the table. It felt smooth and rough at the same time. "I'm worried about Nick getting back okay."

"I know you are." Devan leaned forward and touched her hand, his tired eyes twinkling. "You can admit you like him, Mom. I won't tell anybody."

Suppressing a smile, she clenched her jaw. She appreciated Devan's desire for her to be happy, and that he seemed okay with Nick sticking around, but now that he was in the room with her, she had to know what he thought of Clara. She had already noticed a look on his face, the same look on young couples attracted to each other; she'd seen that a lot when she was still making wedding cakes. She'd noticed Devan's worrying about where Clara had disappeared, the way he kept watching the lake, the way his eyes jumped whenever Clara's name came up.

She took his hand into hers, rubbing his thumb. "Devan, honey." Her lips formed the question she wanted to ask, but her voice stumbled into a sigh. How could she ask him without offending him? "Sweetheart, I've noticed how much you—"

Devan pulled away. "I know."

"You do?" She folded her arms.

Staring into his teacup, Devan lowered his voice. "You don't have to worry about me, Mom. I promise things will be fine."

"We're on the same page, then?" Lilian leaned forward, gaining courage. She could talk about these things with her own son; he seemed more open to it than she expected. "You know what I'm talking about?"

He smirked. "Clara."

It was as simple as that. Lilian held her breath and listened to the crickets chirping in harmony, but she didn't feel harmonious. Devan didn't seem like he did, either. He stared back into his cup, chewing his bottom lip as he clenched the edge of the table. Suddenly, he stood up, his face tight. "I'm not like Dad."

"Honey, I know that. I didn't mean to imply—"

"I know you didn't." He let out a heavy sigh. "I'm an adult, Mom. Trust me."

She swallowed again, feeling as though pebbles were lodged inside her throat. There was a knock on the door.

"Lilian?"

She recognized Nick's voice and stood up.

"I'll get it." Devan headed for the door, and Lilian felt more tightness in her throat. She could hardly breathe. Standing, she told herself her reactions to Nick were ridiculous. She hardly knew him. It didn't matter that she'd slept with him three years ago. It was a mistake—a big mistake since he'd been with who knew how many women before then, and probably even since then.

Nick entered the room, a beautiful woman who had to be Violet beside him. She was tall, like Nick. Lilian crossed the room and took her outstretched hand. "I hope your flight was okay."

"Long, but good." Violet smiled and squeezed Lilian's hand. "Thank you for letting us stay here. Dad says you're wonderful."

Lilian turned to Nick, blushing as her mind stumbled over what she should say and do. She wanted to hug him like they had when he'd dropped off Clara earlier. "You must be hungry," she stammered with a glance at Violet, "both of you."

Devan cleared his throat. "I'll fix some food." He turned to Violet with a weak smile. "I'll show you your room so you can drop off your bags."

Nodding, Violet kissed Nick on the cheek. "Love you, Dad."

He stepped away. "If you see your sister, tell her I'm coming to say goodbye."

Nick waited until Violet and Devan had left, and stepped closer. "My flight leaves for Brazil in a few hours, so I need to get going." His hand touched her, his gaze reeling her in. "Lilian, I need you to know that I ... no matter what stupid mistakes I've made, that I—"

He didn't have to finish. In a firm, tender grip, he pulled her to his chest and closed his mouth over hers, kissing her so fervently that he reminded her of her own nature to rush into things, to put her trust in her instincts and forget everything else. That was what had drawn her to him from the first moment she met him. That was how he had ended up in the back room of her cake shop, making her laugh and smile more than she had in years. She knew he had to see more than just pieces of her—the way he held her so completely.

Kissing him now, she reveled in his taste, the sweet warmth of his tongue against hers, his fingers moving up her back. He pressed her closer, slowly stopping the kiss. "I'll come back as fast as I can," he said with a half-smile. "There are things we need to resolve."

"You mean from three years ago or from when you showed up last week?"

"Both." He licked his bottom lip and cradled her face with both hands. So gentle. So serious. Every movement drew her in closer, and she understood why he'd said he was a good liar. Even if he wasn't being sincere, she couldn't dig through her softened emotions to see it. She melted against him.

"What if you don't come back?" The edges of her mind itched. She wanted to ask him about the woman he'd mentioned before, but she couldn't bring herself to form the words. She'd been able to talk to Devan; why couldn't she bring this up with Nick?

He pulled away, his face clouded like her bathroom mirror. He might have been able to see all of her, but she could only see pieces of him.

She took a step back, wanting to rush into his arms and kiss him again. She wanted to know he wasn't lying, wanted to forget about the guns he'd locked in her safe a week ago, wanted to push away the fact he'd used other women. Most of all she wanted to know the answer to her question lingering in the air.

"I always come back," he said, taking one last look at her as he opened the door. He nodded a quick goodbye and disappeared down the hallway.

Chapter 12
São Paulo

Nick pulled his duffle off the baggage claim and bent down to tie his shoe. Someone was watching him a few feet away. He didn't know who; he couldn't even see them. But he felt their eyes.

Tugging on his laces, he noticed a foil gum wrapper flattened to the floor. He grabbed it, looking back and forth as if in search for a trash can. Standing, he darted through the crowds, finally losing the man he wasn't sure he'd seen in the first place. He could have been imagining it. He caught a cab and gave the address to a building downtown—one of Matheus Ferreira's businesses.

Nick knew Ferreira wouldn't be in the building where the cab was taking him. In fact, he probably wasn't in São Paulo. Or Brazil. Nobody knew where he was except maybe Kyle or Catarina.

Watching the cab's rearview mirror, Nick noticed another taxi several cars back. So he hadn't imagined it. The taxi was too close, changing lanes exactly with his own cab.

Nick sighed. It wouldn't surprise him if Ferreira's men were tracking him. Ferreira had probably stationed men at the airport, waiting for him to show up and do something stupid. Or maybe it was Jeffrey following him.

"Stop here," Nick said. He handed the driver some bills and stepped out with his bag, noting the tailing taxi as it pulled to the curb half a block down. Just what he'd thought. The building he wanted was five blocks down, far enough away to lose a tail.

Nick didn't know what he wanted more—to find Jeffrey or Catarina. Both would be good, and the building five blocks down was the most likely place to find Catarina. He'd spent a week at the inn figuring out where she might be. Research on the Internet, carefully placed phone calls and e-mails, all things he'd done in his room while eating dinner and Rachel's brownies.

He'd eaten too many of those brownies. The humid air pulled beads of sweat from his skin. It rolled down his back and gathered around the waist of his pants. Out of the corner of his eye, a young man in a suit and tie, a baseball hat, and dark glasses, stepped out of the cab. Jeffrey.

Taking off in the opposite direction, Nick kept his pace brisk, but natural. It was obvious Jeffrey had no idea how to tail someone, despite his training. Too little time in the field.

Nick ducked into a clothing store and watched his son-in-law walk by, looking confused. Nick's mind filled with the questions he'd asked himself since Clara told him Jeffrey was probably in Brazil. Was it betrayal? A safety precaution? A trap? Nick groaned and watched Jeffrey stop in the middle of the busy sidewalk. He continued on, and Nick took off after him. If they were going to settle this, Nick wanted the upper hand by surprising him.

A street vendor yelled out as Nick walked through pungent scents of meat and garlic. A group of women slipped by, their perfume and conversation wafting behind them. Jeffrey was gone. Nick kept walking, but gritted his teeth. He'd never lost a lead.

Then he spotted him leaning against the doorway of a restaurant. They locked eyes. Jeffrey nodded once and disappeared into the building. Nick followed.

"It's about time you showed up," Jeffrey said as soon as Nick sat across from him in a quiet corner. It was noon. The smell of cooking meat on a rotisserie hung heavy in the air.

Nick leaned forward, squeezing the sides of the table until his fingers hurt. "What are you doing here? And why did you leave Clara? Is somebody on our tail?"

Jeffrey furrowed his brow and lifted his hands. He had taken off his sunglasses, but kept his cap on. He looked like a damn tourist. "Slow down. I'll explain."

"You'd better. How'd you find me?"

"I saw you at the airport."

"How long have you been waiting there?"

"Two weeks." Jeffrey wiped his brow, as if two weeks had seemed like forever. It probably had.

Nick leaned back and folded his arms, his fingernails digging into his palms as he surveyed the room for the fifteenth time. Nothing caught his eye. Yet. He figured his worst problem was sitting right in front of him. "Any of Ferreira's men there? One tracked me down a week ago."

"I know. CIA contacted me about the dead body in your kitchen. Not theirs."

Nick uncrossed his arms, ready to grab Jeffrey by the collar. "Are you working for Ferreira? Who's with you?"

Jeffrey's eyes darted to the side. "They're not here. You're not a top priority."

"Then why did I have to kill an assassin?" Nick clenched his hands into fists and tried to keep his voice low. "Start at the beginning. Tell me who you're really working for."

"How's Clara? I've been worried sick."

Nick grabbed Jeffrey's arm, squeezing until he winced. "Don't change the subject. Who?"

A defiant glare crossed Jeffrey's face. "Tell me about Clara first."

Fine. If Jeffrey wanted to play that way, Nick would humor him for now. Nick squeezed harder. "Clara's fine, thanks to me. What kind of a husband leaves like that? I had to make sure she and Violet were safe first or I would've flown down here right away to drag you back home."

Yanking his arm free, Jeffrey sighed. "I didn't have a choice. I made the best decision I could at the time. I knew Clara would be okay."

"And what decision was that?"

"The men were looking for her. They were trying to find you and figured she would lead them to you. The second I realized who they were, I decided—"

"How did you know who they were? You didn't even know where I was for two years."

"A lot of stuff passes my desk." Jeffrey rubbed his arm where Nick had grabbed him. "Ferreira is old news—a nuisance nobody can get rid of."

"He's more than a nuisance."

"Yeah, well, the second I heard a CIA officer was missing in Brazil, I pieced two and two together. Clara told me she couldn't contact you for two weeks."

"So you decided to take off with two assassins? What'd you tell them? I'm surprised they didn't shoot you on sight!"

"I told them Clara was missing and their boss had already contacted me." He shrugged. "I mentioned one name and they believed everything I said. I told them I didn't know where you were, but I could find you."

"What name? They believed you?"

Jeffrey's jaw tightened. He stared down at the table. "Kyle Mendez."

He knew it. "Damn you, Jeffrey. How the hell did you get involved with him outside of work? He's not even in your department. I checked."

"Shhh!" Jeffrey looked over Nick's shoulder at the doorway and reached inside his suit jacket. Nick caught sight of a shoulder holster and small pistol. "I'd tell you everything, but they've found us."

Nick slipped his bag over his shoulder and stood. He didn't bother looking back at whoever Jeffrey had seen in the restaurant doorway. Probably two men. Ferreira always sent them in twos.

Nick was surprised at Jeffrey's acting. He truly looked frightened as they rushed down a short hallway leading to the restrooms. Jeffrey turned into the kitchen where several boys, who were cooking meat looked up. "I don't think they're Ferreira's," he said over his shoulder as they slipped past the cooks and out a back door leading to the street.

Nick looked back. Nobody was following them. Yet. They entered the street shaded from the sun by several buildings. Halfway down, he looked behind his shoulder and caught sight of not two, but four men following them. Dressed in cheap suits, they looked calm and professional. Their expressions were cold. No guns in sight.

"They're back half a block," Nick said as he and Jeffrey approached an open square filled with people. "They're being careful." Which surprised Nick. Ferreira's men weren't afraid to kill in public. The police ignored any crime connected with them.

Jeffrey seemed more nervous by the second. His red face and constant glances over his shoulder confused Nick. If he was involved with Kyle and Ferreira, it didn't make sense why he would try and lead Nick away from them—unless it was a trap.

"Where are we going?" Jeffrey asked through clenched teeth.

"Keep moving." The men weren't pulling out any weapons. Obviously, as long as he and Jeffrey stayed in the crowd, they were safe. But that wouldn't last long, and Nick didn't have a weapon.

Jeffrey shook his head. "I don't know why Ferreira would be after me. His men think I'm leading you into their hands. Even if they mistrusted me, this isn't how they take care of business."

"Sure, Jeffrey, believe what you want, but when Ferreira wants you dead, you're dead fast. How the hell could you not know that? We'll be lucky if we make it through the next hour." He looked up the street. Where could he lose them? Hop into a cab? No, too easy to follow. An alley to narrow them in? A park with trees? "There are too many of them," he whispered. "If there were two—maybe even three. But four."

"I can handle two if you can."

Nick sped up, walking straight to an intersection where he hoped to slow the men down. He broke into a run and yanked Jeffrey into the street. Cars honked. One slammed on its brakes, barely missing them. A man leaned out and yelled.

"Are you trying to get us killed?" Jeffrey gasped as they jumped onto the curb and kept at a dead run down the sidewalk.

Nick looked back at the men. Good. They weren't as suicidal as he and Jeffrey. They had stopped on the curb waiting for the traffic to clear. One of the men met Nick's gaze and smiled.

Nick looked at the tall buildings. If he was quick enough, the men might not see where he and Jeffrey entered, but that was unlikely. He needed to pick a place with few people.

He stopped abruptly and pulled Jeffrey through the doorway of a building under construction on its upper levels. The lobby was still open to customers and buzzed with people.

"We'll use the stairs," Nick said.

Jeffrey followed him, still breathing heavily from their sprint down the sidewalk. "Why did we come in here? I thought we wanted to stay in a crowd."

"Not now."

They headed up the stairs. "Now tell me why you're not dead," Nick ordered when they started climbing. He imagined Jeffrey dead, how Clara might react, how he himself might feel. The thought made him cringe. He had a soft spot for Jeffrey, for how he made Clara smile and laugh.

"I knew I was going to die," Jeffrey said as they reached the top of another flight. "When I left Clara in the apartment, I thought I'd never see her again. I wanted them away from her, and I thought I could lead them away and make a run for it, but I didn't have a clue. I just played it by ear."

"Where did they take you?"

"Downtown. We met up with a Brazilian who asked me questions I couldn't answer. But he didn't seem to care. He mostly wanted to know if I could find you and if—"

Footsteps drifted up the stairwell. Nick and Jeffrey stopped dead in their tracks. Jeffrey reached for his gun, but Nick shook his head. "Not yet."

They had arrived at a deserted floor. Down a hallway, drills pounded between the sounds of workmen talking. Sheets of clear plastic hung in most of the doorways, and a web of construction tape blocked the next flight of stairs. Footsteps grew louder. Nick braced himself for the inevitable, his body tense.

"What's your plan?" Jeffrey asked, reaching for his gun again. "You want me to try and shoot them as they come up?"

"No, they'll be ready for that." Nick gave him an irritated look. "Have you forgotten all of your training?"

The footsteps grew closer, and Nick closed his eyes. The thought of killing any of the four men made his stomach turn. Even the assassin he'd killed in his kitchen haunted him, usually late at night when he was trying to fall asleep.

He backed into the open doorway of the landing, locking eyes with Jeffrey. "Forget the upper floors. They'll guess we headed to this floor since the upper ones are taped off."

Jeffrey followed him through the doorway. It led down a short hall to the left and an empty lobby to the right. Jeffrey leaned against the wall on one side of the door, and Nick dropped his bag and took the other side. The open doorway between them felt like an ocean. They would work together for survival, but beyond that Nick felt a threat buried in Jeffrey's strange behavior.

The whispering grew louder. Nick stared up at the ceiling. "Try and disarm them first," he breathed through his teeth, hoping Jeffrey could discern the words. "If there's two of them, we should be fine. If there's four—"

"I'll be fine."

The whispering and footsteps stopped. Nick looked away from Jeffrey and readied every muscle in his body, focusing his attention on the possible scenarios and what he would do in each one. He felt this was the best plan, but he had never seen Jeffrey in combat; he had no idea what to expect.

They came through the doorway, two of them aiming pistols. Nick smiled. They were acting just as he expected.

Jeffrey grabbed the first man's wrist and elbow—an olive-skinned man built like a tank. The second man, so short he only came to Nick's shoulders, entered on his tail.

A low yelp of pain escaped the olive-skinned man's throat when Jeffrey broke his arm and slipped the .45 into his own hands. With an angry grunt, Jeffrey slammed the butt of the gun against the man's neck, right below his hairline. He dropped instantly.

Not bad, Nick thought with a sigh of relief. Following similar protocol, he brought down his short opponent, a dark-skinned Brazilian who made no sound at all when both bones in his forearm snapped with a sickening crack.

Jeffrey straightened his shoulders and smirked. "That was easy."

"The other two," Nick stuttered after glancing down the empty stairwell. Where were they? They couldn't have possibly—

Jeffrey's eyes widened the same moment a muffled gunshot ripped through the air. He collapsed. Nick spun around, aiming the .45 he'd snatched from the Brazilian. Two more men with guns raced toward him. The whites of their eyes gleamed. Why hadn't they shot him in the back? Where the hell had they come from?

Nick thought about a lot of things as he aimed the barrel of his pistol at the closest man's kneecap. Mostly, he thought of Clara huddled in the closet and it took all his effort not to raise the gun to the man's heart. He kept his aim on the knee and fired twice.

The man stumbled, but didn't fall.

Did he miss?

Nick gritted his teeth and aimed again, relieved the gun had a silencer. At least the workmen would remain oblivious as long as nobody screamed or yelled.

Nick's second shot missed entirely. Confused, he caught a brief glimpse of the man's upper thigh where blood blossomed through his tan suit pants. Damn it, he'd missed the kneecap. What was wrong with him?

Now upon him, the men still didn't shoot. Instead, they used their guns to harden their blows to Nick's body. Blocking them all with carefully executed swipes and kicks to whatever limb came at him, he felt his attackers' increasing anger and frustration. He could handle two at the same time. No sweat.

Until the uninjured man forced a dynamic punch to his jaw.

It shook the world around him, but he hardly stumbled, fighting off several more blows. One more to his arm knocked the .45 from his grip. One to the side of his head. Another to his shoulder. A knee rammed into the small of his back. He gasped. What about Jeffrey? He didn't even know if he was still alive.

A surge of adrenaline sharpened Nick's senses and drew more strength to his movements, landing one solid strike to the injured Brazilian's face, right between his eyes. Then a kick to his shot leg. The man stumbled back, shaking his head.

Nick turned his full attention to his remaining opponent. Smaller than his injured partner, and in less pain, the man moved deftly. His fighting style confused Nick—movements he had never seen. His face hit the floor with a jarring smack.

Chapter 13

The darkness didn't last. When Nick opened his eyes, his stomach lurched. A foot kicked him. Blow after blow hit his ribs until the injured Brazilian picked up his bag then yanked him from the floor and dragged him down the stairwell. He shoved his gun into Nick's side and cursed in Portuguese.

Nick looked behind his shoulder to see the shorter man helping Jeffrey down the stairs. So he wasn't dead. But he wasn't in good shape. His left leg was covered in blood, the bullet probably lodged in his kneecap, or just above it. Jeffrey looked like he might puke, and mouthed at Nick: *Not Ferreira's men.*

Nick turned around in time to start down the next flight of stairs. The Brazilian dug his gun deeper. Nick gave him a glare. "I'm not running, all right?"

The man grunted. "You don't even know where I'm taking you." Instead of heading down to the bottom of the stairwell, he turned onto the next landing and led Nick through a similar doorway as the floor above.

Deserted, the lobby and hallways echoed Jeffrey's moans as they stumbled down to the back of the building. The Brazilian shoved Nick through a door that led outside. The sun blazed. Nick hurried down the stairs and stopped on the last step. The Brazilian grabbed him by the arm and rammed the gun into his ribs again. "Get in." He motioned to a black van parked at the bottom of the stairway. Two men, one holding a rifle, had already opened the back doors. They waited for Nick and Jeffrey to climb inside.

Completely empty, the back of the van offered no comfort to Nick's sore body. He kneeled in the center as one of the men tied his hands behind his back, then shoved him to the side and tied his ankles. They did the same with Jeffrey's hands, but left his ankles alone. The blood from his wound had soaked most of his dark pant leg from the bottom of his thigh all the way down. The drenched material gleamed in the sunlight until the two new men climbed inside and shut the doors. The van's engine roared and started to move. The only light came from two small tinted windows on either side of the van. Nick stared at Jeffrey across from him. He had fallen onto his side and was at least taking the pain well. No tears.

"Look at me," Nick ordered in English. The other two men, one with a gun pointed at Nick, scowled through the darkness.

Jeffrey looked up and smiled. "Not what you planned, huh? I didn't see them until it was too late. They came up another stairway, I guess. Or the elevator, I don't know."

Nick shook his head. "You'll be fine." He glanced at the two men, but they didn't seem to care that he was speaking. "Start talking, Jeffrey."

"What do you mean?" Jeffrey's voice was barely above a whisper. He winced and rested all his weight on his shoulder. The blood from his leg dripped to the floor of the van. Nick could smell it. Still nauseous, he tried to ignore the smell and focused his attention on Jeffrey's face.

"Don't be stupid. You must know as well as I do Kyle's as slimy as they come. How are you involved with him? From work?"

"I haven't had time to explain anything," Jeffrey whimpered. "I'm not sure this is the best place—"

"This place is fine. If I'm going to die in the next twenty-four hours, I want to know if my son-in-law is a traitor. Tell me about Kyle."

Staring at the floor, Jeffrey said, "You're not going to like any of this. But you have to understand I meant well. Everything is for you and Clara."

Nick was silent. Whatever Jeffrey was about to confess, it couldn't be as bad as Kyle's betrayal. A trusted colleague, a solid year of lies. He kept his eyes on Jeffrey, sure his pained expression wasn't from his wound.

"I know I told you I moved from the Air Force to the DEA for classified reasons, but now I can tell you they were never classified. Kyle is the reason. I met him in college, and we were good friends for a long time before he talked me into it. He worked for the San Diego division. It sounded like a nice place to live, and I'd be making a lot more money."

Yes, money. Nick knew Jeffrey loved it. He always had. Over the years he had given Clara everything she wanted. Nick had thought it was great until now.

"Then you introduced me to Clara. You know the rest of that story."

"Yes." Clara had been going to school in San Diego. It only seemed natural to introduce them. Nick waited for Jeffrey to start talking again. Minutes passed as the van made frequent stops, apparently stuck in traffic.

Jeffrey closed his eyes. "Then Kyle showed me a way to make more money."

"Oh?"

"I started selling."

"Selling what?"

"Drugs."

Nick's stomach twinged. "I hope to God you're not using. If you—"

"Hell no! I'm not that stupid."

"Nobody caught you selling? The DEA is pretty damned strict."

"Kyle was higher up. He knew his way around the system. I didn't have to worry."

Nick squeezed his hands into fists and slowly let them loose. "How did you explain this to Clara?" He glanced at the two men in front of the double doors. Apparently bored, the gunless man had closed his eyes. The other kept his rifle aimed.

"I never explained anything to her," Jeffrey answered. "I told her I'd earned a raise, and we moved into the apartment we wanted. We went on trips. We started looking at alternative possibilities for a baby."

"A baby?" Nick's mind spun. "Clara didn't tell me you were trying."

"We didn't want to tell you yet."

"What do you mean alternative possibilities?" Nick said, confused.

"We tried for a while, but we found out she can't have children."

Nick's heart sank. He'd always dreamed of grandchildren, of making up for all the time he'd missed with Violet and Clara. He'd talked to Clara every week. Even the past few days she could have told him. He recalled the four-day trip to West Virginia, all the meals Clara had quietly eaten, picking at her food, sipping her soda as her nervous eyes avoided him. It wasn't like her to keep things from him. It reminded him of her mother. Behind a wall.

Jeffrey was pale, almost colorless. "Clara and I haven't been on the best of terms lately."

"What do you mean? Did she find out about the drugs? How long have you been selling?"

"A few years. I don't do it all the time. I know it's stupid and wrong, but I got used to the money, and I was afraid if I didn't do it, Kyle might make things hard for me."

"Money. Bullshit. I trusted you! Clara trusted you. You've put drugs and money in criminal hands all so you could, I don't know, buy more things? I don't understand." He glared at Jeffrey. "Look at me, damn it."

Jeffrey squeezed his eyes shut. "You're right. I knew you'd react this way. I guess you might as well know the rest."

"There's more?"

"You have no idea how hard this is for me to—"

"Spit it out. I'll get it one way or another."

"Fine, fine." Jeffrey was almost panting. His words came out slow. "Clara's been distant lately—like she doesn't want to be with me anymore. Off and on, like she's trying to make up her mind about something. She'll be happy for a few months, then quiet. I've tried to give her things she wants, but that hasn't helped. We settled on an expensive procedure to try and have a child, but then she backed out of it. She's done that twice now."

Maybe Clara knew more than Jeffrey thought she did. If so, Nick couldn't blame her for having doubts. He wondered, with a sharp pain in his chest, why she hadn't asked her own father for help. But he already knew the answer.

Jeffrey sucked in a shaky breath and continued. "A year after I started selling—about two years ago now, things were bad between me and Clara. Kyle suggested I leave her. He told me there were opportunities to make more money. He said I could be in charge of groups of men. Power. Wealth. That sort of thing."

"That sounds like him. What was he asking?"

"I don't know. I never agreed so he never told me."

Nick had a good idea of what Kyle might offer. Drug cartels, probably. He recalled scattered white buttons on the bunker's stained concrete, Kyle kneeling over Catarina's half-naked body. Sweat beaded his shaved head, his smooth skin black as licorice.

Nick almost fell over as the van swung around a corner. He stared at the pool of blood below Jeffrey's knee. He might never walk easily again, if at all.

"Keep going," he urged. "So you told Kyle no and he left you alone?"

"Not exactly. He just ... left."

"Of course," Nick muttered. "He came here. That's about the time he said the DEA sent him over."

"My boss said something about Kyle and an assignment, but it was hush-hush. I didn't talk to Kyle again until a week ago."

"When you left with Ferreira's men?"

Jeffrey gasped, his leg twitching as he held his breath. He finally opened his mouth. "Yes, when I left."

"Tell me again why you came here. How did you even get here?"

"They flew me on a private jet. And I told you why I came. I wanted to lead them away from Clara. They thought they could get to you through her."

"That's why you came all the way to Brazil?"

"No, that's why I left the apartment with them. I came to Brazil because I thought you'd either be here already or you would come back."

"Why would you figure that?"

Jeffrey looked Nick directly in the eyes. Nick had never seen him so earnest. "I thought you might come back to try and clear your name. You didn't murder Ferreira's wife. I know you."

He said it with such conviction that Nick's anger subsided. He stared at the ceiling of the van and wrestled with the fear of where they were going. The van slowed to a stop and sat idling. No traffic. No muffled talking up front.

"Do you know where we are?" Jeffrey asked.

"No."

"Then what's wrong?"

Lowering his eyes to Jeffrey's leg, Nick gulped. Blood dripped steadily. The crimson pool had shifted back and forth during the drive, sending Nick's thoughts straight to his kitchen floor. Crisp red on the white linoleum. He twisted and puked across the floor of the van, angry he couldn't wipe his mouth.

"Are you all right? Does blood bother you?"

"No, it doesn't."

"Are you hurt, then? You're turning pale."

"You're not one to talk. I've seen dead men with more color. You're losing a lot of blood." He turned to the man with the rifle and asked in Portuguese, "Why are we stopped? Where are we?"

The man glanced at Nick's puddle of vomit and wrinkled his nose.

"Hey!" Nick yelled. "Why are we stopped?"

The van's engine turned off. Two doors slammed and the back of the van opened, flooding the interior with sunlight. The two guards in front of the door jumped down and Nick squinted as a woman stepped into view. Catarina.

Chapter 14
West Virginia

Lilian picked up a smooth stone and rubbed it between her fingers as Devan walked beside her. The lake lapped along the shore, leaving sand between gaps in the rocks. Devan's boots, a pair of hand-me-downs from his father, made an impression of a pair of spread eagle wings from toe to heel.

Straightening her shoulders, Lilian kept her pace. The stone in her hands was cold in the late afternoon warmth. "Devan," she said quietly, "I wanted to take a walk so we can discuss something." She waved her hand in the air when Devan slowed his pace and gave her an annoyed look. "I don't mean Clara. I mean your dad. We never talk about your dad."

Stopping in his tracks, Devan turned to face her. The sun glinted in his eyes, making them bright. "Is everything okay? Did he call you?"

"What? No, he never calls me." Lilian had resented that at first, how Chris hadn't seemed bothered by the divorce at all. He wasn't supposed to be, she knew that. But it hurt anyway—to end a twenty-seven year relationship and imagine him so happy about the whole thing. He called Devan, of course. They met all the time, but Lilian never heard any details.

"Do you want him to call you?" Devan tilted his head, his expression confused. "What's this about?"

Staring at the lake, Lilian watched the sunshine reflect off the ripples. It was beautiful and calm. She wanted to feel that way, but turmoil had been building inside her since Nick had left for Brazil. She'd been thinking about Chris more, about how something so stable could end so badly. Seeing Nick again had opened up old wounds she'd thought were healed. She felt if things worked out with him, Chris would always be a shadow blocking her sunlight, reminding her nothing good ever lasted. Or maybe she and Chris were never good in the first place.

Devan blinked. "Mom?"

"I'm sorry." She started walking again. "Maybe I just needed a walk. I don't expect you to understand."

"Understand what?" Devan's hands took her shoulders and pulled her into an embrace. Surprised, Lilian hugged him back. "I know you're hurting," he said softly against her face. "The divorce hurt me, too, but I'm

123

here, okay? Dad still loves you in his own way. He talks about you sometimes and he misses you."

"He does?" Pulling away, she stared at the ground. Her feet had sunk into one of Devan's footprints, right between the wings. Chris missed her. Somehow, that didn't ease her ache one bit. It made it worse.

"Of course he misses you. He just says things had to change. You changed."

"I didn't change. He's the one who thought I wasn't good enough anymore. Things were fine." She stared at the ground again. Her feet were sinking deeper into Devan's footprint.

"I don't know, Mom. I don't know what happened." Devan's voice was deflated. "I'll let you be alone. I think I need to be alone, too." Lilian felt his touch on her arm, and then he turned away and Lilian dropped the stone in her hands. She watched him walk up the shore. He was right. This wasn't something he could fix. She wasn't even sure what needed to be fixed.

Frustrated, she left the lakeshore and picked her way through the undergrowth to the road, telling herself over and over that Nick had nothing to do with Chris. She ripped the blades from their roots. A soft humming drew her attention away, and a slim figure appeared around the road bend. Violet.

She was dressed in a pair of tight jeans that showed off her long legs and tiny waist beneath layers of a button-up shirt and camisole. From her heavy-duty boots and soiled backpack, Lilian guessed she was out for a hike looking for insects.

"Hello," Violet said softly as they stopped in front of each other. She smiled and adjusted the backpack across her shoulders. "I came out to collect samples."

"Of bugs?"

"Beetles. Carabids—cicindelidae, specifically."

Lilian wrinkled her brow and Violet laughed.

"Ground beetles."

Lilian lowered her eyes to Violet's backpack and noticed three beetle pins pushed into one of the straps over her shoulders. They had rainbow-colored backs. Colorful, like Violet. Despite her gray eyes and dull brown hair, she seemed more vibrant than Clara.

"So that's what you do?" Lilian asked with a raised eyebrow at the beetles on Violet's backpack. "You study those nasty-looking creatures that scuttle across my floor in the middle of the night?"

Violet laughed again. "I wanted to ask you about the butterflies since my dad used to bring us up here when we were kids. We saw a small migration of them once."

Now they were on comfortable turf. Lilian could discuss butterflies. Maybe. She shivered in the warm air. "Yes, they come through here a lot. It's not normal for them to stop in the exact same place every year, but a lot of them rest in this area on their way to Mexico. They like the trees or the flowers, or something."

"So that's why you built the inn?"

"I didn't build it. It was an old house from the forties. Nobody wanted it until I came along."

Violet looked behind her shoulder where the inn, white and blue from reflections of sky in the windows, glittered through the trees. Looking at it now, Lilian's chest swelled with pride. She switched her mind back to beetles. "Come on," she urged, and motioned Violet down the road. "There's a riverbed up ahead where I think you might find some beetles. Lots of them."

Violet nodded and followed closely. "Beetles are good, but I'm feeling nostalgic for the butterflies. I didn't see my father much when I was a kid, but butterflies remind me of him ... and my mother. She loved the butterflies. That's why my dad kept bringing us up here to the mountains to see them."

Lilian nearly stopped in her tracks as she made the connection between Nick and butterflies. Instead, she quickened her pace. "Why these mountains specifically?"

"My grandparents are from here, and I grew up in Charleston and lived there until—" She gave Lilian a weak smile. "You know about my mother, right?"

"I know she passed away." She couldn't bring herself to say it any other way. She remembered what Nick had told her. The pills. The alcohol.

Violet crouched and started digging in the dirt with her manicured fingernails. "Yes, she died ten years ago. I moved away after that."

Lilian wasn't sure if she should ask why. Violet peered at the dirt, holding her breath as she overturned a rock and a long black beetle scrambled away from her fingers. She scooped it into her palm and stood up, the insect racing from one hand to the other.

"Where did you move to?" Lilian asked.

"England. I had an offer from a university there to be a research entomologist and decided I should take it." She smiled. "A big step for me since I'd never lived anywhere but here."

"So what about your sister? What did she do?"

"Clara was still in high school. Dad stayed home until she graduated."

Lilian refrained from asking too many questions. Mostly, she needed to know why Nick had come to her when he was in so much danger. Was it because he was in love with her? Or was it the inn and its seclusion? It seemed absurd that he would remember her after all those years if he had been involved with so many other women. Then she remembered the butterflies, the one connection between her and Annabelle. If he had memories of Annabelle here with the monarchs, he would naturally be drawn to a spot where he had been happy.

"Violet," she asked in a hushed voice. "Where did your mother die?"

Violet leaned down to set the beetle back onto the ground. "She died in France while we were traveling." She stood and brushed the dirt off her hands. Her gray eyes were so much like Nick's that Lilian had to look away. "With all of you there? I thought Nick said he was away."

"Yes, it was just me and Mom." She returned her focus to Lilian and frowned. "That's when she told me about the divorce. But I, I'd rather not talk about it. I'm sorry." She turned away and slipped the backpack from her shoulders. "I need to collect more samples. I've got to get something done while I'm here."

Violet pulled a Mason jar from the backpack, unscrewed the lid, and set both on a flat rock. She started searching the ground again.

"I'll see you back at the inn," Lilian said softly.

"Oh, I'm sorry." Violet straightened. "Thanks for talking with me. Sorry if I'm not the best conversationalist." She laughed and her smile looked like Nick's, too. Lilian wondered why Nick never talked about her since they were so much alike.

"It's all right. You're welcome here anytime, whether you're a great conversationalist or not."

Violet's smile faded. "Thank you, but I hope you're not bothered by Clara. She likes to attach herself to people. I've tried talking to her, but we don't, well, I don't know. Anyway, I'm sorry."

"Stop apologizing, please. I promised your father both of you are welcome here, and it'll stay that way."

"Well, in that case, there's something I want to show you. She's beautiful."

"She?"

"The monarch. She just broke from her chrysalis yesterday. Clara didn't care, but I thought you might."

"Yes, I'm very interested."

Violet shoved the Mason jar back in her bag, and they headed out of the trees to the road. Lilian sensed her excitement. She was sure both of them had seen the butterfly cycle a hundred times before, but it was always a miracle.

When they reached the inn, Lilian entered Violet's room, noticing that every flat surface except the floor and the bed was covered with jars. The jars were lined on the bottom with dirt and twigs, the glass glowing in the sun from the windows. Beetles, mostly, some grasshoppers, a praying mantis, a lot of spiders.

Lilian shuddered. "Did you find these inside?"

"Just those two." Violet motioned to two jars on the window sill. One contained a beetle the size of her thumb, trying to climb up the glass. The other one looked empty.

"Why are you keeping them?" Lilian asked and wrapped her arms around her waist. A hundred roving eyes stared at her.

"Where is she? Oh, I put her over here." Violet lifted a jar, larger than the others, and held it up to the sunlight. "Don't worry, I'll let them all go before I leave. I'm just taking notes and drawing sketches. Easier to do when they're confined, you know?"

"Sure." Lilian didn't ask where Violet had collected all the jars. Probably Rachel.

Violet laughed. "I'm sorry. Would you rather me not keep them inside?"

"No, no, it's all right."

"Well, here. You're not afraid of butterflies." Violet motioned her over. "This is a female. See? No spots on the hind wing vein."

Stepping over to the jar, Lilian peered inside at a monarch perched on a tall twig. Its wings were closed. Most people who hadn't seen a monarch before were surprised how large they were, almost four inches across. The monarch in the jar looked as if it might not have room to spread its wings if it tried. "You're going to release it soon, right?"

"Of course. I wanted to see if you have any tags, though. I know it's a little early, but since it's the beginning of August, she's probably a fourth-generation."

"Which means she'll migrate." Lilian nodded. "Yes, I think I have some tags. The scientists always leave some when they come to study them."

"How many scientists come up?"

"Three or four a year." She frowned, thinking of the articles she had read. "I guess the populations were doing really well, but they took a hit two years ago. That's normal, fluctuations and everything, but the reports keep saying it's worse this time." A sudden heaviness weighed down her shoulders.

"Oh, I know. There's illegal cutting down in Mexico. They can't live without the cover of the trees."

Lilian tried to control the shaking in her voice, but it came through loud and clear. "Your father told me he thinks it might have something to do with somebody in

Brazil. That's all he said. And he gave me an article he read on the plane when he went to get Clara."

Violet looked at her hands. She seemed to be holding her breath. "Did my dad say anything to you about me? I mean, anytime you were with him? Before he left?"

Lilian shook her head. "He told me not to check you and Clara into the computer. He said you'll be safer that way."

"Right. Safer." Violet snatched the monarch jar and brushed past Lilian. "C'mon. Let's see if she'll fly. The weather's perfect."

"I'll get a tag and write down the number first."

When they stepped onto the porch, Lilian looked along the lakeshore for Devan, but he had disappeared. Violet unscrewed the lid of the jar covered with a piece of stretched nylon and reached in to retrieve the monarch. Cupping it in her palm, she held its wings closed and tilted it to Lilian, who carefully attached the tag. Violet lifted her arm and held the monarch to the sun. "Fly," she whispered, flicking her hand. "Come on."

The butterfly tipped, almost falling, but clung to Violet's skin with its wings folded tightly.

"I killed my mother," Violet said, her voice monotone as she kept her eyes fastened to the butterfly.

Lilian stiffened and blinked. "What?"

"That's how my mother died. I thought my dad might have told you."

"No, he never said that." Lilian processed the information slowly.

"Yes, I'll tell you the whole story sometime. You know, I don't think she's going to make it."

"The monarch?"

"Yeah." She flicked her hand again, this time hard enough to send the butterfly spinning into the air. It tumbled for a minute, a falling orange leaf plummeting to the ground. Lilian gasped, surprised at Violet's cruel release of the insect. And then, with a sudden burst of spirit, the butterfly opened her wings and glided into flight. She soared on the air and disappeared into the forest.

"Lil?"

Lilian turned around to see Rachel leaning through the open doorway of the inn.

"That new guest just called. He's almost here. You wanted him in room three, right?"

Lilian smiled. "Oh, the scientist. Yes, put him in the east room."

Violet leaned against the porch railing, screwing the lid back onto the jar. "So one's staying here?"

"Yes, he's new, though." Lilian turned to see a dark Toyota emerge from the shaded road. It pulled into the parking lot and a tall black man stepped out, running a hand over his smoothly shaved head.

"He's a handsome one, isn't he?" Rachel said with a smile. "I'll go get his reservation ready."

Lilian wrinkled her nose. He was very handsome. He pulled some bags from his trunk and headed to the porch, smiling when he met Lilian's eyes.

"You must be Lilian," he said, grinning so wide his teeth gleamed like pearls. "Robert Allen." He shook her hand.

She remembered his name from her phone conversation with him a week earlier, and nodded. "I'm happy you're here."

"So am I." He pulled her hand closer and squeezed. His smile was lopsided. "I'm very happy to be here."

Chapter 15
Brazil

She looked different than she had in the jungle. Her makeup covered the bruises Kyle had given her on both cheekbones, and her sand-colored hair was shiny and clean. The loose waves bounced as she stepped closer to the van, lowering her eyebrows.

"Cut their bonds," she ordered the men standing behind her, giving Nick a quick smirk. Two dimples in her cheeks deepened, innocent and childlike. But they didn't last.

"Catarina," Nick growled, blinking from the sun. He was surprised at the gruffness in his voice, but the smell of Jeffrey's blood reminded him Catarina wasn't what he had thought.

Her face grew cold, and she turned to her men before walking away. "Take the injured one upstairs to Gibson. You know what to do with the other one."

With his hands and feet finally free, and no gun pointed at his head, Nick wanted to run, but he wasn't that foolish, and he couldn't leave Jeffrey. The men led them around a corner where a white stucco house stood inside a perimeter of tall concrete walls and a grove of trees. The two-story house was larger and more privately secluded than most Nick had seen in São Paulo—red tile roof, barred windows.

As soon he was inside, Nick threw out the idea of escape. Everywhere he turned, a mass of muscle holding a rifle stared back at him. Jeffrey, still hanging on his captor's arm, turned to Nick. His voice trembled. "I'll be fine, right?"

Nick kept his expression calm. "Of course." He wanted to add, "Don't do anything stupid," but two men pulled him down a hallway before he could open his mouth. They pushed him into a tiny windowless room with blue walls and a small bed and nightstand.

"She'll be in soon," one of the men said in Portuguese before he shut the door. Nick heard it lock. Great. He could try and break it down, but now wasn't the time. He paced the room instead. It smelled like dryer sheets and garlic. He looked at the quilt on the bed, handmade. A small vase of flowers on the night stand. He guessed this was Catarina's home. One of them. Seeing her again made him angry.

He missed the quiet days he'd spent researching the right lead, befriending them over months and sometimes years, working under some boring cover career that usually involved a desk and a quiet office. It all paid off when he made the right contact and got valuable information to the U.S. government, possibly saving lives. But fighting armed men in empty hallways and running around in the jungle with dead termites pasted on his skin wasn't his forte.

Sitting on the edge of the bed, he buried his face in his hands and closed his eyes. What did Catarina want? She'd been a mystery to him since the first time he met her in the jungle. It was still so clear in his mind, the birds still singing loudly in his ears.

He followed Kyle into the cold, damp bunker. The stench of urine was so strong that bile rose up his throat. Four bodies lay strewn across the cold cement—all shot in the head and chest multiple times. Two wore bulletproof vests beneath their cotton shirts that were riddled with bullet holes and oozing blood. Nothing like an AK-47 at close range to rip through Kevlar.

Nick looked away from the dead faces. He saw blood splattered across the cement in a violent, sweeping spray, and immediately searched for Catarina. There she was, curled on the floor against the back wall.

With his steel-toed boot, Kyle kicked him forward. "In the corner," he growled in Portuguese. The other men, busy pulling the dead bodies out of the bunker, grunted and glanced at Nick with nervous expressions. It was obvious they knew what Kyle had planned all along. How had he not seen it? Of course, there had been nothing solid to tip him off. Nick had thought Kyle played his loyalty to Ferreira too well—but for how long? Their friendship had seemed genuine the entire year Nick had known him.

His mind spinning in circles, Nick sat down next to Catarina. She had sandy hair and creamy white skin. White? Wasn't she supposed to be Brazilian? He had imagined a bronze-skinned beauty with big black eyes and long thick hair. That's how everyone described her, but nobody he'd met had ever really seen her. Ferreira was well-known from photos taken of him before his terrorist acts—a tall, fair-skinned devil with white hair and distinguished creases around his vicious, gray eyes. There were no photos of Catarina.

With her arms tied behind her waist, she stared at the cement wall. Her dirty, frizzy hair reached down to her shoulder blades. She seemed to be crying, but Nick couldn't see her face. He looked up at Kyle. "What? You're not going to tie me up?"

"Oh, I will in a sec." Kyle kept his rifle aimed at Nick's head.

Pressing his tongue against the backs of his dirty teeth, Nick kept himself from doing or saying anything stupid. Six men with rifles against one unarmed, angry man. His odds were not good. He didn't stand a chance.

A low groan came from Catarina. Her body flinched, and she finally looked up at Nick with hungry, thirsty eyes. They were beautiful eyes—bright green. Maybe if he played his cards right things could still work out. He could be on her side now—more than before. He was a victim, too.

"What happened?" she asked in a cracked whisper.

Nick's eyes widened. English? A slight Texan accent? Who was this woman? "You're Catarina?" he asked quietly with a glance up at Kyle, who was giving orders to his men.

"Yes," she said quietly. "They've captured you? You were with them?"

He nodded, surprised at her observance.

"You were going to kill me?" she asked.

Nick looked up at Kyle, who was still distracted. Apparently they thought a guard was hiding somewhere outside the bunker. He took the chance to lean closer to Catarina and look her in the eyes. "No, I was going to take you back to your husband." He wasn't about to tell her he wanted to bribe her into espionage and wring every ounce of information out of her. He smiled softly. "Your husband sent us here to get you back."

Her lips tightened into a straight line. She fastened her attention to the wall.

"Catarina," he whispered. "You've been here for several weeks. How many men have guarded you?"

"Six."

Four killed in the bunker and the guard Nick had shot. That left one more, just as the others were discussing. One man loose wouldn't be good for any of them. Himself included.

Kyle returned his attention to Nick after someone threw him a ball of black nylon rope. "Turn around; hands behind your back."

Nick did as he was told. "Why don't you just shoot me?" he asked as Kyle yanked the rope around his wrists so tightly it ripped into his flesh. Nick kept his expression emotionless.

"Because Ferreira has plans for you," he laughed. "He doesn't like people trying to find him. Really pisses him off. Damn, you were easy to fool."

"I trusted you. I thought you were my friend," Nick muttered. "Trusted the CIA and DEA reports, the background checks I did myself, the whole lie." He squirmed as warm blood trickled down his fingers. "How long?"

"Oh, it's all recent."

"Who bribed you, then?"

"None of your business. Turn around."

Nick turned, leaning his shoulders against the wall. Kyle stared down at him with a smug grin. The cap on his head cast a shadow over his eyes. "Can't wait to see Ferreira's face when we hand him both you and his wife." He looked at Catarina and wet his lips. "After I've had my fill, of course."

Nick's stomach turned. "You wouldn't."

"No?"

"Ferreira would kill you."

Catarina shifted her body across the cement and shook her head. Her eyes squeezed shut with a pained expression. "He won't care," she muttered to the wall in Portuguese.

Smiling, Kyle tapped his dirty fingers against the trigger of his rifle. He twisted his expression into an evil scowl. "Both of you will wish you were dead before we get out of here." His laugh echoed off the walls as he nudged Catarina with his toe. "Sit up." He rocked her back and forth, digging his toe into her ribs. She opened her eyes and waited. "Sit up!"

With a jerk, she lifted the upper half of her body from the floor and turned to face Kyle, pulling her knees close to her chest as she stared straight ahead, her eyes dilated from the weak light. Her face was blank. "They hurt you?" Kyle asked.

"Who?"

"Felipe and his men."

"No, they didn't hurt me." Sarcasm tinged her voice.

"Stand up."

With her hands still tied behind her back, she struggled to get to her feet. Kyle offered no help. Finally, she faced him. "Did you come to take me to my husband?"

"Yes."

She stepped forward and stuck out her chin. "Did he order you to take me to him?"

"You could say that." Kyle snapped his fingers at Renato, who threw him a canteen of water. Catarina stared wide-eyed as Kyle unscrewed the cap and took a long swig. "Thirsty?" he asked.

She narrowed her eyes and Kyle chuckled. Keeping his attention on her, he tossed both his rifle and the canteen back to Renato. "Come with me." He grabbed her by the arm.

She didn't struggle as he pulled her a few feet away where several bamboo mats and wool blankets lay rolled out across the floor. Nick ground his teeth when Kyle ordered Catarina to lie down. She dropped to her knees, and with her hands still tied behind her, struggled to lower herself onto her back. Kyle kneeled beside her. "You aren't afraid of me?" he asked.

"You're no different than any other man."

Kyle pulled a large knife from the belt on his hip. He waved the blade above her face. "We'll see about that."

Nick struggled to stand, his heart reverberating in his ears. "Leave her the hell alone, Kyle. If Ferreira wants her back, just take her back."

Kyle snapped his attention to Nick, his dark face still covered with mud, his white eyes glowing in the sunlight that fell on him from the blown doorway. He removed his cap and ran his hand over his head. A wide grin spread across his face. His teeth looked like pearls. "You have no idea what you're up against. Face it, Nick, you're done."

Then his grin faded, replaced by sadness and anger. A long moment stretched between them, something solid, but unidentifiable. "What?" Nick asked, confused.

The sadness deepened on Kyle's face. "If you could get your wife back, I'll bet you'd go to a hell of a lot of trouble to do it."

Nick blinked. What was he talking about? Annabelle? What did this have to do with Annabelle? Kyle had never had a wife, unless he'd lied. Or maybe it was about his son.

Shaking his head, the sadness gone now, Kyle turned to Catarina and grabbed the top of her blouse. With a violent jerk, he ripped it open. White buttons flew left and right, rolling across the floor until they stuck in a pool of blood leftover from the shooting. Catarina's naked breasts were paler than the rest of her. She stayed still. Kyle lowered his knife to her collarbone.

Nick had seen enough. Finally on his feet, he lunged forward, angling his elbows for Kyle's face. They hit with a loud thump, and Kyle grunted. Nick felt himself fly backward, a sudden pain in his chest. He turned to see the butt of Kyle's rifle aimed straight for his head. Everything went black.

The sound of a door opening brought Nick back to Catarina's blue-walled room. He lifted his face from his hands to see her standing in the doorway, looking angry. "So," he said, glaring. "Was all this necessary?"

"No, but from what I understand, you two turned it into a fight." Catarina shut the door and walked to the center of the room, hands on her hips. "You shouldn't have run."

"I had no idea they were your men. Now my son-in-law has a bullet in his leg."

"He'll be fine." She glanced at the ceiling. "He's upstairs with my surgeon right now. I trust Gibson with my life."

Nick guessed she was speaking from experience. He rubbed the healing wound on his temple.

"This is your own fault," Catarina said with a toss of her head. "I told you to stay away from my husband." She stepped closer.

"I didn't come back for Ferreira." Nick stood and faced her, his heart pounding. His emotions felt obscure, like looking through thick glass.

Catarina wrinkled her brow. "If you didn't come for Matheus, then why are you here? For Kyle?"

"I came to find you."

Her eyes widened. "You didn't think I was dead? All the reports confirm it. They're everywhere."

Nick nodded, remembering his plane ride back to the U.S., how he'd almost spilled his drink when the story streamed through his headphones. "I heard about your murder, but my name isn't out there yet. They're assuming it's some CIA officer gone off the deep end, but I know all the fingers will end up pointing at me." He also knew the CIA would never divulge his identity until he was convicted. And even then they'd deny everything.

Catarina flicked her hand. "Names don't matter to Matheus."

"Exactly. I didn't think you were dead—Ferreira wouldn't knock you off for something so trivial. I know, because Kyle received a phone call from him when you were kidnapped. I was on the other side of the room and could hear him yelling into Kyle's ear—sounded pretty frantic to me. A man that distressed about his wife doesn't murder her on a whim."

Catarina squeezed her eyes into slits. "But how did you think you could find me? Unless I said something the night we ..." Her voice trailed off. Her eyes grew dark. "What did I tell you?"

Nick frowned. He couldn't think about that night. Not now. He held his breath and pushed the memories away. "I've wanted to get close to you for two years. It was just my job until now. Now it's personal."

"Personal?" Her expression softened, eyes flashing again. "So that's why you came back." She stepped closer and touched his arm with the tips of her fingers. "I thought so."

Nick's instincts told him to play along, but then he thought about Jeffrey and his blood in the van. Catarina was the cause, and he felt a repulsion toward her that made him push her hand away. "That's not it." He noticed Catarina's mouth twitching at the corners, almost smiling. Her emotions looked stitched at the seams, pushing, stretching.

"Personal?" she asked. "You mean because you think Matheus set you up for my murder? He didn't do it."

"Then why is he telling the press you're dead?"

"Because some idiot murdered his mistress instead of me. We look a lot alike, and for the longest time he has made sure I don't exist in the public eye. To everyone else, she is me. Or was, anyway. It's easier for Matheus, anyway, if everyone thinks I'm dead. She was Matheus' idea—for my protection. Looks like he was right." Her fingers twitched when she said the words. "Matheus thinks you did it. The evidence against you is flawless."

Nick's mind reeled. He had no doubt Kyle was behind all of it. He wasn't careless enough to murder a look-alike mistress instead of Catarina, but one of his men might have made the mistake. Either way, Kyle was the only one who could have set him up so well. The only one who knew his habits and schedule, who was close enough to steal hair, fingerprints, even blood. The CIA might let him off for a murdered mistress, a nobody, but Catarina was a powerful figure, like Ferreira; murdering her would be reckless—extra fuel for Ferreira's ongoing threats to the U.S., and the CIA would never overlook such a bad move by one of its own. It made sense why Ferreira was trying to disguise the murdered mistress as his murdered wife instead. Why not use it to his advantage?

Catarina cleared her throat. "You know who did this."

"Kyle. But it must have been a mistake."

"I'm sure it was."

"But Ferreira won't believe Kyle's after you. He's his right arm, apparently." He looked into Catarina's face, his mind clouding. "Why does Kyle want you dead?"

"I don't know." She looked away. "I like you, Nick," she whispered. "I want to help you. But not without payment."

Of course. There was always a catch. He was willing to pay, though, if it meant getting what he needed. "What payment?"

She stepped away and glanced at the bed. "Let's not worry about anything until you've slept. I'll be back in the morning. How do you like your coffee?"

He lowered his eyebrows. "Black, I guess. Why?"

A scream pierced the air and Nick's heart jumped. It was Jeffrey's scream. Another, and another. They grew louder and more intense. Nick bolted for the door.

"No, Nick."

Catarina dug her fingernails into his arm. Fighting the instinct to kick her across the room, Nick stepped aside.

She opened the door, where two armed men were waiting. "I know you're not stupid enough to try and get out of here," she said over her shoulder. "Get some rest." She slammed the door and Jeffrey kept screaming.

Chapter 16

The mattress was hard and cold. Even if it had been comfortable, Nick knew he wouldn't be able to sleep. He pulled the thin blanket up to his chin and stared at the sliver of yellow light around the doorframe. Shadows crossed through at regular intervals.

Hours had passed since Jeffrey's screaming. Nick's wristwatch was broken from the fight, so he had no idea what time it was, and his body ached, every bruise pulsing hot. He squeezed his eyes shut. Sleep. He needed sleep. He couldn't remember the last time he'd slept well. His mind always filled with bursts of memories, like bullets coming at him every time he closed his eyes.

He was eager to think of something else and concentrated on Catarina's hard mattress beneath his aching back. The familiar smells of São Paulo surrounded him, then the jungle, the smell of blood when consciousness crept back to him. He opened his eyes.

The bunker was mostly dark except from the other end of the room. On top of a rusted card table in the corner, insects surrounded a small lantern.

Nick considered his chances of escape. From the blown doorway, cool night air drifted past two of Kyle's men, one of them Renato. They sat facing each other on either side of the doorway, asleep, their heads lolled back against the concrete, rifles slack in their hands. Wouldn't be hard to get past them.

Nick squirmed, feeling the slow itch of bug bites across his face and neck. The mud was wearing off. He imagined the mosquitoes having a heyday with the blood still oozing out of his wrist wounds.

Squinting, he turned to the mats where he had last seen Kyle and Catarina. She wasn't there now, just four men: Kyle and three others, all of them sleeping.

That was careless of Kyle, Nick thought smugly. He tried to sit up and groaned. Shit. They'd tied his feet, too. Where was Catarina?

He looked around, finally realizing she was right next to him, completely silent. On her side, she faced him, her head mostly in shadow. She blinked and twisted her lips into a half-smile.

"It's about time you woke up," she whispered in English. "I've been waiting for hours."

Confused, Nick looked at the rest of her. She wore nothing but her dirty linen shirt that hung open around the top half of her body. Along her legs, dark blood coated her skin. "What did he do to you?" he asked, trying to hold back his anger.

"What do you think he did to me? He cut my leg open. It's nothing." She stretched her arms, which were still tied around her back. "Listen, I think I can get out of these bonds if you help."

Nick guessed Kyle had done more than just cut her, but she didn't seem to care. Her nonchalant attitude about everything surprised him. It made him wonder what else she'd been through before this. "Did they mean to fall asleep?" he asked as she fought to sit up.

"The ones on the mats, yes. But the two at the door are supposed to be awake." She gave him an annoyed glare. "Obviously."

Well, yes, obviously.

Finally on her knees, she turned her back to him. "Turn around and see if you can get these knots undone."

He saw what she meant. The nylon rope around her wrists looked loose. On his knees, he turned his back to her and grasped her ice-cold hands in his.

"How did these get so loose?" he asked quietly as their shoulder blades brushed against each other. "Didn't Kyle retie them?"

"No. The men who brought me here untied me once a day so I could eat and drink, but they never tightened the knots. They weren't stupid enough to fall asleep at the same time, either."

Nick smiled and grasped the tightest knot in his fingers. "It's a good thing these guys are stupid, isn't it?" As he worked on the knot, the rope around his own wrists dug deeper into his flesh. He tried not to wince.

Catarina chuckled. "I didn't want to give Kyle the satisfaction of a struggle, but I figured it would give me the chance to work at a few of the knots."

Nick's stomach turned. "He didn't notice what you were trying to do?"

"He was a bit distracted."

Nick's throat tightened. Although he had expected Kyle to hurt Catarina, he hadn't expected him to torture her. "Did any of the other men touch you?"

"No, Kyle wouldn't let them. He finished with me and threw me back over here." She twisted around to look him in the face. "Why the hell would you care? Because I'm bound and half-naked? Please."

He thought he saw her eyes roll before she turned back around. "Who are you?" he whispered, still working on the knot. She wasn't even trembling.

"What do you mean—who am I?" Her body tensed. "Who the hell are you?"

"Nobody important."

"If you're close to Kyle, you're somebody important. How'd you get taken so easily?"

Nick kept working on the knot, worried his fuzzy mind would make him give something away. If his plan was going to work, he'd eventually tell her everything, but not right now. "I'm a little out of my element," he said softly, almost done with the knot now.

Catarina sighed. "Who do you work for? CIA?"

He didn't answer. It didn't matter if she guessed right. The knot, now completely undone, slipped from his fingers. Only two more remained. His skin turned cold with a realization. "What kind of work do you do for your husband?"

"That's none of your business." She tried to yank her wrists apart. "Hey, keep going! Why'd you stop?"

"Because I'm not stupid." Nick stared at the lantern on the table, wondering what he'd landed himself in. If Kyle's betrayal had taught him anything, it was to see Catarina had something up her sleeve.

Her shoulders slumped. "What? You think I'm going to leave you here once I'm free?"

"That's exactly what I think." He turned around and watched her do the same until she faced him. Even in the dim light, he could see she was livid.

"I suppose you're right, Nick," she snapped. "Isn't that what Kyle called you?"

Looking away from her breasts exposed near the open folds of her shirt, he fastened his attention to her face and kept it there.

"Yeah, it's Nick."

The anger in her eyes increased as she fussed with the knots around her wrists. "I'll untie you, I promise. Just get me loose."

He smiled. "I'm supposed to believe that?" He followed her gaze down to the cut on her leg. "How long has that been bleeding?" He couldn't tell in the shadows, but he was sure the mosquitoes were feasting on the blood.

She winced. "A while. I'm not sure it's going to stop. I didn't think Kyle meant to cut it so deep ... at first." Pausing for a breath, she yanked her wrists against the rope.

"Then?" Nick urged.

"He started talking." She looked up, frowning. "That's when I realized he wants me dead." She cursed in Kyle's direction, her voice so soft he barely heard her.

"Kyle can't want you dead. Your husband will kill him if you die."

Her eyes narrowed to slits. "You have no idea what Kyle's up to, do you? I was fine here with the other men. All they wanted was a bigger share of Matheus' drug trade. None of this double-crossing shit."

Nick closed his eyes and tried to think. Catarina was strong, but he was sure if he helped her free she would collapse in the jungle, leaving him here to die as well. By the looks of things, he knew she was right about bleeding to death. A small lake of blood already shimmered across the concrete floor where Kyle had thrown her.

152

"Catarina," he whispered, "if I let you free and you get me out of these ropes, I can help you."

She threw her head back and laughed silently. "How could you possibly help me?" Clamping her lips shut, she yanked on the ropes again and lowered her eyes to the floor. She stopped struggling and chewed on her bottom lip. Nick guessed she was close to undoing another knot, and after a moment she yanked free.

"That feels good," she said, and stood up to look down at Nick. "I knew I could do it eventually. Thanks for your help." She stretched her arms and inspected the cuts on her wrists.

Nick gritted his teeth. "You're really going to leave me here, aren't you?"

"You bet."

She turned and walked straight to Kyle. His snores grew softer as he turned onto his side. Catarina froze, waiting for him to grow still. Nick thought about waking up the men, but decided against it.

Creeping forward, Catarina snatched her jeans lying next to Kyle. Then she walked past Nick and took a canteen of water sitting next to the lantern. Now closer to the light, Nick saw bruises across her face. Had those been there before? He couldn't remember. Eyeing the canteen, he watched her take several swigs and then sit down on one of the folding chairs.

"What are you doing?" he hissed. "Why aren't you leaving?"

"My leg." She peered down at her inner thigh before pouring some water over the wound, revealing a long, deep cut across her pale skin. Pink water speckled with drowned mosquitoes splashed across the chair. It cascaded to the cement already stained with blood.

"That'll get infected," Nick whispered. "If it ever stops bleeding." He watched fresh blood spread across her crimson-stained skin. "I can help you if—"

"Shut up."

She glared at him before grabbing a handful of her shirt. She yanked at the hem, but it resisted. With a final, angry tug and a few curses, she ripped off a long strip, balled it up, and shoved it against the wound. She held it in place and looked at the two guards in the doorway.

"You won't get far," Nick whispered, emphasizing every word. "You've lost too much blood. I can help you with that cut, and I know my way back to the main camp where there's a truck." That was assuming he could get rid of Kyle and the others so they couldn't hunt them down.

"I'll be fine." Catarina pulled the ball of material from her wound. The bleeding seemed to have slowed. At least the wound was insect-free. She stood and tossed the bloody material onto the table, then grabbed her jeans and pulled them on. "Besides," she said, yanking on the zipper. "I don't want help from some second-rate CIA agent who can't even save his own skin." She grabbed the canteen and looked around the bunker.

Landing her eyes near Kyle's feet, she crept forward and made her way to a pair of dirty tennis shoes.

Kyle didn't move as she stepped over his legs, grabbed the shoes, and headed back to the chair. When she sat down, Nick noticed her tightened jaw and what appeared to be a suppressed scream of pain. He was impressed by her strength.

"I could at least take care of the guards there for you before Kyle wakes up. We'd have two rifles, then, and all the supplies in their packs."

She finished lacing up one tennis shoe and started working on the next, her face growing whiter by the second. "I can take care of the guards myself. I told you, I don't need your help."

She stood, and with a final angry glare, turned from him and marched to Renato. Her limp was gone, or at least she was hiding it well. She grabbed hold of the rifle, flipped it around, and smashed the butt into Renato's temple. Instantly limp, the man slumped on his side. Catarina spun around and did the same to the other guard, snatched his rifle, too, and swung it over her shoulder. She muttered something in Portuguese and bent over to push the man onto his stomach. In less than twenty seconds, she pulled off his backpack, stripped him and Renato of any visible weapons, and left the bunker with nothing more than an irritated sigh.

Nick stared at the empty doorway. His time was running out.

Still on his knees, he inched toward Renato until he reached his feet. There had to be a knife clipped to one of them. He hadn't seen Catarina take anything from either of the men's feet, and since he had seen all the men stash knives on their boots, his hopes soared.

Finally, he caught sight of a clip on the left boot and immediately turned his back. Leaning over, he rolled Renato's leg enough to pull out the knife and balance it in his palm. Now all he had to do was prop up the blade somewhere sturdy.

Ten agonizing minutes later, he had his hands free. Kyle stirred. Nick hurried faster, slicing through the rope around his ankles. He cursed whoever had tied them and finally stood up. Kyle still looked asleep, his cheek pressed to the bamboo mat. A string of saliva dripped from his open mouth. Nick thought about kicking him in the head, but wasn't sure how effective it would be. The man was a tank. Slit his throat, maybe? Nick didn't feel up to killing anyone else, but he didn't want Kyle on his tail, either.

He crept closer, a foot away from Kyle now, the knife a heavy stone in his hand. What he needed was his silenced AK-47. He looked around, but couldn't see it anywhere. Or his pack. But Kyle's pack was closer. Nick knew it had more medical supplies than anyone else's, and a GPS and satellite phone. He lifted it quietly from the floor and slung it over his shoulders. He lowered the knife to Kyle's neck. He'd never slit somebody's throat before. He didn't know how loud it might be, if Kyle might have time to scream or gasp.

Renato stirred, and Nick froze. He had to leave. If one of them woke up, the rest of them would wake up. Kyle was holding his rifle. He'd shoot Nick the second he saw him loose.

Nick turned and left the bunker as fast as he could.

Chapter 17
West Virginia

Devan woke early every morning to meet Clara at the dock. This morning the air was cooler than usual. Clara, dressed only in her swimsuit, stood in the blue dawn light with her arms wrapped tightly around her waist.

"I'm not used to this," she said with a shivering laugh when Devan reached her. "I'm used to a heated pool and the San Diego sun. Or a warmer day at least."

Devan shrugged. "We can go hang out in the kitchen. Rachel's making croissants."

"Nope, gotta swim every day no matter what. It's my routine." She leaned close to Devan's face, smiling. "It's why I beat you every time."

"We'll see about today." They both jumped into the lake, laughing. The water was cool, but it didn't take Devan's breath away. They swam for a solid hour, stopping twice for a short break. Devan liked someone next to him, another body beating in rhythm with his. He liked the silence beneath the water. He liked that Clara could outswim him.

She reached the farthest shore, grinning smugly when he got out of the water. "And yet again!" she yelled triumphantly. "Jeff always wins, so this feels good."

Frowning, Devan wiped his face. "He swims with you?"

"Yeah, every night after work. When he's home." She looked at the forest down the shore, squinting even though the sun wasn't over the trees yet. "Sometimes I forget how good things used to be."

Devan waited for her to continue, but she pursed her lips and headed for the trees. She stopped at a boulder where Devan had stashed a bag he'd brought up with his truck the day before. Bottled water, towels, clothes, and shoes. Today he wanted to show Clara the river.

They dressed and started up the trail as the sun broke the horizon. Clara sipped at her water, stopping a few times to look up at the trees. "That's a marbled orb weaver," she said, pointing to a black and yellow spider with red legs. It sat in the middle of its web between two branches. Sunlight sparkled through the dewy strands as Clara took another sip of water and pressed on.

"So you know a lot about spiders?"

"Not as much as Violet, but yeah. I used to love bugs. Spiders mostly"

"Oh?" Devan stopped, and Clara turned to him, shadows dappling her face. She was wearing pants, but hadn't pulled on a shirt over her swimsuit. Devan tried to keep his gaze from wandering to the deep crevice between her breasts. He knew he shouldn't look, but it was useless. His fingers itched to touch her, and he realized how careless he had been to spend so much time with her alone.

"I wouldn't have pinned you as a bug lover," he said, lifting his gaze to her face. "Or anything like Violet. You two hardly talk."

Clara shrugged and started walking. "I don't listen to her anymore. This is the first time we've seen each other since my wedding."

Moving alongside her, Devan matched the rhythm of her stride. "Is there a reason you don't like each other?"

"Yeah."

Her steady breaths were almost drowned by the music of the forest, everything coming alive as sunlight bloomed through the foliage. Chirping birds, a woodpecker's knocks, rushing water in the distance. Devan studied Clara out of the corner of his eye, noticing her clenched jaw and the dented water bottle in her tight grip. "You all right?"

"I'm fine. Is the river close?" She stopped and stared ahead, then spun around to face him. "Where is your father?"

"He lives in Charleston. Why?"

"Is he with somebody? Rachel told me he had an affair."

Devan sighed. A year of tension. Silence. Clothes heaped high. His mom had separated the laundry those last six months, doing only hers and Devan's. His dad's dirty pile grew taller and taller. Some of his shirts smelled like perfume his mother didn't wear. "Yeah, he had an affair," Devan grumbled. "They got married."

"How do you feel about that?" Clara's expression seemed fragmented, a puzzle shifting out of order. Her eyes roamed to Devan's arms and chest. "I mean, how do you feel about the affair? Do you think it was wrong?"

Devan reached out a hand to steady himself, fingers grabbing rough bark. "Of course it was wrong. He broke my mom's heart. He left us." He didn't add that his dad blamed his mom for the breakup, that he claimed he did it because she stopped loving him long before he looked at another woman.

Clara's expression fell back into place. She started hiking again. Fast. Devan ran to catch up. "You can't just stop there. Why did you ask me that?"

Clara shook her head, stopping in her tracks as the river came into view. "It's beautiful."

Nodding, Devan looked at the water cascading down the gentle hill. It jetted over mossy rocks, almost velvety. The smell of wet earth and wood hung heavy in the air. The river was wide at this point, but narrowed as it reached the lake. Here, a fallen tree was the only way across. It stretched over a deep section of the river where an eddy swirled around a group of boulders.

"Do you want to cross?" Devan asked.

"What? The river?" She stepped back, shaking her head. "I don't like heights."

It was the first time Devan saw panic on her face. "I'll help you over," he said, reaching out to touch her shoulder. She glanced at his hand and backed away.

"No, I told you. Heights. Me. Not good." She held her water bottle close, squeezing until another dent appeared. She wasn't like this every day, distant and jumpy. If anything, Devan thought he had helped her get away from her worries. She was smiling more, and he'd noticed her taking second helpings at dinner—a huge turnaround from the first two days when all he'd seen her eat was a roll.

"I promise I'm strong," he said with a sarcastic twinge in his voice. "You're not going to fall."

"I know. The forest's the same over there as it is here."

Devan glanced across the river. He'd crossed that log a hundred times. "No, it's not. Most of the monarchs are on the other side. There's a lot of milkweed and flowers."

"Oh?" She took another step back.

"I'm not going to make you," he said, trying to hide the disappointment in his voice, "but I think you'll like it." He held out his hand. "Please?"

A smile flickered on her lips, sending relief through Devan's heart. She trusted him. That was more than she felt for her husband. Every time she said Jeff's name her face turned cold—and Devan guessed it wasn't because he was missing. Something ran deeper in her relationship with Jeff. Devan could sense it, but didn't dare bring it up.

"Promise I won't fall?"

"Promise."

They set their water bottles down at the same time, and she put her hand in his. It was the first time he'd touched her in days, and he tried not to squeeze too tightly as they walked to the log. Clara climbed up and stood straight, teetering. "This is bad," she whimpered. "I fell and broke my leg when I was ten. I haven't gotten over it."

"It's all right." Devan stepped up behind her and settled his hands on her waist. "See, I've got you. Keep going."

"Alright."

He inched along with her, tightening his grip. She felt delicate, different from her confidence in the water. She took a deep breath, and Devan felt it all the way up his arms. Her footsteps slowed as she stared into the whirlpool below them. "You asked about Violet," she said so quietly Devan almost didn't hear her. "We don't get along because I'm mad at her. And she's mad at me for being mad at her."

"Okay."

Her footsteps stopped. "You know about my mom, right?"

"A little bit. She died, didn't she?"

"Yeah, because of Violet."

Tightening his hold even more, Devan inched closer. She was trembling. "Maybe we should talk about this when we get to the other side."

"No. This is the first time I've been able to say anything. It's weird." She suddenly relaxed. "My dad blames Violet, too, but she doesn't care. She talks about it like it's nothing. She's forgiven herself, but I can't forgive her."

"What happened?"

"You know how divorce feels. I saw it in your face when I asked about your dad."

Devan squeezed his eyes shut. "Yeah."

"I didn't find out my mom wanted a divorce until after she died. But Violet knew. Dad paid for a vacation to France—just Violet and my mom. I was still in high school, and I had a boyfriend. Dad must've thought that trip would change Mom's mind. Time away from him or something. She always seemed happier after a good vacation."

His eyes still closed, Devan thought of his dad slumped on the couch, a beer in his hand as he stared at the television. *Your mom doesn't love me anymore, Devan. Just like that, and I'm going to lose her. Not my fault. None of this is my fault.*

Devan opened his eyes when a soft breeze blew Clara's sweet scent around him, richer than the forest air. She took a step forward. "Mom told Violet about the divorce when they got to France. They went to a bar and they both got drunk. Violet says she barely remembers what happened when Mom took her sleeping pills in the hotel that night. I guess she took half the bottle."

"You're blaming Violet for that?"

"Yes. If you knew my mom you'd understand. She was dependent on people, emotionally, and she got depressed a lot. I think that's why she had such a hard time with Dad's job—because he was always gone. Violet knew better; she shouldn't have let her be so careless."

Devan moved his hands down to Clara's hips, pulling her closer to him. She was tense again, her breaths coming faster. He knew it wasn't because of him. "There's more to this, isn't there? Ten years is a long time to be so angry with her. It sounds like it was a simple accident."

Clara's body stiffened. "I suppose it's a long time, but it doesn't feel long. My mother preferred me, and Violet knew it. So I fought for Dad's affections, and I won. It's obvious I'm his favorite, especially since Mom's death. He'll never forgive Violet for letting it happen, and I won't either."

Devan shook his head, confused. "But ten years, Clara. You're married. Violet has moved on, and you should too."

"I can't." She hung her head and wiped away a tear. "Dad stayed home, until I graduated. He drank a lot, and he stopped talking to me. He was like a stranger." She shuddered. "And he was mean."

"Mean?"

"Angry. All the time."

"Did he hurt you?" Devan had a hard time imagining Nick hurting his own children.

"He hit me once when he was drunk. Just a slap, and he apologized. He felt really bad." Her body relaxed again, this time into Devan. "Violet made a huge mistake, and then she ran away. She went off to England and left me to clean up the mess. Except I couldn't. I tried. How could she do that to me? To Dad? I can't forgive her for it. I can't." A soft sob interrupted her words, and Devan nudged her forward until they were on solid ground. He pulled her into an embrace and held her as she cried.

"I'm not usually like this," she stuttered through her tears. "Jeff heard it all when we were dating, and I've never dared tell anybody else."

"You keep it bottled up, I understand." He stroked her shoulder, still trying to imagine Nick hitting her. The thought made him sick. A strangely familiar emotion washed over him.

"I like your dad," he said as Clara's sobs died down. "But I guess I don't know him real well. I mean, he was only here for a week."

Clara sniffed and tensed her shoulders. "He wasn't always angry. I didn't mean to make him sound bad."

"It's okay. My dad's not bad, either. He made mistakes."

The familiar sensation grew stronger, like being torn in half. Devan loved his dad. He loved him more every time he saw him, every time they talked about airplanes and dreams and Devan leaving the inn. His dad understood his need to move on, to let go. But there were things he didn't understand. He wondered if Clara felt that way about Nick.

She pulled away from him and wiped away her tears. "My dad made mistakes, too, but he changed after my wedding. He started calling me every week, even when he moved out of the country."

"That's good."

"Yeah." Her chin trembled, and she looked away as new tears rolled down her splotchy cheeks. "He's trying to make things better, but I don't think he's coming back. Just this feeling. It's kind of freaking me out. That's why I'm crying all the time."

Devan tried to pull her into his arms, but she stepped away. "Let's go look at that spot you were talking about. It's amazing, right?"

Closing his fingers around air, Devan dropped his hands. "It is. C'mon."

As they walked, Clara squared her shoulders and breathed long and slow. It was like when she swam, working her way through the water—through her pain—coming out ahead once again. When they reached the grove, she gasped.

Devan always forgot exactly how beautiful it was, especially in the morning. The tall deciduous trees stood close together, but they didn't cast huge shadows. Instead, sunlight filtered down in soft golden cones, warming the blanket of flowers spread along the ground. White, pink, yellow, blue, like a smudged painting.

"Wow," Clara whispered. "Is it always like this?"

"Pretty much. Mornings are best."

She walked forward, her steps deliberate and silent. The air was so peaceful, even the chattering birds fell quiet. When Clara reached the center of the grove, she turned around. "Aren't you coming? This is amazing. It's so warm." Looking up at the canopy, she spread her fingers wide and smiled. Devan folded his arms. She was even more beautiful with her tranquil expression, her body as still as the trees. A monarch flitted past her face, and she laughed. "They're really here!"

"Look down."

She lowered her eyes. "What? Where?"

Grinning, Devan walked to her, careful not to crush any flowers. He motioned her to crouch down and pointed to a milkweed plant. "They're usually on here somewhere." He turned over a half-chewed leaf, then another. A black and yellow caterpillar inched its way to the pale green stem. "See? This one's close to the pupa stage. It's huge."

Clara leaned forward to watch it. "I've never seen one before. Only butterflies."

"I thought you said you loved bugs."

"I do!" She straightened. "But I haven't studied them as much as Violet has. I never took classes or anything. Most of the time I just helped her study for tests. But this." She motioned to the flowers around them. "This is why she likes what she does. All of it working together. No fighting. No lies." Her eyes turned watery and she looked into her lap.

Devan rubbed at a spot on his knee, trying to keep himself from holding her again. "Clara?"

She looked up. Their knees were almost touching.

"Why did you say you didn't want your dad to find Jeff? Is it because you don't want to be with him?"

She kept her eyes on his face. "I don't want to be with him most of the time. It's complicated."

"Most things are complicated." He leaned forward and touched her knee. "Is there a reason you keep spending so much time with me?" He breathed in the heady scent of the flowers, Clara's skin, her breath. Their lips touched, soft as velvet.

Clara stood up and backed away, smashing a cluster of pink flowers under her feet.

"Devan, you can't. I can't ..."

Running past him, she left the grove and disappeared through the trees. Devan chased after her, cursing under his breath. The birds were squawking again. He stopped in his tracks, the image of his dad filling his head. Empty beer bottles. Laundry piles. When he looked up, he saw the fallen log across the river. Clara ran across it at a dead sprint.

Chapter 18

"Each phase is called an instar," Robert Allen explained as he pointed his pencil at a caterpillar inside a plastic cage. He had filled the cage with milkweed and five monarch caterpillars of varying sizes. Lilian smiled as Lois, a guest's ten-year-old daughter, giggled.

"I like stars."

Robert laughed. "Well, that's not what I meant, but you get the idea—growing bigger every time they shed. Phases. Instars." He straightened and looked back at Lilian, who had just stepped onto the porch from inside.

Robert still didn't strike Lilian as the scientific type. Most of them had beer guts or were rail thin. One scientist who visited every fall liked to stick butterflies on his bushy white beard to make the kids laugh. But the children liked Robert well enough. Lois, especially.

Lilian smiled at him as she took the last bite of a brownie. Lately, she was attaching herself to anything that reminded her of Nick, like looking into Violet's gray eyes more often than she should, constantly watching news reports about Brazil, eating too many of Rachel's triple-chocolate brownies. If she didn't stop soon she'd gain ten pounds just from missing him.

"Having fun?" she asked Robert and brushed the brownie crumbs from her hands.

"Loads of fun," Robert said with a wink at Lois. "I have quite the attentive student here."

"You know so much!" Lois said, beaming, and then turned to Lilian. "When can me and Erin go out with the butterfly nets, Mrs. Love?" Her freckles looked like brown sugar sprinkled across her nose.

"Call me Lilian, remember? Take the nets anytime you want. Just make sure your parents know where you are."

"Oh, I will." She looked up at Robert. "Thanks for telling me all that stuff. I'm gonna go find Erin now!" She dashed off, and Robert grinned.

"Are all of your guests so charming?"

"Most of them."

"Do you get a lot of families up here?"

"We used to." Lilian ran her finger across the top of the cage, staring at the caterpillars as they chewed their way through the leaves. "Business is slow this year."

"Do you think it has to do with the monarchs?"

Lilian looked up as Robert folded his arms and focused on her face. She thought about how he ran around the lake every morning—nearly three miles—took his time eating breakfast, and twiddled away the afternoon on the porch reading a book in front of his caterpillar cage.

"I think the monarchs have something to do with it," she said, looking away from a bruise on his cheek. It was barely visible beneath his dark skin. "We get negative reviews when guests don't see any."

"I'll bet." He rubbed his chin and nodded to the cage. "Have you thought of raising them? That way you'll always have them close by. I thought for sure you'd already have a hundred cages up and going."

Lilian looked away. "We need to do that again, but we were doing so well. There didn't seem to be a need. There weren't many last year, but that's normal isn't it? Aren't they supposed to pick back up?"

"Not necessarily." Robert's mouth twitched at the corners. "It's sad, I know, but I don't think they'll be around much longer. Everything I've studied lately points to extinction."

Lilian's heart thumped. Robert was a respected scientist. He had sent her links to his articles; he had even won awards, so his opinion meant a lot to her. "Not everybody's so sure," she said, trying to keep her voice steady.

"Not everybody knows all the facts." Robert's eyes turned cold.

"What facts?"

"Nothing." His eyes softened, and he leaned forward. "I don't mean to worry you. It probably won't happen for a very long time."

Now that he was closer, Lilian studied his bruise again. Faint. Healing. The shape of a strawberry. "We've had bad weather this summer, too," she mumbled. "That kills a lot of them. They're so fragile."

Turning to the lake, Robert tapped his pencil on the porch railing. He had set his novel on one of the tables behind them, right next to his unfinished breakfast of croissants and fruit. Lois must have interrupted him with all her questions about the caterpillars. A breeze swept through, fluttering open the novel's pages. Robert ignored it.

"A lot of things are fragile," he said in a distant voice. His back was to Lilian now, and she watched his shoulders tense. His tapping grew faster and the pages kept fluttering. Then everything stopped, and in the sudden stillness Robert took a deep breath. "I like fragile."

Lilian found Violet kneeling in the dirt by the boathouse. "Find anything good?"

Violet looked up and smiled. "Not yet. But dinner smells amazing. Is it ready?"

"Yes, roast chicken." Sitting on the steps, Lilian watched Violet part a clump of grass.

"Rachel's a great cook. How long has she been here?"

"Since I opened. She used to work with me at my cake shop. She takes a week off here and there when we don't have bookings." She chuckled. "The food isn't as good when I cook."

"I'll bet your cooking's fine." Violet leaned closer to the ground, her nose brushing the grass. "I saw him a minute ago. Where did he go?" She had brought out two Mason jars. They were on the steps, and Lilian picked one up and fiddled with the lid.

"I have a few questions about Robert," she said, trying not to sound too eager. She'd noticed Violet and Robert talking quite a bit.

"Robert?" Violet straightened. "What about him?"

"Something's bothering me. I don't want to sound rude, but he's different than the others. You're familiar with people in his field, right?"

Scrunching her nose, Violet pressed her hands to her knees. "He's nice. Really nice. But sometimes I'll ask him stuff every scientist in his shoes should know, and he gets this blank look on his face. I didn't think too much about it."

Lilian unscrewed the jar and ran her finger along the rim. "Have you read his articles? Do they sound okay?"

Violet nodded. "From what I've read, he'll do a great job with his research here."

"But that's just it. He's not doing a lot of research, is he?"

"Sure he is. He told me yesterday the third-generations are doing well. That means the fourths should be fine. So it'll be a good migration and it'll all pick up."

"That's not what he told me."

"Really?"

174

They stared at each other and Lilian felt something click. She tightened and loosened the lid until her fingers hurt. Should she mention the bruise? Had Violet noticed it? Suddenly, it seemed larger in her mind.

"I got one!"

Lilian looked up to see Lois and her little sister, Erin, skipping across the front clearing with two butterfly nets in hand. "Look, Mr. Allen! See!" Lois ran up the steps of the porch and out of Lilian's sight.

"They've been trying to get a monarch all day," Violet said as she stood and brushed her hands off. "They even skipped lunch."

"So did I." Lilian stared into her lap. She had spent most of the afternoon in her room searching the Internet for information about Robert. Everything she found seemed fine.

"I didn't eat lunch, either," Violet said with a flick of her hand. "I started thinking about England."

"You miss it?"

"I left in the middle of a project. Nobody knows where I am, and Dad told me not to call anybody. What if they fire me?"

Lilian squeezed the jar in her hand. Fire her? The distress in Violet's voice made Lilian wonder if her job was her main concern. She hadn't mentioned her parents since the morning with the butterfly—nothing about her confession of killing Annabelle. It must have been an accident. Nick wouldn't lie to her. Or would he? She picked up the other jar and stood up, noticing the coldness in Violet's eyes. Maybe Nick was so angry about Annabelle he didn't care what happened to Violet. Maybe he wasn't coming back. These thoughts frightened her. It meant she hardly knew Nick.

"Your father brought you here to keep you safe," she said, looking sternly at Violet. Her next words were a shaky mess. "Aren't you worried about him at all?"

Violet stared over Lilian's shoulder. Her chin trembled. "Of course I'm worried about him, but I grew up with this, and I've learned to hide it. So did Clara and Mom. We had to." She turned toward Lois and Erin bounding down the porch steps. Robert followed, laughing as the girls circled him with their butterfly nets.

"I think it's time for dinner," he yelled out as seven-year-old Erin begged for a piggyback ride.

"Daddy's always busy," she whined. "Puhhleease?"

Robert's face lit up, and he crouched down. "Alright, I'll carry you to the table." He gave her a teasing glare as she climbed onto his back. "As long as you eat all your dinner like your mom keeps telling you."

"Yep!" She wrapped her arms around his neck, and he stood up. Lois followed them inside.

"You know," Violet said, narrowing her eyes. "He seems pretty nice, but I don't know."

Lilian pressed her lips together and stared out at the lake. Maybe she was being completely paranoid about Robert. It seemed far-fetched to suspect him of—what, she didn't even know.

A hawk soared into view and circled the lake, its wings spread wide, feathers sleek against the sky. Lilian squinted to see its sharp, shiny eyes. It looked focused, like it might fold its wings and dive any second. Its beak was made for killing, but the creature still struck beauty into Lilian's heart.

"If you're worried about Robert," Violet said, "I can keep an eye on him." She smiled, but it looked shaky. "I think we're on edge because of what's happened with my dad, that's all."

Lilian turned to look at the hawk again, but it was gone.

Chapter 19
Brazil

Nick woke to the smell of rain. He turned on the lamp next to his bed and rubbed his scruffy jaw, wincing from the tenderness still there. It was his second morning in Catarina's home and she hadn't come back since she'd left him in the bedroom. The only human contact he'd had was with her men who brought him food twice a day. Every time they opened the door, he reminded himself how escape was possible even past the guns and muscle—if he planned it right. But he would have to leave Jeffrey behind. A brief knock on the door made him jump.

Catarina walked in wearing a pale blue dress. The heady smell of lavender drifted from her, and Nick shut his eyes. Lilian. Why did she have to smell like Lilian?

"Follow me," she said. He followed her into an airy dining room to a table spread with bread, fruit and coffee.

A tall glass vase stuffed with straight stems of lavender caught Nick's attention. Strange. He wasn't sure lavender grew in Brazil, but the stems were fresh, and the smell was strong as he sat across from Catarina. She smiled and spread a cloth napkin over her lap.

"I hope you're not angry with me," she said, smirking as she reached for a bowl of sliced fruit covered in clear syrup. "I told my men to move you to a better room, but I think they're afraid of you." Her smirk broke into a grin as she shifted her eyes over him. "You have quite the reputation from a few days ago—it took four of them to bring you down."

Nick scowled and leaned across the table. "I want to see Jeffrey. Now."

"You will. Eat first then I'll take you to a nicer room where you can clean up. You look terrible."

Nick sat back in his chair and stared at a bowl filled with small loaves of bread. He'd eaten the same type of bread every morning for the past two years in Brazil. His mind flooded with memories of the dead-end days he'd spent behind a desk as an executive of an agricultural firm based in São Paulo—his cover the CIA had set up. But Ferreira thought it was a cover for his dealings with drug cartels and industrial terrorism.

"Your husband thought my name was Goncalo," he said slowly as he picked up one of the bread loaves. It was freshly baked and steam rose to his face as he broke it in half. He reached for the butter, wondering exactly how much Ferreira knew about him now. Probably everything.

"That sounds familiar." Catarina handed him a butter knife. "He might have talked about you before. He talks about Kyle all the time." A strange expression crossed her face, a cross between fear, sadness, and anger.

Nick buttered his piece of bread. He wasn't hungry. He took a bite anyway, chewing as he thought of Kyle's covers, similar to his own. Kyle was supposedly one of the DEA's top agents. He'd proven it by ascending faster in Ferreira's chain than any other man Nick had seen. That was why Catarina knew about him and why the DEA hadn't pulled him out of Brazil when Nick rarely saw them leave agents in a mission so long.

"I have to know," Catarina said between bites. "Was it you who killed my assassin in West Virginia?"

Nick swallowed before his mouth dropped open. He stood up and the lavender vase teetered. "That was your assassin?"

"Of course it was." She took another bite and narrowed her eyes. "Sit down."

"No." Nick gripped the table and leaned forward. Catarina's lips looked sticky from the fruit. Next to her plate Nick spotted a small sharp knife for taking the skin off mangoes. For an instant he thought about pressing it against her throat, but then he thought about the cut on her leg and his stomach turned. Kyle had been so vicious. He couldn't turn into that, no matter how much he wanted to help Jeffrey.

He looked into Catarina's pained eyes. Everything about her squeezed his emotions tighter, like an angry fist inside his chest. He thought she wanted him, but maybe he was wrong. He needed answers. "Why the hell would you try to kill me? To protect your husband? Every rumor, everything you said in the jungle, even when you say his name. It all points to the same thing—you hate him."

Licking the sugar from her lips, she nodded. "I was delirious in the jungle. I should never have let you go after we escaped the bunker. I realized I had no idea what I'd told you—things that could lead you to him."

Nick almost grabbed her arm, but straightened instead. "Matheus must be found and dealt with. That's been my job, my mission. Isn't that what you want? Freedom?"

Looking away, she muttered, "It's complicated. I didn't want to kill you, but everything with Matheus is more important right now. There's more." She looked up. "Come on, I'll take you to get cleaned up if you're not hungry."

She led him to a room decorated in blue organza and silks. From the frilly pillows on the bed to the lacy curtains and soft rugs, Nick knew it was her room. She opened the bathroom door and waited for him to enter. "You can shave and shower. Take your time."

"And Jeffrey?" He turned to her, grabbing her shoulders to pin her against the door. "I still don't know if he's all right. I want to see him." He was sure no matter how threatening he became, she wouldn't cave.

"You'll see him," she said, searching his face. "I promise."

Nick tried to read her expression, knowing the fragile trust between them could go sour any second.

She left and Nick turned to the mirror. He removed his shirt and wet the razor Catarina had set out for him. The bathroom smelled clean. It was bright white. Standing in the middle of it, Nick felt like a dark stain, as dark as the blood oozing from his skin when he cut himself with the razor. He shut his eyes. He was tired of feeling wrapped in lies and disappointment, nothing but a shadow to everyone around him—not a real person, not himself. It was nothing he could worry about at the moment. Now he had to figure out Catarina. She had a weak spot—he knew that from the jungle.

Stepping into the shower, he focused his mind on the night he'd left the bunker. Water slapped his face, and he leaned against the cool tiles.

That night had been cool, too, the beam of his LED flashlight an eerie blue on the dark soil. Catarina's footprints were easy to find, leading half a mile from the bunker. He found her doubled over in pain against a tree.

"Let me carry you," he said, shining the flashlight in her direction.

She snapped her attention to him, lifting her own flashlight. "How did you ..." A gasp interrupted her, and she dropped the flashlight to clutch at her leg. "Damn it, they'll find us in two seconds with these lights. How did you get out of there?"

"My second-rate abilities," he said with a frown, and stepped forward.

Catarina swung one of the two rifles off her shoulder and aimed it at his head. "Don't come near me. I can handle this myself. You are on your own."

"What?" Nick almost laughed out loud, but stopped himself. She had to be joking. She couldn't even walk.

"I said you are on your own. I don't need you." The rifle lowered, and she gasped again, falling to her knees. "Damn it," she hissed through her teeth. "Damn it."

He approached her, slipped her bag and rifles from her shoulder, and scooped her into his arms, expecting her to protest. Instead she grabbed hold of him and buried her face in his neck.

"Carry this," he said, hoisting her bag on top of her abdomen. "And shine one of these for me." He gave her the two flashlights and stood up after slinging the two rifles on his back. He felt like a packhorse, but it wasn't anything he couldn't handle. He'd have to create some false trails first, make sure he wouldn't be followed. He didn't have his machete, but that would make it too easy for Kyle to follow them anyway. He stuck with the best natural paths he could find, and knew which direction to go with Kyle's GPS—when it decided to work; it was picky with the heavy foliage above. From what he'd found so far, the main camp was miles away near a road. If they made it there fast enough, he could get a truck.

His progress was slow. Catarina smelled of sweat and cigarette smoke, her body relaxed and limp. Her face was cold against his neck.

"I'm sorry I left you in the bunker," she said through shallow breaths. "I thought I could get away alone. I thought the bleeding would stop. I thought ..." Her head rolled back, eyes closed, but she'd propped the flashlight well enough for Nick to see. He pressed forward, hour after hour. Catarina stirred, but didn't come to until Nick found a small clearing and propped her against a rotting log. She moaned and opened her eyes. "Where are we?"

"Nowhere. We need to rest and I need to do something about your leg." He pulled the rifles and backpack off his shoulders. His entire body ached. "There should be a lamp in here somewhere."

Catarina stared at her bloody jeans. "Did I pass out?"

"You're in shock." Nick pulled the rifles close and knelt down next to her, the damp earth seeping through his pants as he took an energy bar from the bag. "How long has it been since you ate or drank?"

"I don't know." She took the bar from his outstretched hand and dropped it in her lap before taking a long drink from the canteen. Nick dug through the backpack. Blanket, food, first aid kit, a small LED lamp. He switched it to the lowest setting and set it on the ground between them. Catarina stared ahead, her eyes glazing over.

"Would you please eat?" He snatched the bar from her lap, unwrapped it, and shoved it into her hands. "When you're done, I need you to take off your pants."

He thought she might object, but wasn't surprised when she nodded and took a bite of the bar. As she ate, he pulled out the blanket and unfolded it.

"What are you doing?" Catarina swallowed the last of her food.

"You'll need something to sit on." He helped her stand and unrolled the blanket out across the soil and dead vegetation. Rotting. It was always rotting in the jungle. The wet smell of it hung thick in the air.

Nick turned away, and Catarina unzipped her pants. The sound echoed off the leaves. "Shit," she growled. "Hell, th-that ... h-hurts!"

Nick cringed at the thought of pulling denim from a drying wound.

"Okay, I'm ready."

Turning around, Nick saw her sitting on the blanket, her dirty jeans balled at her side. She leaned against the log and bent her knee up and out so he could inspect the cut on her inner thigh.

"Hold this." He handed her one of the flashlights and she lowered it to the wound.

Nick couldn't see past the caked blood. He grabbed a sterile wipe from the first aid kit and swatted away the bugs dancing around his fingers. Catarina reached for the wipe. "Give me that. I can do it myself."

He pushed away her hand, squinting to see the cut. She had no underwear on.

"Stop blushing," Catarina said.

He moved his hands to avoid touching between her legs. "I'm not blushing." But he was—his cheeks felt hot. He didn't know why. It wasn't anything he hadn't seen before.

"Yes, you are. Do what you need to, I don't care."

He kept wiping away blood, upset for feeling embarrassed. "It's a clean cut, but deep," he said, slowing his breaths. "It's clotting. That's good."

"It hurts like hell. Is it infected?"

Nick dropped the bloody rag and ripped open an alcohol wipe. "I can't tell yet. I'll do what I can, okay? This is going to hurt."

Her leg tensed when he touched the wipe to the cut. She didn't even gasp. He used up one wipe. Then another and another.

"Is it infected?" Tears streamed down her face.

"Your skin's inflamed, so probably. But if I keep it clean and get you out of here soon enough, a trip to the hospital will—"

"Get me out of here?"

"Yeah, you know, back to your husband." All sorts of things ran through his head—visions of getting her on his side in the next few days, convincing her to tell him how to find Ferreira in return for what might appeal to her: money, freedom from her husband, whatever else might make her happy. He needed to find out those things fast.

"I thought this was a one-way ticket to prison. Or worse." She glared at him, looking thoroughly confused and angry. "I don't trust you."

"And I don't trust you. Yet." He gave her a soft smile as he prepared a clean dressing for her wound. She stayed silent, tears trickling over her bruised skin. Nick saw an ache in her eyes that wasn't there before and leaned closer to apply a butterfly bandage to one end of the cut.

He suddenly wanted to feel her warmth against him, wanted to wipe her tears away. "Hold that secure while I get another one," he said, backing away as she pressed her fingers over the bandage. When he fastened the next one, Catarina brushed her hand over his, lightly caressing his skin until his heart skipped a beat.

"Do you want to trust me?" she asked in a breathy voice.

Nick stared down at her hand on his. She had lovely, slender fingers. "I think we'd both benefit from that."

"Good." She leaned forward, practically falling against him, and kissed him sloppily on the mouth.

Holding her steady by the shoulders, he kissed her back. He liked the way she felt, the way she seemed to throw everything out the window on a whim. Maybe it was because she was delusional from loss of blood. He didn't care. He hadn't been with a woman for so long—not since the cake shop and Lilian Love three years ago. At that moment, kissing Catarina, he wondered if Lilian had been more of a curse than anything, the memory of her a reminder of what he really was.

Catarina pulled away and looked into his eyes. "You're not second-rate." She collapsed into his arms, completely limp. Nick thought she had passed out, but then she stirred. "I need someone like you," she whispered, and started crying again, this time with tiny gasps and chokes. Nick lowered her head to his lap so she was lying down and pulled a part of the blanket over her legs.

"You need to rest," he said, stroking her hair.

"I don't want to rest." Her eyes stared into the darkness. "Everything's floating. Everything's beautiful." She sniffed and wiped her nose with the back of her hand. "I wish I was free like that."

Chapter 20

When the bathroom door opened, Nick turned around. The shower curtain rustled, and Catarina stepped inside.

"May I join you?"

Nick let the jungle fade from his memory, the blood and tears and smell of rotting leaves, how Catarina had needed him. Sunlight from a high window above the tiles fell across her skin in golden light, accentuating the exquisite warm tones of her body.

Nick slid his eyes down to her legs, trying to see the cut Kyle had given her, but it was too far up her inner thigh for him to see. Then he stopped. Along her hips, silvery stretch marks glistened beneath rivulets of water. He hadn't noticed those in the jungle. The light had been too dim, not like the brightness here that exposed everything no matter how slight.

Nick stepped closer, his breath catching in his throat as his fingers brushed across the stretch marks. Shaking her head, Catarina stepped back. "I'm sorry. You want this, don't you? I might not remember anything I said in the jungle, but a woman doesn't forget a kiss like that." She lifted her hand to his chest and caressed his wet skin. Heat rushed straight to his toes, the familiar pleasure of losing control—fast. He took her by the arms and squeezed her to his chest.

"It's clear you're not out to kill Matheus," Catarina said breathlessly, pressing herself even closer. "That's why I'm here. I want to give you something."

He guessed she didn't mean her body. Her voice had changed, more direct, and his breathing slowed. He moved his arm around her to feel the velvety cool skin of her waist, different than Lilian's. "You're going to tell me how to find your husband?"

"I am."

"And you'll help me clear my name."

"Possibly."

Sliding his hand down to her lower hip, he rubbed his thumb along the shallow dips in her flesh. He thought of Annabelle's same scars, then Lilian's, all reminders of their sacrifice to a child. A physical reminder. Something he didn't have except on his heart where nobody could see. Even now they seemed to fade.

"How do I get your husband?" he asked. He was a centimeter away from kissing Catarina before she pushed away.

"There are names I'll give you—for your loyalty." She knotted her eyebrows, her expression annoyed and distracted from her earlier passion. "Let me clear some things up," she said sharply, and stepped back to look down at her slender thighs, opening them wide enough for Nick to see the dark stitches in her flesh. "You know Kyle cut me. He was going to let me die."

"So you think he's still after you?"

"I know he is." She looked down at her feet. "My men have tried to find him, but he's disappeared. I can't hide here much longer, and it's too risky for me to be with Matheus, so we'll have to start moving."

"We? You mean you and your men."

She chewed on her bottom lip and squeezed her eyes shut. "You know, I thought he wanted to betray Matheus, just like he's betrayed you, but now I don't know. I have an idea why he wants me dead, but thinking about it makes me sick. You can find him and get him off my tail—you know him better than any of my men. And I want Matheus out of the picture, but not killed, especially by you. That's what the names are for. They're the perfect way for the U.S. to find my husband and clear your name at the same time."

Nick shook his head, confused. "The U.S. can still kill him. I can't prevent that. If they stick black ops on him he's as good as dead."

"That's a risk I'm willing to take. It would at least be out of my hands." She ran a finger down his jaw. "I at least have more control over whether or not you kill him. If that happened, I'd never forgive myself."

"Why does it matter? I'm not an assassin, anyway."

"It matters." She looked down, and Nick squeezed his hands into fists. Besides a further explanation about 'the names', there was something else she wasn't telling him. He would let it slide. For now.

Lifting her chin with his hands, he looked into her eyes.

"What do you plan to do once Kyle and Ferreira are out of your way?"

She pulled away. "I thought it was obvious," she said with a wicked smile. "I'll take Matheus' powerful position ... although I have plans of my own regarding where things will go." She turned to open the shower curtain. "I'll be on the bed."

Nick's jaw dropped. Nestled between her shoulder blades, a tattoo resembling a pair of upside-down wings stretched across her skin. They didn't look as if they belonged to anything except maybe a bird, pale at the top and gradually turning to an intense, dripping red as if slashed with a knife and left to bleed to death. Although they were probably supposed to be bird wings, the shape reminded Nick of a drooping butterfly.

"It can't be," he said aloud. Not another connection. He remembered the butterfly article he had given Lilian and the suspicions he had that Ferreira was a large practitioner of the illegal logging in Mexico. One of Ferreira's businesses was located in that area. He stared at the tattoo, still shocked by its uncanny presence, but even more shocked when he noticed the scarred flesh around it. Raised snake-like bumps. Whip marks.

"Did you say something?" Catarina turned around, still holding the curtain.

Nick opened his mouth, but couldn't speak. His heart was speeding. He stepped forward and pulled Catarina back into the shower, touching the scars on her back even more tenderly than he had touched her stretch marks. These felt like heartache, sacrifice, unnecessary torment.

He smoothed his hand over them, wishing to make them disappear. Had she lived this way her entire life? Beaten and manipulated, left to bleed like the set of dying wings on her back? The thought sent a strange burst of guilt through him, and he kissed her so hard she moaned and hooked her leg around his hip, squeezing him closer. "The bed," she mumbled.

Now that her leg was wrapped around him, his desire hit full force. He pushed his hips against her, cupping the back of her head in his hand, rubbing circles in her hair. He wanted to do what she asked, carry her to the bed and please her, forget his own pain for a moment, so he followed her, knowing her silk sheets would smell of lavender. He thought of Lilian the entire time, and when they finished, Catarina held onto him tightly and whispered his name over and over. He squeezed her close.

"I'm sorry about what happened in the bunker," he said softly. "About Kyle."

"What do you mean?"

Nick ran his fingers over the scars on her back. "He raped you. Cut you."

"Raped me?" Catarina sat up and looked him in the face. "He didn't rape me. He only cut my leg, like I told you."

Nick's jaw went slack. He'd been certain Kyle was sick that way, taking whatever he wanted. He had even hinted at it in the bunker: *after I've had my fill, of course.* "I thought for sure that's what he'd done," Nick said, frustrated for having jumped to conclusions so quickly. "But that wouldn't make any sense, would it? To set me up for your murder and leave evidence that he'd harmed you himself."

"Exactly."

Another whiff of lavender drifted under Nick's nose. He squeezed his eyes shut and loosened his hold on Catarina. She squeezed him tighter and nuzzled her face against his neck, whispering his name again before he pushed her away and slid off the bed. He walked quickly to the bathroom.

Everything was wrong. Catarina. The bruises on his jaw. His cracked watch. He glanced at it on the counter, the hands frozen at noon as the years he'd been with the CIA flew by in a furious wind of lies. Noble lies. Justified. But the lines were always blurred.

He bent down to tie his shoes as Catarina, now in her dress, entered the bathroom. "Nick, I never said we had to do that. I thought you wanted to."

"I did." He stood up, hesitating to get close to her again. He was still attracted to her—her soft skin, her smell, the need in her voice when she'd whispered his name on the bed. He guessed she'd been with as many men as he'd been with women. They both used others to get ahead, to try and dull the pain. A perfect match. "I'm sorry if you expected more than that," he said as she stepped closer. "I thought I—"

"I'll give you the names if that's all you want." Coldness swept across her face, and she turned to leave the bathroom, her dress unzipped down to her waist, exposing the stark red wings.

Nick touched her shoulder, inching his fingers to the tattoo. "Catarina, what is this really about? What do you want?"

She spun around, her eyes wet. "You're different from any other man I've met. I thought ..." She turned and walked to the bed, where she slipped on a pair of flats the same color as her dress. "I don't know what I thought. I was wrong."

Nick didn't know what to say. Watching her back, he wondered how he was different. Whatever it was, he'd disappointed someone yet again. No surprise there. He stared at the tattoo, at how bright and strange it seemed on her skin. "Did your husband give that to you?"

She didn't turn around. "Give me what?"

"The wings. What do they mean?" Nick approached her, reaching out to touch the wings, but grabbed the zipper instead.

"They mean loyalty," she mumbled as he pulled the zipper up, careful not to catch her hair. The wings disappeared. "They're supposed to bind me to him. All of his men have them. Some are small on the shoulder or arm. Some are bigger, like mine."

He didn't recall ever seeing the tattoo on Kyle. Then again, he'd never seen Kyle shirtless. "Are you bound to him?"

"Only by one thing, and not the tattoo." She turned around, her expression changing to sympathy. "Your daughter must mean a lot to you."

"My daughter?"

"Jeffrey's wife—Clara or Claire? He wouldn't stop talking about her as soon as we put him on the morphine. You know, he's not what you think."

Nick tensed as he remembered Jeffrey's lies. He definitely wasn't what Nick had thought. "I know all about that."

"Oh?" She wrinkled her brow. "But your daughter must love him, anyway. And you must love both of them, right? Especially your daughter."

"I have two daughters. I love both of them, yes." Although he sometimes wondered how he really felt about Violet.

"I knew you'd love your children," Catarina said softly. She smiled, but it fell into a frown the next moment. "I love my child, too."

Nick straightened his shoulders and nodded. He had guessed right. "So that's why you don't want me to kill Ferreira. You don't want to be directly responsible for his death because of your child. Am I right?"

She chewed on her bottom lip and nodded. "Yes. I could never forgive myself. Matheus will turn Alejandro—my son—into a monster, just like him. I can't let that happen, but he loves his father so much. He would never forgive me if he found out I could have prevented his death. With your help I can at least keep him away from Alejandro."

"Where is your son now?"

"In the city. But I'm putting him on the plane with you and Jeffrey. His father wants him back, and I can't argue. I'm sending you home." Her face grew dark. "If you're going to cooperate."

"Right. We never outlined those terms, did we? You want your son safe, but what else do you want? Treason? Information? I won't be with the CIA anymore. I won't have access to—"

"You'll find a way." She tilted her head, smirking. The tenderness he'd seen in her a moment ago melted. A malicious glare crept into her eyes. "Do you want Jeffrey or not?"

Nick waited for the small jet to start its engines before he turned his attention to the silver briefcase in his lap. Remembering the code Catarina had told him, he spun the digits below the handle, landing on the correct combination five times before opening the case. When he did, he slammed it shut.

Papers. That's all it was. Names. Locations.

He held his breath, trying to forget that if he was found with this briefcase before placing it in the right hands, he was a dead man. No questions. No trial. No prison. Others would find him long before then, and that was why Catarina had seemed so eager to hand it over to him. She had told him she had risked her life just gathering the information. The sooner he got rid of it the better.

Out his window, he saw Catarina standing next to the SUV they had driven to the private airstrip. Her hair whipped across her face as she spoke to three burly men in suits—men Nick hadn't seen before, more professional than the others. Colder.

A thin, pale boy who had shown up minutes earlier with the three men stood next to her. Alejandro. He was twelve or thirteen with bright green eyes, like hers, and a hardened expression. Catarina wrapped her arm around him, squeezing until he squirmed away from her. He shook his head as the men walked him to the plane.

"Would you like a drink, Mr. Avery?" a female voice asked in Portuguese.

Nick looked up at the flight attendant in front of him. Dressed in a white, low-cut blazer and short skirt, she leaned forward to flash her tanned cleavage. "Catarina says you're welcome to anything you wish. It's a long flight."

A drink sounded nice, but he knew better. One drink would lead to three or four. He was too stressed to control himself. Running a hand over the briefcase, he shook his head. "No, thank you. Club soda is fine."

She smiled and leaned forward even farther. "Anything else I can get you, then? A blanket? Magazines? Books? Movies?"

"You can bring my son-in-law out here."

Her smile fell. "I think he's more comfortable lying down in the front. He's drifting in and out. I'll let you know when he's awake."

She left and he turned back to the window. Standing alone, Catarina looked at the plane, her hair still blowing around her face. She was too far away for him to see her eyes in any detail, but he thought they looked wet.

Alejandro stepped onto the plane with the three men who led him to a seat across the aisle from Nick. "My mom told me about you," the boy said as he sat in one of the double seats. He lifted his spindly legs and set them on the other set of facing seats. "She said I'd like you." He grunted and folded his arms.

Nick smiled, trying to hide his discomfort. The boy's black hair was slicked close to his head. He had pale white skin, and from what little Nick had seen of Ferreira in photos, he would be a spitting image of his father if his hair ever turned white. Except for the eyes.

One of the suited men sat behind the boy, glaring at Nick as he cracked his knuckles and leaned back in his seat. The other two men exited the plane and it started to move.

"It's nice to meet you Alejandro."

The boy frowned. "Don't call me Alejandro. My mom calls me that," He rolled his eyes. "Call me Alex."

"Alright, fair enough. Alex."

The jet's engines grew louder, silencing the conversation. When they were in the air, the flight attendant approached Nick again. "He's awake."

Carrying the briefcase with him, Nick stood and followed her to the front of the plane. Jeffrey, lying on a cot, smiled as soon as Nick slipped past the curtain. "We're going home. I thought she was going to keep us there forever."

"No, everything's fine." The air reeked of vomit. Nick knelt next to the cot and placed a hand on Jeffrey's arm. "How are you feeling? They gave you too much morphine, I think."

Laughing, Jeffrey rubbed his fingers on his forehead. "I've puked thirty times, but other than that I'm all right." He scrunched his nose. "It hurt a lot, I think, I don't remember much. Whose plane are we on?"

"Hers." Nick leaned forward. He hadn't spoken with Jeffrey since before he was shot. His list of questions was long. "Listen, Jeffrey, have you told me everything about how you ended up in Brazil?"

Jeffrey raised his head. "I told you about the mistakes I've made. You think that was easy?"

"I'm sure it wasn't."

"Then trust me." He looked at Nick's hand resting on his arm, and smiled. "I had lots of chances to kill you in São Paulo. The stairwell. The hallway. But I didn't."

"What are you talking about?"

"I told them I'd get rid of you. That was the deal."

Nick's shoulders fell. "Well thanks for breaking it." He chuckled, but his tone was serious.

"See? You can trust me." Jeffrey wet his lips and stared straight ahead. "I'll see Clara when we get to West Virginia? She'll be there, right?"

"I hope so."

"Good. I need to see her." His eyes rolled to the back of his head, and Nick stared at him, remembering the first time he'd met him inside a cramped office in Langley. He remembered the smell of peppermint from Jeffrey's mouth as he had sucked on a piece of candy from the lobby, his words sloppy and precise at the same time as he gave Nick information about a possible agent he'd dealt with during an investigation.

Nick had noticed Jeffrey's toned arms and thin waist, his dry hair and the faint smell of chlorine on his hands when he handed Nick a stack of papers. He had to be a swimmer, like Clara, and even more intriguing, Jeffrey's smile reminded Nick of Clara's smile—a deep dimple in his left chin when he laughed. They were perfect for each other.

Nick stood. He wondered if he'd acted too quickly, made too many assumptions to try and ease Clara's loneliness. She'd been so sad since Annabelle's death, and finding her a husband seemed like a good solution. It hurt him to think of her alone—more than it hurt him to think of Violet alone. She'd moved far away, seemed caught up in her bugs and old dusty journals filled with long articles and pencil sketches. Annabelle's death hadn't seemed to affect her like it had affected Clara. Clara had cried, but Violet—she'd had no tears at the funeral, only a blank stare, like one of her glassy-eyed bugs.

Chapter 21

The airplane cabin smelled of shrimp and garlic, not a good combination with Jeffrey's vomit up front. Nick made his way up the aisle and sat back down in his seat, briefcase in his lap. Alex looked up from his food. Nick gave him a weak smile. "Hungry?"

"Mmmm." Alex chewed slowly, like a cow, and rolled his eyes in exaggerated pleasure. "I don't think they have enough for you," he said after he swallowed. "At least I hope they don't."

Nick stared at him, confused. "You don't want me to have shrimp?"

"I don't want you to have anything." Alex folded his arms and squeezed his eyes into slits. "I don't want you to talk to my mom anymore. I'm going to tell my dad all about you."

Nick grunted. "I think your dad already knows about me."

The slit-eyes widened. "How? My mom acted like you were some big secret."

"Really?" Mimicking the boy, Nick slitted his own eyes. "A big secret, huh?"

"Yeah. A big secret." Alex lowered his eyes to the briefcase, but didn't say anything else. He finally turned back to his food and popped another shrimp in his mouth, licking his fingers with three long slurps of his tongue.

Nick closed his eyes and rested his head on the back of the seat. Alex's loud chewing annoyed him, but the airplane's hum made him sleepy. He tried to concentrate on something besides food and the smell of Jeffrey's vomit. He replaced them with the smell of rotting mud on his face, once again.

Most of it had worn off by the time Nick woke up the morning after he'd bandaged Catarina's leg. She stirred, still lying in his lap, her hair strewn across his arms in a mess of dirty curls.

"You smell," she whispered, and yawned as she stretched her body. "Ouch!" She clutched at her leg.

Nick patted her shoulder and helped her sit up. "Let me get you some pain meds. I'll be surprised if you can walk at all."

Looking around, Catarina's eyes widened. She scooted away from Nick and stared at the blanket covering her naked legs. "Where the hell am I? What the ... oh." She laughed. "I remember. Why is your face always covered in mud? How did we get here? I thought I left you in the bunker."

Nick pulled out some aspirin from Kyle's bag and handed Catarina the pills and his canteen. There wasn't much water left. He estimated that if they drank minimally, it would last one day at most—unless he gathered more somehow. He'd seen Kyle's men doing that once after it had rained, carefully tilting leaves to their mouths or canteens.

"Catarina, we need to get out of here fast. I don't know where Kyle is or if he's trying to track us or what. I didn't mean to sleep so long." He didn't feel any immediate threat, but he wanted to get moving anyway.

"You didn't answer any of my questions."

Nick helped her stand and handed her the pair of dirty, bloody jeans. She bit her lip as she pulled them back on. From what he could see, her cut had stopped bleeding.

"The mud is a mixture of dead termites, paint, and dirt," he explained as he handed her a pack. "Camouflage, and it helps keep the bugs away. I carried you here, don't you remember?"

"Carried me here?" She gave him a dark look. "I would never let—" A light turned on in her eyes. "Oh."

"So you do remember." Chuckling, Nick swung the other pack and the two rifles over his shoulders and they left their tiny camp. Catarina stayed close to him, limping. "Do you want me to carry you?" he asked.

"No."

"Do you need another drink? Something to eat?"

"No."

"Then follow my footsteps. Walk lightly, in muddy spots like this." He showed her how to step in spots that would quickly hide their tracks as the water filled them in again. "You're going to get dirty, but you are already."

"Thanks."

"I didn't mean it that way." He turned to look at her, a smile playing on his lips. Her face looked sallow, her eyes dry and red. He was sure she was in some sort of half-conscious daze, and stopped to make her take a drink. Then he gave her an energy bar. There were only two left that he could see.

"Damn mosquitoes," Catarina said after the fourth hour of walking. She slapped at her face and neck and gave Nick a questioning look. He peered up at the trees for a termite nest, but didn't see any. They continued on for another hour as Catarina kept slapping at her skin.

"They're not even bad yet," Nick said. "Wait until dusk. I don't have any traditional mosquito repellent, so if you want any you'll have to use bugs."

"Fine." Sweat had broken out across her brow. Sunlight reflected in her eyes, and Nick looked up at a break in the trees. Good, he could use the GPS.

"Let me see exactly where we are then I'll find some termites." He could already feel bites on his own skin as he dug in Kyle's bag for the GPS unit. He turned it on, quickly noting how far they were from the camp. He was taking a roundabout way, avoiding the original paths he and Kyle had made. He hoped to God he could make it back there before Kyle did.

"Should you be turning that on?" Catarina asked with a nod at the GPS unit. "Can't Kyle locate us?"

"Not this fast, no. This is the only one we had, anyway, and I have his phone." He also had his own cell phone, he remembered. It was in one of his pockets, turned off.

"Phone?"

"Satellite phone."

"Oh." Catarina was quiet, her breaths steady and heavy. Even though she was limping, she walked more quietly than Nick. "Shouldn't we call someone, then?"

"Call who? Unless you have someone standing by with a helicopter, I don't see how that's going to help. And, honestly, I don't know who the hell to trust anymore. I don't know who's watching the calls on that phone."

"Actually," she said between heavy breaths. "I do have access to a helicopter."

He stopped in his tracks. "What?"

"A helicopter—you know, something that'll get us the hell out of here faster than this hiking shit."

Birds chattered around them. It was the hottest part of the day, and Nick's back was sopping wet. His toes were cold, his fingers numb. A sharp pain in his stomach kept reminding him how hungry he was. Maybe Catarina was right. He'd thought of using the phone to contact other agents he knew in the field, but he would have to get in touch with CIA headquarters to do that, and every instinct inside him fought against that idea. It might have been because he was in trouble, needed rescued, he didn't know. It didn't feel like a matter of pride; it was something stronger.

"Fine, make the call," he said, pulling out the phone from Kyle's bag. He got it ready and walked around until he found a good signal, hoping this wasn't a mistake. He still wanted time to try and get information out of Catarina, but he didn't want to end up double-crossed by her, or even worse, dying in the jungle if he refused to let her call. If it came to death, Catarina would go long before him. That was what scared him. The thought of dying alone made him shiver, even as he stood in a pool of sunlight. Bugs floated around him, their wings reflecting the light, their bodies slowly moving.

He shook the tension out of his shoulders and laughed out loud. Damn, the jungle was getting to him. He wasn't going to die here. He was too good for that, even if this was out of his element.

"There's a small clearing three miles from our location," Catarina said when she finished her phone call. "It's big enough for the helicopter to pick us up. They'll be here by morning." She tossed the phone back to Nick and limped past him, obviously determined to make the three-mile journey in good time. After they stopped to squish termites onto their skin, she collapsed from exhaustion, and Nick scooped her into his arms.

She squirmed. "I can walk, just get me a drink."

"I'm carrying you whether you like it or not."

"Put me the hell down!" She stretched her body out, and he almost dropped her, but tightened his hold and ordered her to wrap her arm around his neck. She did.

"So what's with the Texan accent?" he asked after she relaxed.

"What accent?" She hid it this time, applying the perfect Portuguese edge to her English words.

Nick smiled and kept silent. He'd ask her again later. When the sun went down, he let her walk again, and then checked their location. The clearing was a few yards ahead.

"Do you think Kyle's following us?" Catarina asked when they reached the clearing. Nick studied the area. The helicopter wouldn't have room to land, but it could drop a rope or a ladder. He could at least see the stars. That was a relief.

"Not that I can tell," Nick said as he set up the lantern and pulled out what food they had left. He spread the blanket out for Catarina, and she sat down with a heavy sigh. "Then he must be waiting for us somewhere," she said, and rubbed at her temples. "Or he's hoping we die out here. He'd like that, I'm sure."

"You're not going to die out here," he said softly as he handed her an energy bar.

"What about all the animals?"

"I've got the rifles. Not a problem. They haven't bothered us so far."

She took a bite of the bar and chewed, her face blank. "And what about you?"

"Me?" He bit into his own bar, pleased with how the conversation was moving. Catarina was exhausted, and that made her vulnerable.

"Yes, you. You're out to kill someone, and it's not me," she said, still chewing. "It's Matheus. You're after him."

Nick nodded. "I'm trying to find your husband, yes."

"Well, you won't."

"Not if you don't want me to. But, do you? I've heard you're not happy, Catarina. I can help you, if you want. I can make things right for you."

"Right? For me?" Catarina laughed loudly, grabbing her sides. "Nobody can help me," she said through the laughs. They grew harder, more strained by the second. Then she doubled over, dropped her food and started crying. Moving closer, Nick wrapped her in his arms. He cursed himself for making her cry, but he was sure it had more to do with her health than his words. He squeezed her to his chest, and she relaxed against him, still sobbing.

"What can I do?" he asked, stroking her hair like he'd done the night before. "Does your leg hurt? Do I need to look at it again?"

"No, it's not that. It's you. Nobody's ever said anything about my accent before. Nobody's ever noticed."

"And that's making you cry?"

She pulled away and wiped the tears from her face. "Nothing makes me cry. I don't know what the hell is wrong with me."

Nick was quiet for a few moments. "Were you born here?"

"No."

"Texas?"

She nodded and picked up her food. "I haven't been there since I was thirteen." Her shoulders slumping, she looked at Nick's lap. "Can I?"

Nick helped her lie down, resting her head on the soft part of his thigh. She stared ahead, nibbling on the end of her energy bar. "I'm so tired," she whispered. "I'm tired of everything, and I don't want you to kill Matheus. I remember when I was Alejandro's age. I remember when they came and killed my father and brought me here to Brazil. I remember ..."

"Who killed your father? The drug lords?" He leaned over to look at her face, but she'd closed her eyes. The energy bar fell from her fingers and her breaths came deep and slow. This time Nick didn't fall asleep.

Chapter 22

West Virginia

Devan noticed the scent of freshly baked brownies when he and Clara entered the inn.

"She makes those every night," Clara said after they entered the library. Devan had just finished helping some guests on the lake, and he was dying to talk to Clara alone. He'd kept his mouth shut about the kiss in the butterfly grove yesterday morning and Clara seemed to have chosen to do the same. But the silence couldn't last forever.

"My mom keeps asking Rachel to make them," Devan said with a weak laugh. "You know, because of your dad."

"Yeah, we ate a lot of chocolate desserts when he was around." She turned to him. "Is there a reason you wanted to come in here?"

Devan's words stuck in his throat—if he even had words to say. He knew the library was always empty and he would have her attention. Shrugging, he bent to look at the caterpillars. The scientist needed to get more milkweed and clean the bottom.

"I want to apologize," he blurted to the caterpillars instead of Clara. "For yesterday. I'm sorry." He straightened when Clara touched his shoulder.

"I ran from you because of Jeff," she said, the sunlight from the window illuminating her eyes. She blinked. "I know he's not good for me. He's not good for anybody. But I love him." She looked down. "I'm afraid he won't get out of this, though, and it makes me want to run from everything. Sometimes I want to hurt him back."

"You mean he's cheated on you?"

"No, nothing like that. I wish it was that."

Devan's heart sank. He started to sweat.

"He would never hurt me, but sometimes I don't even know who he is. Not like you." She curled her fingers around his hand. "I know everything about you is good, and I've never had that. Jeff and I pretend so many things around each other, and it all gets so blurred. Sometimes I think he loves me, and other times I have no idea if it's one big show because it's what we're supposed to be—in love. How do you know when it's real?" She hung her head and shut her eyes so tightly her face turned pale. "How do you know when to give up and move on or just keep pretending until it's real?"

Devan moved forward as she looked back up at him. "Clara, I'm so sorry." It was okay to comfort her; he wasn't doing anything wrong.

"Stop," Clara said when he closed his arms around her waist. She darted her gaze over his shoulder and he turned to see the scientist watching them from the doorway, his hands full of fresh milkweed. Devan ripped away from Clara. "Mr. Allen."

A smile played on the scientist's lips. "You can call me Robert, you know. Everybody calls me Robert except those two little girls. Crazy things." He headed for the cage, his mouth twisting into a grin. "I hope I'm not interrupting anything."

"Not at all." Devan moved away from the cage. It was his own fault for bringing Clara into the library where anybody could see them, but Clara seemed to think differently. Right now her jaw was rigid as she glared at Robert's back.

"Where did you say you're from?" she asked. "California?"

"New York. I've never been to California." Robert lifted the cage lid and began moving caterpillars to the bottom. "I'd love to study the monarchs in San Diego. You live there, right?" He straightened. "With your sister?"

"No, Violet lives in England."

"So it's you and Jeffrey in San Diego."

"Yeah." Her voice was quiet.

Devan looked back and forth between them. Silence. Yet something was said. Robert opened his mouth and then clamped it shut. Turning back to the cage, he pulled out the chewed plants. "I'm sorry I interrupted you two. I need to head out for more milkweed, anyway."

Shifting from her right foot to her left, Clara sucked on her bottom lip. The tightness between her and Robert stretched until she stopped shifting and put her hands on her hips. "So how long are you here?"

Robert turned, towering over her. Devan moved closer to wrap an arm around her waist.

"Until I get what I need." Robert looked Devan in the eyes and grinned wide. Everything about his expression looked overdone. "I have a lot of work ahead of me. Have fun, you two."

Clara stayed stiff until he left the room, then relaxed and turned to bury her face in Devan's shoulder. He clutched her close. What had just happened? Warm tears soaked his T-shirt, but Clara was silent. No sobs. She wasn't even breathing hard. Was she angry? Frightened? Completely nuts?

"Tell me what's going on," he said with a glance at the empty hallway.

"I know him," she whispered. "He works with Jeff. I saw him at a company dinner two years ago."

"What?" Devan pushed her away. Her eyes were barely wet. "That's a good thing, right? Maybe he knows where to find Jeff."

"Weren't you listening? No, it's not good! It's been bugging me for days. I thought I recognized him when he got here, but when he asked me about Jeff just now, there was something in his eyes. I don't remember telling him Jeff's name. He knows him."

Devan gave her a questioning look. He wasn't following her logic. "You mean he's looking for Jeff? Why would he have to be all sneaky about it?"

Staring at the dead milkweed on the desk, Clara shook her head. "I don't know if he's looking for Jeff, but it's all wrong. It feels wrong. If he works with Jeff at the DEA, why is he here posing as a butterfly scientist?" She narrowed her eyes and said barely above a whisper, "We have to search his room. That'll tell us—"

"What!" Devan backed away. She had gone from wanting to kiss him to being completely paranoid. The guy was just a scientist. At least that's what Devan wanted to believe, but Robert's grin burned in his memory.

Clara pushed her face an inch from his. "What I've found out about Jeff scares me to death. This guy isn't here for the butterflies." Her tears were gone now as she stood rigid. "We can't call the police."

"Are you sure Robert doesn't just look like the guy you saw? Is his name even Robert?"

"I don't know who he really is, but I remember seeing him. He's not Jeff's boss, but he's over him somehow." She clenched her fists. "I wonder if he's looking for Dad. Maybe it's all connected." She glared at the empty doorway across the room. "I have to search Robert's room. He's gone outside to get more milkweed. I can hurry." She brushed past Devan, and he grabbed her arm.

"Wait a sec. How do you think you're getting in there?"

"You'll give me a key, of course." She looked up at him, her jaw clenched, her eyes narrowed to slits. "Trust me. We need to know what he's up to."

"But searching his room? If he is dangerous, that's not a good idea."

"But I have to do it. If you don't help me, I'll pick the lock." She broke out of his hold and marched out of the library. Rushing after her, Devan caught her by the shoulders and pressed her back against the wall. His heart pounded. She felt strong, but he saw the fear in her eyes now. If she was dead-set on spying, he wasn't going to let her do it alone, or at all. He would do it. He slowed his breaths.

"Let's be smart about this, okay? I'll get the key. You go stay in your room. I have more reason to search than you do, so if he catches me I'll tell him I was doing maintenance." He could feel Clara's heartbeats against his chest. She didn't struggle under his hold.

"Do you know what to look for?"

His mouth went dry. "I don't know. Guns?"

"Check his bags. Look for papers, anything weird that doesn't fit who he says he is. And Devan?"

He tried to focus on her, but his thoughts were too busy racing through what he was about to do.

"I'm not overreacting."

When he let himself into Robert's room, it looked untouched. No wrinkles on the bed. Bags zipped, set by the door. Even the curtains were pulled neatly shut, making the room darker than normal. Devan closed the door behind him and slipped the key in his pocket. His heartbeat drummed in his ears as he turned and locked the door.

Staring at the room in front of him, he thought of his dad, the way he had lived so long with lies and secrets. Guilt. Was this how he felt, his head swimming with fear that someone would discover him? It was a strange feeling, one Devan hadn't felt much in his life. He always lived inside the lines—and a part of him was dying to cross them.

He closed his eyes, trying to push back his fear that Robert would burst in any second. He went into the bathroom. A razor was set by the sink, placed at a precise ninety-degree angle, a washcloth folded beneath it. The guy even flossed. Several strands were coiled in the otherwise empty trash can. The mirror was spotless, but the cleaning staff wasn't due until tomorrow.

Devan checked the cupboards under the sink, then left to search the rest of the room. No personal belongings. No books. No shoes. Everything had to be in the bags by the door. Could he go through them? Would Robert notice later?

Devan's fingers twitched at the thought of rifling through the man's stuff. But he had to. What if Clara was right? Robert's evil grin flashed through his mind again. It was evil. He wasn't imagining that, at least, and that made unzipping the first bag even harder. He cringed at the sound.

Neatly folded clothes, nothing else. Devan searched the corners, the pockets, between the shirts. Then finally, at the bottom, he found a book. He slipped it out and read the title. Something about monarch butterflies. Okay, that seemed normal.

Flipping through the pages, he looked for extra papers, notes, anything. A small photo fell to the floor and Devan snatched it up. Just some kid with pale skin and slicked hair. Almost menacing. He had to be twelve or thirteen.

Devan turned the photo over. Nothing. This was it? Unless Robert kept more stuff in his car, Clara had to be dreaming things up. He put the photo and book away, and stood up, looking around the clean room. Why would somebody live this way? His own room was a mess—he never made his bed, always left wet towels on the floor, shoved pants into his drawers. Even his mom wasn't this meticulous.

Then he remembered the chewed milkweed Robert had left in the library, and the dirty bottom of the caterpillar cage.

The brownies smelled even stronger when Devan entered the kitchen for dinner. Two staff members sat next to him, chatting. His mom, across from him, stared at her plate with a blank expression.

Still tense from spying, Devan tapped his foot under the table and stared at his own plate. Nobody had seen Robert since he'd left for more milkweed an hour ago. Clara, now in the dining room with Violet and the other guests, seemed upset that he hadn't found anything.

"Is he back yet?" Devan asked Rachel when she walked in from the dining room. She brushed past him, glaring.

"For the fifth time, no, he isn't back." She set down her serving tray and turned to his mom sitting across the table. "Did you want me to serve strawberry pie or brownies for dessert?"

"I don't care."

"Then I'll serve pie. We've had brownies every night this week."

"That's fine." Lilian rested her chin in her hand and picked at her roll. Maybe she was worried about his behavior with Clara? She hadn't brought it up again, but he was sure it was still bothering her. She didn't understand. Just as she had with his dad, she made assumptions and closed her eyes to everything else.

He wanted to open her eyes, tell her more about Clara, about Robert, but his mouth refused to open. She looked so sad and worried, and for the first time in days, Clara melted from Devan's mind. He felt the butterfly in his hand again—sugar caged in his fingers, delicate wings so easy to crush.

"Mom," he finally managed to say. She looked up from the roll, her eyes red and puffy as if she hadn't slept for days. He hadn't noticed that before. "Can we go talk somewhere?"

She glanced at the two staff members engrossed in their conversation. "Not right now. Rachel, you said Robert's still working outside?"

"I think so. The girls said he was going to play checkers with them tonight, so I'm sure he'll be back soon."

Twisting to look at Rachel, Devan knotted his eyebrows. She hadn't told him that. She gave him another glare and turned back to cutting pie. He'd been so absorbed with Clara that he'd missed that Rachel was upset with him.

"Thanks for dinner, Rachel." Lilian stood up from the table and straightened her shoulders.

Devan opened his mouth to say something, anything. She had never ignored him before. It felt foreign, made his head light and empty as she silently left the kitchen. He stood up to follow her, but thought it might be better to give her some space. If he lost himself in a book, that would help. He went to his room. An hour passed. He didn't read a word, but instead stared at the poster on his ceiling, thinking of Clara's persistence that he search Robert's room. But she was wrong. The man was just a clean-freak who looked like someone she knew.

A knock on his door made him jump. "Devan?"

It was Clara's voice. Devan rushed to the door and peeked through the crack. He'd already taken off his shirt. Not that Clara hadn't seen him mostly naked before, but not in his room. The thought made his body flush with excitement as he opened the door a little wider, cursing himself at the same time.

"This is stupid," Clara said, staring at her feet. "But Robert just came back and I'm worried."

He opened the door wide enough to let her in. Dressed in thin cotton pajamas, she slipped by and looked at everything in the room but him.

"Are you all right?" he asked when she stopped her gaze on his messy bed. She turned to look at him, her face cold and blank.

"I don't care if you didn't find anything in his room. He's going to hurt someone, I can feel it."

Devan felt himself tense. "Did he say anything about his room? Is he acting weird?"

"No, he's playing checkers with the girls. They're eating pie and laughing. It's freaking me out. He's good. Too good." She narrowed her eyes and leaned closer. "He reminds me of Dad."

His skin cold now, Devan snatched his shirt off the floor and pulled it on. "How does he remind you of him? Is that supposed to be a bad thing?"

"Just how everybody likes him. He's good at lying. I have no idea what he's really thinking or going to do." She started pacing in front of his bed, sucking on her bottom lip. "Violet would understand. Maybe I should talk to her. I'm afraid she'll laugh at me, but if this is what I think it is, she'll get it. I think."

"Do you want me to come with you?"

"No, she had a headache and went to her room. I'll go in the morning." She stopped pacing and looked up at him with pleading eyes. "I don't want to be alone. Not with him here."

"You're afraid he'll do something tonight?"

"Not really. I told you it was stupid." She stepped closer and Devan fought back the urge to touch her. In the back of his mind, his mom's eyes glared at him. Then Rachel and Violet and Nick. But his dad's eyes were the angriest, and Devan couldn't shove them away. His dad must have felt this way, knowing that if he took what he wanted he would hurt people. Three years later, and Devan still saw the pain in his mom's eyes. That was why Devan stayed.

"Can I stay with you?" Clara asked, touching his arm.

He took a step back. This was why she had come to him, using Robert as an excuse. He remembered her crossing the log, clearly brave enough to face her fear. Running. She didn't need him. She wanted him. She had that look on her face again, her lips parted, practically begging.

"Maybe you should stay with Violet tonight," he said, working his words past the lump in his throat.

She wrinkled her forehead. "Violet? Why would I stay with her?"

"I don't know. I want you safe. It's just—"

He swallowed his words, almost choking when Clara leaned forward and kissed him. Her mouth was stiff, nervous. Devan sank into his instincts and wrapped his arms around her, squeezing gently as she relaxed. It was as if all her worries puddled to the floor, leaving her soft and malleable.

"I'm sorry," she whispered when they stopped for air. "I can't help it. You just, you're so not like him."

"Who? Jeff?"

She backed away, touching her mouth. "Yes, Jeff, and right now all I want is you. When I kiss him it's like he's a million miles away." She grabbed his waist and pulled his shirt up to feel his skin.

Devan watched her. He felt distant, unlike he'd ever felt, and decided he would give in. She wanted him, and he felt too tired, too confused to fight his emotions anymore. Trailing a finger along the top of her pants, playing with the button, he wondered if she would be like any of the girlfriends he'd had in college. None of them had made him feel this way with just one touch. Dizzy with need. She lifted his shirt higher.

"Are you sure?" he asked, smiling. He tried to fight his growing excitement. He wanted to be annoyed, angry, anything but excited. This was wrong. His dad's voice screamed it at him once again.

"Help me forget everything," Clara said, gazing into his eyes as she pulled his shirt over his head. "Just for awhile."

"I'll talk to my mom about Robert tomorrow." He touched the smooth bumps of her spine, feeling the thin material of her shirt, the clasps of her bra. She kissed him again, and he realized he'd known all along he could lose himself in her, move in harmony like they did through the water.

But there was something he couldn't shake, and he closed his eyes as her words from the library rushed into his mind—*I know he's not good for me. He's not good for anybody. But I love him.*

Chapter 23

Lilian kept her wedding photo shoved in the back of her sock drawer. She hadn't looked at it for at least a year, but now it wouldn't leave her mind. Embarrassed she was even thinking about Chris, she locked her bedroom door and sat on the edge of the bed facing her dresser. She breathed deep, taking in the faint smell of brownies from a plate on her dresser. Her heart twisted at the thought of Nick. Then her stomach growled, and she gripped her knees.

She hadn't eaten anything for twenty-four hours, not since she and Violet had spoken about Robert. Her anxious suspicions had erased her appetite, making her more and more nervous until she'd decided she had to act on her instincts.

As soon as Rachel had told her Robert was still outside during dinner, she'd left the kitchen to sneak into his room. Just a quick look. But the man was the cleanest guest she'd ever seen, and she'd found nothing. It made her squeamish. Confused.

Her fingers itched to call Nick, but he had told her not to contact him or the police unless it was absolutely necessary. She was surprised that with her feelings of fear and confusion, Chris was the person she kept thinking about for help. Maybe it was because she knew he was strong and capable and might help her if she asked. Or maybe Devan could ask. Chris would definitely help Devan.

She walked to the dresser and pulled open the sock drawer, pushing her hand to the back until she found a small framed picture. Chris stared up at her from behind the glass, dressed in a tuxedo with his arms curled tightly around her waist. She threw the picture on the bed, scowling at all the memories. Twenty-seven years. So many smiles and laughs, tears the day of Devan's birth—happy tears. She had been so happy. Then cakes and keys to a business that turned her art into too much work. Chris thought he knew what she wanted, always pushed things onto her, and she'd never been brave enough to tell him no. Instead, she grew more distant, building a wall until Chris gave up. But the inn was hers; the butterflies promised her freedom, and she'd taken it.

Now all she could see was dead wings falling to the ground, Nick's soft assurance that he would come back, her cell phone by the bed begging her to call him for help. But she didn't know if this was an emergency. Maybe she was overreacting again. Could she trust her instincts about Robert? Violet seemed to suspect Robert, too, and that was enough. But was Chris her last resort for help? Although she hated to bring back all that pain and anger, she had to admit that Chris felt safe to her. She asked herself why, when she'd spent so much energy blaming him for everything wrong in her life. Her fingertips tingled. Her mouth went dry. Something in her mind twitched, nagged.

Grabbing Chris' picture, she shoved it back into the drawer. She didn't need him. Devan could help her. He would be enough.

She left her room, Robert's laughter echoing down the hall, mixed with the giggles of the two girls. When Lilian reached Devan's door, she hesitated to knock. She'd never felt so nervous to talk to her own son before.

Finally, she knocked twice. Nothing. She had assumed he'd gone to bed early since she hadn't seen him on her way to and from Robert's room on the other side of the inn. Her heart sank. He was probably with Clara outside. Or maybe he was asleep. The light was off. She knocked again. If he was asleep, she could wake him up for something this important.

"Devan, honey? We can talk now."

The handle twisted, and Devan cracked open the door. "I'm sleeping. What do you need?"

"I thought you wanted to talk." She stepped back.

Devan started to close the door. "I'm too tired. We can talk in the morning."

"But Devan, there's something I need, I mean, you're awake now." He had almost closed the door when a thought occurred to her. She narrowed her eyes and blurted, "Are you alone in there?" before realizing how bad it sounded.

Devan's mouth dropped open. His cheeks turned beet red. "That's none of your business." Before he closed the door, Lilian caught sight of his bed and the silhouette of a thin figure sitting on the edge. Bare shoulders, hair down. Clara. The door closed, the lock turned, and Lilian stared at where Devan's face had been.

She put a hand to her chest, her skin damp with sweat. This couldn't be happening. It was worse than she'd feared. She rushed down the hall to the front door.

The evening was calm. The sun had set, leaving the sky a dusty blue that would soon turn black and show the stars. She reached the dock and leaned over to grab her knees, gulping air like a fish as the wood planks beneath her swirled into a blur. She closed her eyes and took control. Calm, get calm.

"Nick," she whispered to her feet. "This is going to hurt you the most." And that twisted her disappointment even tighter. She wondered if he would blame her, if there was any more she could have done. She had gently warned Devan, voiced her concern, hoped beyond reason Nick would return before things got too bad. Now she felt a distance open up between her and Devan, wide like the lake stretching beneath her, and she asked herself if it had anything to do with Clara at all, or if every mother felt this way at some point—clinging to her child's innocence that had long since disappeared.

She straightened to stare at the sky as it slowly grew darker. Suddenly cold as ice, she wrapped her arms around her waist and wondered where Nick was at that moment, if he was safe, if he needed her, too.

"Lilian?"

His voice made her jump, and she spun around.

"R-Robert."

He stepped forward. It always surprised her how big he was, and when he reached her, she backed away. Two more steps and she'd fall into the lake.

"I saw you run down the hall," he said, tilting his head to look at her more closely. "I thought I'd come see if everything's all right."

Looking away, she fought to steady her breaths, tried to ignore the bruise on his cheek, his thick arms the size of small tree trunks.

"I'm fine," she stuttered. "I needed some fresh air."

He took a step back and looked across the lake. "Yes, it's nice. I don't blame you." His eyes glazed over as he crossed his arms. "I've enjoyed my stay here. It's a beautiful place."

Lilian wasn't sure what he was getting at. Wrinkling her brow, she looked behind her shoulder at the water's glassy surface. The forest reflected in the water, a dark strip of shadowy cones. She turned back to Robert and straightened her shoulders to make herself taller. He didn't look like a threat, staring into the distance with a soft smile. His eyes looked as smooth as the water.

"It must be nice having families here all the time," he said, turning to her. "And your son. You must never feel lonely."

She squinted, her mind spinning. Never lonely? She'd never been so lonely in her life, aching for Nick to come back to her in one piece, hating Devan's decisions, remembering her happiness with Chris and how it all fell apart.

"Sometimes I'm lonely," she whispered, surprised the words had come out of her mouth.

Robert's expression softened in the dim light. "How?"

Lilian wasn't sure how she should answer. It was none of his business, but he did seem genuinely concerned. He was studying her, and the longer he looked, the more he seemed to be willing an answer out of her. He stepped closer, closer, closer. Lilian felt her heels touch the edge of the dock.

"Robert, I—"

"I think you miss someone," he said, moving his hand toward her. "Someone who might return soon."

Lilian almost took a step back, but reminded herself she'd fall into the water. She held her ground, fear erupting inside her. "I'm going inside now." Her voice came out weak, not strong like she wanted. She tried to move forward.

"Wait." With lightning reflexes, Robert snatched her wrist in a loose grip. His eyes drilled into her, making her hot and clammy at the same time. "I know you're waiting for him," he said, gripping her tighter when she tried to yank away. "I can see it in your eyes."

"Who?" She tried to pull away again, but he held his grip, this time so hard her fingers turned numb. She was right. Violet was right.

"He was supposed to be here. How soon will he be back?" He shook her arm. "Tell me!"

"Who?" But she wasn't stupid. Nick. He wanted Nick. She could see it stamped all over his face, practically hanging on his lips.

He let her go and spun around, walking quickly off the dock with his hands balled into fists. Lilian looked at the underside of her wrist where two fresh bruises blossomed across her skin.

Biting her lip against the dull ache, she told herself she was in shock. Too many things at once, her suspicions proven, everything in danger. She watched Robert march up the hill, his body framed inside a checkerboard of yellow lights.

She chased after him, her footsteps loud on the dock, but he was quick. She was only halfway up the hill when he reached the inn and slammed the screen door behind him.

Lilian's lungs burned. She crossed the clearing, but before she reached the steps, Robert reappeared carrying his two bags. He stomped down the stairs, avoiding her glare as he headed straight for his car.

Devan opened the screen door. "Mom? Where's he going? What happened?"

She stopped dead in her tracks and stared at Devan, sloppily dressed, his hair ruffled. "Robert," she said between heavy breaths. "He's here for Nick. He's not—"

Tires screeched from Robert's dark sedan. It peeled out of the parking lot, kicking up a thick dust cloud when it reached the dirt road leading down the mountain.

Chapter 24

Despite his mother's distress and Robert's sudden, unexplained departure, Devan couldn't get Clara out of his mind. He could still smell her, always like sweet grass and water. He could still feel her soft skin against him. Being with her in his room, finally having her, had been surreal, especially with his dad screaming at him in his head the whole time. But he'd never needed anything more in his life, and suddenly understood things he'd never wanted to understand about his dad, why he was yelling at him in a silent, intense haze. He had never admitted to Devan how quickly the guilt could start eating at him, how good and bad it could feel at the same time.

Now, watching Clara from across the library as she argued with Violet about Robert, Devan ordered himself to forget what had happened. It didn't work.

Violet kept rubbing her temple and squinting from the bright lights of the library. Devan turned to the wall and switched them off. Several lamps around the room bathed the walls in a soft orange glow.

"Thank you," Violet said with a glance in his direction. She turned back to Clara. "If you would have come to me earlier we could have figured something out together. If you'd get off your high horse once in a while maybe we could actually communicate."

"What are you talking about?" Clara flung her hands in the air. "This is why I can't talk to you. You're always judging me. You think this is about her, and it isn't. It's about you. It's always about you."

"We aren't talking about me. We're talking about Robert. We don't know where he's headed. What if he finds Dad, and we never see him again? Have you even thought of that?"

Clara's bottom lip trembled. Devan wanted to hold her, but kept his distance. "Of course I have, but how is it any different than all the other times he's left? He always comes back."

"Well maybe he won't this time. This is different. We've never been part of it before."

They stared at each other, standing far apart, both tense and angry. Devan looked at his mom sitting on the sofa at the back of the room. She was biting her nails, her eyes squeezed shut. He knew she was listening, worrying, wondering what to do. None of them had decided to call Nick yet. The decision hung in the air, nagging at Devan stronger and stronger. Finally he began to forget about being with Clara. Somebody had to call Nick—if he was even reachable. Devan knew Clara had tried to contact Jeff even though she wasn't supposed to, and nothing had come of it.

"Stop arguing, you two." Lilian stood and marched across the room. She put her hands on her hips, trying to look stern, but Devan knew better. She seemed tired, almost solemn. He hadn't seen her look that weak since the divorce, and it hurt him. He wanted to put an arm around her, but then he remembered the anger in her eyes when she'd asked him if he was alone in his room.

"Sorry," Violet answered, and sat down on the matching chair opposite Clara's. She folded her arms. "This is why everything's gone bad. We can't be around each other, not since—"

"I know this is about your mother, but just forget about her for now, please. Think about Nick." Her voice caught in her throat. "I mean, your father. We need to call him. Whose phone are we going to use? I'm assuming it would be best to use one nobody would recognize."

"Rachel's got one," Devan said, already heading out of the library to find her. He felt strange inside. He wondered what Nick would do if he discovered what had happened between him and Clara. He wondered if he'd found Jeff by now, if he would bring him to the inn, if Clara would decide to stick with the marriage, if all hell would break loose when Jeff found out what was going on. If he found out.

Devan had no idea what Clara would tell him. He had to admit he hardly knew her, for how physically close they'd been.

But he had to focus. He had to remember the danger Nick was in and that Robert was heading down the mountain to find him.

"Devan, where is everybody?"

Rachel rushed toward him from the end of the hallway. She was in her bunny slippers that he always laughed at, her hair pulled into a mess on top of her head.

"We're in the library. I thought you'd be in bed."

"I was, but Erin knocked on my door."

Devan looked at the little girl trailing behind her. Eyes wide, cheeks flushed, she looked like she might burst into tears.

"M-my sister left," she spluttered. "But I didn't want to tell Mommy or Daddy. We're supposed to watch each other."

"She left?" Devan squatted down to look her in the eyes. Lois couldn't have left with Robert. Devan had watched him leave the inn. Alone. "What do you mean?"

"She says she's looked everywhere," Rachel explained. "So I was going to get her parents."

"She never goes away," Erin whimpered, twisting her hands together. "But Mr. Allen stopped playing checkers with us and she left."

"What?" Devan stood up to look Rachel in the face. "Do you think she went after him?"

"How should I know? I didn't even know he was gone." She narrowed her eyes. "What's happening? Why are you all in the library?"

He glanced at Erin. "I can't tell you here, but I think we need to find Lois as fast as we can. Go get her parents and bring everybody to the library."

Searching his face, she leaned forward. "Does this have to do with Nick?"

"Just do it. And bring your phone."

When he returned to the library, Clara stood up. "Where's Rachel?"

"She's coming. Mom, there's a problem. Lois is missing."

"What?"

The room fell silent. Devan knew everyone was thinking the same thing—how Lois had attached herself to Robert, how his leaving might have upset her, how much they couldn't afford such a distraction at the moment.

"She's not anywhere in the inn?" Violet asked. "There are a hundred places to hide here. I've searched every corner and closet for bugs."

Lilian gave her an anxious look. "Why don't you go look? Clara, you can help."

"I'll go with Devan," Clara answered, stepping away from Violet.

Lilian folded her arms and looked up as sheets of water pelted across the roof. "If we're going to search anywhere outside, we'd better do it now. Where are Jason and Jenny?"

"Here."

They entered the library. Jason, Erin's dad, carrying her in his arms. She was crying and biting her bottom lip.

"We'll help search, too, of course," he said. "I'll help look outside."

Devan stepped forward, stumbling over his words. "No, you can't go out there."

Jason wrinkled his brow as he passed Erin to his wife. "Why not? She's my daughter. I'm sure as hell not going to sit around here while someone else tries to find her. And where's Robert?"

"He had a family emergency," Lilian said softly. "He left alone."

Devan was surprised at how well she was able to lie. He was also surprised at Jason's sudden interest in his daughter. He had ignored her his entire stay so far. Devan thought hard. He needed more lies he could pass on to the unsuspecting parents, but Robert was the only person who kept coming to his mind. What if he turned around and came back? What if he brought others with him? What if he got stuck on the road in the rain and marched back up here with guns from his car?

Not that Devan could imagine why he would want anybody here. He wanted Nick or Jeffrey. Still, Devan didn't want to leave Clara and his mom without someone to protect them. He knew the area much better than Jason who hadn't stepped foot in the forest since they'd arrived.

"I think Lois might be hiding somewhere in the inn," he said as calmly as he could. "I'll go look outside. It's dark, and I know where to go."

The rain pounded on the roof even harder. Devan imagined himself out in the darkness, hunched over with a flashlight looking around wet branches, rotting logs, boulders, streams. Now that it was raining, he hoped Lois was smart enough to head back to the inn.

Violet's voice broke his thoughts. "I know the woods, too, Devan. Everybody here can search the inn while me, you, Rachel, and Clara go search outside. We can split into two teams."

"Then I'm going with you," Jason said, his face bright red with concern and panic.

Lilian cleared her throat and stood tall, obviously intent on taking charge. Her voice came out steady and strong. "Everyone can search outside. Jenny and Erin can stay here and look." She marched to Devan, her eyes no longer tired. A fiery resolve burned behind them. "But I need to make a call first."

Devan handed her the phone, and she disappeared down the hallway.

Chapter 25

West Virginia

The jet landed just after eight. Startled awake by the wheels touching down, Nick looked around the lit cabin. Alex had spread himself out on the seats, a blanket tucked up to his chin as he slept. He looked almost angelic in the low light, his features not as sharp with his hair ruffled around his face. Nick caught a glimpse of Catarina in his relaxed countenance—a hint of dimples waiting for a genuine smile.

"Alex," Nick whispered after gathering his bag Catarina had given back to him and the briefcase. "We've landed. You might want to wake up." He gently shook the boy's shoulder, but the boy didn't open his eyes.

"We're flying on from here," Catarina's man grumbled in Portuguese. Still sitting behind Alex, he had his nose buried in a Playboy magazine, his eyes drowsy as he slowly flipped the pages.

"Here in the states or overseas?" Nick asked, doubting the man was stupid enough to give away such information.

"None of your business." He tossed aside the magazine and stood up, towering over Nick. "Catarina said you should find that briefcase a home pretty damn quick, understand?"

"Sure, I understand. Give Ferreira my best." Nick grumbled curses under his breath as he headed down the aisle. The man had no clue what was inside the briefcase. If he did, he would know that the more quickly Nick got the names to the CIA, the more quickly Ferreira and his top men were going down.

Sorting through the names earlier, Nick had seen several of Ferreira's locations detailed in the pile. It would only be a matter of time before he was found and arrested—or black ops took him out. For Catarina's sake, Nick hoped that wouldn't happen, but as far as he was concerned, his original mission was almost complete. He just had to get to Langley, no matter the outcome. Dragging this out was making things worse.

He stopped at the open door as two flight attendants pushed aside the front cabin curtain, Jeffrey between them. Looking groggy, he had his arms wrapped around their shoulders as he limped along. He smiled at Nick. "Ready to go home?"

Nick shrugged. He was starting to feel numb inside, especially as he looked at Jeffrey. He felt so divided when he looked at him, sure that he loved Clara, but wondering if love was enough. Love never felt like enough these days.

Taking Jeffrey's bag from a flight attendant, Nick helped Jeffrey down the stairs into the cool night. The jet had taxied away from the main terminals and parked in a quiet, low lit area. The sun sank in the sky, making everything a soft reddish orange. As they reached the bottom of the stairs, two men in suits stepped out of a dark car.

"In from Brazil?" they asked, eyeing Jeffrey's bloody pant leg.

"São Paulo," Nick said. His stomach twisted as Jeffrey's weight grew heavy against him.

"Passports?"

"Mine's in my bag," Jeffrey said, turning to take a crutch from a flight attendant behind them. He pulled away from Nick, who bent down to drop his bag to the ground.

"Where did your bag come from, anyway?" Nick asked, confused. "You never had one before."

Jeffrey cleared his throat. "I left it at the airport in a locker. Catarina's men went and fetched it."

"How nice of her." Nick glanced at the men watching him. They looked like government types, stiff and proud as they waited for Nick to fish out the information. He found Jeffrey's, too, and handed it all over. The man on the left flipped open the passports, studying them for a minute before he gave his partner a quick nod. He pulled out a phone and faced the terminals. "Everything's fine out here. They just need to refuel."

"Smooth," Nick said after the men handed him back his papers and drove away.

Jeffrey leaned on his crutch. "What was that about?"

"Just protocol. Catarina's got it down to a science." Nick grunted and turned to the flight attendants still standing on the stairs. The one in the low-cut blazer flashed him a sweet grin as the other one handed Jeffrey his other crutch.

The jet was back in the air by the time Nick and Jeffrey reached the parking garage where Nick had left his rental. He winced, wondering how much of a bill he'd run up on the damn thing or if the CIA had found it by now.

"That one," he said, motioning to a tan SUV, glad to see it still there. The garage was dark and quiet.

Jeffrey let Nick help him into the front seat and let out a long sigh as they drove out of the garage. "Hope you've got cash because I don't."

"Catarina gave me some." Nick looked at the clock. Almost nine. "I spent most of mine on flights and this car. It's a good thing I had it stashed back at the house before any of this started." His hands tightened around the wheel. He wanted to call Lilian and see if everything was okay, but although Catarina had given him and Jeffrey back most of their things, she'd kept their phones. She'd probably had them destroyed to keep anybody from connecting her to them. Nick stopped to pay for parking and breathed a sigh of relief when they reached the freeway. "Alright, it's time to talk."

Jeffrey stared out his window. "About what?"

"Don't play stupid, Jeffrey. I want to know what your connection is in all of this. You haven't told me everything."

"I've told you enough." Jeffrey started to pick at a small tear on the door. Yanking the wheel, Nick pulled onto the shoulder and skidded to a stop. The car shook as traffic zoomed by.

Jeffrey twisted around. "What are you doing?"

Red taillights zipped into a blur. Nick couldn't stay here too long or a cop would pull up, but he could at least scare Jeffrey into talking. There was a secret hanging in the air, and it was nagging at him as fast and intensely as the cars driving by. "I'm going to head straight for Langley if you don't speak up. They're going to wonder what you were doing down in Brazil with Ferreira's men."

"You wouldn't tell them that."

"You wanna bet?" He gunned the engine and the car lurched forward. When he slammed on the brakes, Jeffrey grabbed his leg as it hit the dashboard.

"Okay, okay! But why do you want to go to Langley? Aren't they looking for you?"

"Catarina gave me information to find Ferreira, and now that I know she's alive, I can work my way out of some of the mess."

"So she's willing to declare herself alive? 'Cause I don't think my testimony would be enough." Jeffrey lowered his voice. "I'm not sure that would be the best idea anyway. Right now."

His jaw tense, Nick stared at him. "Why not right now? I think once Ferreira's taken care of, Catarina will help me out.

Maybe." Nick's hands went limp around the steering wheel. Saying it out loud, he realized how stupid it sounded. Catarina had already told him she wanted to take Ferreira's place, and if that happened, she'd steer as clear from the U.S. government as she possibly could. There was no way she'd step forward and blow her nonexistence—a perfect cover.

Unless he was wrong.

Nick closed his eyes, thinking of Alex, his hardened expression and coldness to Catarina. Her words from the bedroom came back to him: *It's not what you think.*

"If you have to know everything," Jeffrey said quietly, "I'll tell you. I was going to tell you, but things went south."

Nick looked at the briefcase he'd slipped under his seat, the corner gleaming in the darkness. "Start talking, then. All of it."

Checking the road, Nick waited for a break in traffic and merged onto the freeway. As he watched the speedometer inch higher, Jeffrey took three deep breaths and rubbed at a spot above his wound.

"I've been working for Ferreira since the Air Force. It was a huge mistake, and I tried to get out of it. That's how I ended up with the DEA—Kyle told me Ferreira might leave me alone if I wasn't in a position to hand over information. So I left."

"And Ferreira didn't seem to care about that?"

"Kyle said Ferreira would leave me alone if I kept my mouth shut."

Nick focused on the slow car in front of him. A week ago he would have thought Jeffrey capable of nothing worse than yelling at a co-worker. Now he wasn't surprised by anything. "How did you get in with Ferreira in the first place?"

"I told you before. I knew Kyle from college, and when the right situation presented itself, he talked me into joining him and Ferreira's team. He made the whole thing look easy. Lots of money. Nobody would get hurt. He didn't tell me they'd give me this."

Nick glanced over to see Jeffrey turn his back to him. Lifting up his shirt, he pointed to a tattoo—the wings.

Nick gritted his teeth. The tattoo looked like Catarina's, only on the shoulder blade and smaller.

"So that's why she said you weren't what I thought," Nick muttered under his breath. He touched the briefcase with his foot, wondering if Jeffrey's name was in there. He had flipped through all of the papers, but he could have missed it. Fear crowded his thoughts. What other things had he overlooked?

Jeffrey lowered his shirt. "What did you say?"

"Nothing. Keep going."

"When a guy showed up at my apartment to give me the tattoo, I recognized it from high school. There's a gang that wears one like it. I started having regrets right away, but I stuck with it. I'd seen enough in my job to know how lopsided things are, and for some reason I thought I could make a difference. I didn't do anything for them for a long time. They wanted to know I was serious, and they wanted to train me, but they were careful about it. Men would show up at my door now and then. I think a year went by before I sold my first piece of information. Three days later, two of our planes were gunned down over Iraq."

A lump formed in Nick's throat. "That's murder, Jeffrey. Not even self-defense. Not even part of your job. What did you think would happen?" He glared ahead. "And how the hell did the Air Force not catch this?"

"You have no idea how careful everything was planned, how worried I was that would happen. But, I just ... I told you it was all a mistake. I'd screwed up some investigations at work, received warnings and whatnot. My girlfriend had just left me. It was a bad time for me and, well, it was a lot of money."

"That's why you got into drugs in California? You didn't have enough? Are you completely stupid?"

"I told you I was helping Kyle. If I didn't help him, things would get worse. Once you're in with Ferreira, you don't get out." He turned to Nick, his eyes widening. "Do you have any idea what I've been living with? Clara saw some drugs I was holding for one of Kyle's clients, and that's when things got bad between us. She stopped trusting me. She started snooping around, tracing my phone calls, digging through my files. That's why she doesn't want to try any procedures for a baby. She's afraid of what kind of father I'd be. She's afraid of me. I honestly don't know why she hasn't left me."

Nick was quiet, waiting for him to continue. It was coming together, but something still nagged at him.

Jeffrey leaned forward, gripping his seat. "Ferreira's ruined my life. I tried to ignore his ties to me, move away from it all, but nothing will ever change. That's why when Kyle's men showed up and told me I had to get down to Brazil to help find you, I thought it might be my chance to fix things. If I could somehow get to you and warn you, we could work together."

"What are you talking about? You think I can get you out of this?" Nick shook his head, almost laughing.

"No, but I hoped we could make something good come out of it. They didn't give me much of a choice. I had to go with them."

"Wait a minute." Nick moved into the other lane, finally fed up with the slow car in front of them. The nagging was stronger now. "Catarina looked at your tattoo. She knows about your connection with Ferreira."

"Yeah, I remember her lifting up my shirt when they gave me the morphine. She asked me if you knew about it. I thought she might have told you."

"No." Well, she had hinted at it.

"She asked me what I'd done for Ferreira, but when I explained Kyle and the DEA, she said something about me being unimportant."

That was good. Jeffrey's name wouldn't be in the briefcase, not if Catarina hadn't made a big deal out of him. That left one last thing to figure out. "Did you see Kyle at your apartment or when you got to Brazil?"

"No, but I'd met a few of his other men before, the ones who came to get me."

"Why do you think he wanted you down in Brazil to help find me? What's the point of that?"

"He couldn't find you. That's all I understood from what his men told me." Jeffrey shifted in his seat. He was still gripping the side, his knuckles white enough for Nick to notice.

"That's not a good enough reason to drag you down there and risk you messing things up. Does he trust you that much?"

"I guess so. I've never gone against him. He's too close to Ferreira."

"But you're not that qualified to find someone like me and kill me—your own father-in-law. No offense, Jeffrey, but you don't have that much experience in the field, and Kyle must know that."

"What are you saying?"

Nick wasn't sure. He stared at the dark road ahead, a blur of white, yellow and black. His thoughts felt the same—a complete blur, but at least moving forward.

Kyle knew how much family meant to Nick, that all he had left close to him were Violet, Clara and Jeffrey. But he also knew Nick's career had created deep rifts between him and his daughters. He would know Nick wasn't stupid enough to run to them unless their safety was on the line.

But why wouldn't Kyle have taken Clara? The men could have easily killed Jeffrey and found her in the closet. She would have been easy leverage to lure Nick.

He tapped his thumb on the steering wheel, his body growing colder by the second. The answer was right on the edge of his thoughts, but he couldn't think clearly. Heavy raindrops started splattering across the windshield. Great, now it was going to storm.

"Kyle knows you want out of this, right?" he asked Jeffrey.

"Yes, I told you that."

"So he would have known I would go help Clara, and that she'd tell me where you'd gone. She said the men weren't keeping it any secret that they were taking you to Brazil. He must have known I'd go find you, and that you'd side with me."

"I guess so." Jeffrey's voice softened, almost shaking.

"And that I'd run right back to where I've put everybody for safety. He wants the most leverage he can get."

"Leverage for what? You think he's following us to the inn?"

"I think he's already there."

Chapter 26

Lilian took one look at the rain and knew it was one of those storms. It was worse than the night Nick had arrived. She felt it in the intense drops slamming onto her head, her shoulders, even her toes. Her clothes were already soaked through, and she had only been outside a few seconds.

Devan and Clara headed down to search the lakeshore for Lois. Rachel and Jason went north where Lois and Erin usually played with their butterfly nets, and Violet and Lilian walked south to the road.

"Give it twenty minutes," Lilian said loudly through the rain. "Nobody will be able to get up or down the mountain."

"You still didn't get a hold of him?" Violet gave her a worried look as she switched on her flashlight.

"No. It won't go to voicemail. It just rings forever."

"Weird. Do you think Robert went to find him?" She hunched her shoulders and kept her flashlight close to her body. Its yellow beam didn't shine far.

"I hope not."

Although Lilian couldn't imagine what else he would be doing.

They stopped at the edge of the road. Small muddy streams had already swept away Robert's tire tracks. The road was steep for a few yards, then leveled out. Beyond that, the forest bent over the road.

"That little girl's in a lot of danger," Lilian said with a heavy heart. "I'm afraid Robert took her." Her voice caught in her throat on the last word. For the first time since meeting Robert, she was able to imagine him harming Lois. Her stomach twisted, and she pulled her hood closer.

"You said he left alone. You saw him."

"I did. But what if Lois was in the car when he left? I was down by the lake. What if he told her to get in his car before he came down to talk to me?"

Tightening her grip on her flashlight, Lilian started down the road. Violet stayed close at her side.

"Are ten-year-olds that stupid?"

"She was really attached to Robert. She might have done anything he told her to."

Lilian swept her flashlight across the road, into the trees. This was impossible. If Lois had headed down the road after Robert, she would be closer to the bottom by now. It would be quicker to take the Jeep, but Lilian wasn't foolish enough to brave the road. She'd been stuck on it one too many times to even try.

"How long do you think we'll be able to keep the truth from her parents?" Violet asked. She slipped, and Lilian reached out to steady her.

"As long as we can. I wish they had checked out yesterday. I wish I would have sent them into town the second we suspected Robert. What was I thinking?"

"Don't talk like that!" Violet kept sweeping her flashlight across the road, crossing Lilian's. The two yellow beams revealed nothing but wet trees, falling rain, and moving mud. "You didn't know what was going to happen. If anybody should have done anything, it was me. I'm the one who understood the danger, and I ignored my instincts. How far are we going?"

"I don't know. If it wasn't raining, we would see tracks or something." She stopped and lowered her flashlight. "Maybe we should call the police. We don't have to tell them about Robert's connection to Nick. He could be a child molester for all they know. It won't endanger Nick."

"I guess not. Do you want to go call? I can keep looking."

"Sure. I'll come back down in a minute."

Lilian headed up to the inn, her boots slipping. Nick wasn't here to catch her if she fell. Not this time. She wasn't sure he would ever be there for her again. She reached the brightly lit balcony and pulled out Rachel's cell phone. She had to try Nick one more time. It rang and rang. Nothing.

Dialing the police, she squinted to see Clara and Devan's dark forms along the shore. Their flashlight beams crossed and uncrossed. Their shoulders touched as they bent their heads down in the rain. Lilian sucked in a sharp breath.

"Everything all right up there?" the dispatcher asked when Lilian introduced herself. "The rain's gonna shut down your road again."

Lilian looked away from the lake. "I know. We've lost a guest in the woods, or town, we're not sure."

"Oh, dear. Are you searching? Do you need help?"

"Possibly. I was hoping you could send out a call to keep an eye out for her in town?"

Lilian gave the woman Lois' name and description, then Robert's, trying to keep her voice steady. The more she thought about him with Lois, the sicker she got. Her damp forehead felt like it was burning. "He's driving a dark sedan. A Toyota."

"Do you have the plate number?"

"It's a rental, but I can grab it from the system if you need."

"Alright. Let's wait and see what happens in the next hour." The dispatcher cleared her throat. "So you think she's with this Robert Allen?"

"I don't know." Lilian swallowed a sour taste in her mouth and started giving vague details about Robert.

"We'll send somebody up as soon as the rain clears a little," the dispatcher said when Lilian finished. She tucked the phone away and turned to the stairs, stopping in her tracks when she noticed the caterpillar cage sitting on a table near the railing. The milkweed was starting to shrivel. On the bottom, the caterpillars lay curled and stiff, their black and yellow stripes glowing eerily under the balcony lights.

"Lilian!"

She opened her eyes to see Violet motioning her toward the road, a smile plastered on her face. Then she turned and started running. Had Violet found Lois? Lilian caught sight of two dark forms. One was hunched over, hanging on the other's shoulder and arm. Nick. As Violet approached him, he looked up but didn't smile.

When Lilian finally reached him, he was hugging Violet with his free arm. His bag was slung around a shoulder. The young man leaning on him had to be Jeff. Drenched in mud, his left leg looked limp; he supported no weight on it at all.

"Lilian," Nick said as Violet pulled away. "Lilian."

She rushed into his embrace and kissed him in place of her words, then stepped back. His eyes were wide, reddened from lack of sleep or something else as he glanced at Violet. "Are you two safe? Why are you both out here?"

"We lost a guest." Lilian wasn't sure where to begin. "There's a man looking for you. I tried to call, but—"

"What does he look like?"

"He's black, shaved head, strong like you."

"He said his name's Robert Allen," Violet said before he could answer. "He said he was a scientist."

"Where is he?" Nick stepped forward, practically dragging Jeff with him.

"He left." Lilian stepped out of his way. He looked vicious, keeping his pace even though Jeff stumbled to keep up.

"How long ago? What was he driving? Did he have weapons?"

Lilian took Jeff's other arm to help him keep up. He was trembling and kept opening his mouth as if he wanted to say something. They reached the stairs, and Nick helped Jeff up each step.

"He didn't hurt anybody," Violet said. "He was nice until he left. But now a little girl's missing, and we don't know if he took her."

"What?" Nick turned to look at both of them. Jeff gasped as his leg twisted. He bounced on his other foot to straighten out.

"One of the guest's children who took a liking to him," Lilian explained. She kept her voice steady despite the panic creeping into her chest. Nick looked like he was about to kill something. "She's ten. We've all been looking for her."

"How long has Kyle been gone?"

"Kyle?"

"That's his real name. When did he leave?"

"An hour and a half, maybe."

Nick turned and opened the door, pulling Jeff inside with him. They crammed into the entryway, dripping muddy water. A musty stench filled the air. Lilian looked up as Erin and her mom, Jenny, appeared from down the hall. Their eyes were wide and wet. Jenny dared to smile as she looked at the screen door closing behind Lilian.

"Did you find her? Is she okay?"

Air drained from Lilian's lungs. "Not yet, I'm sorry. Jenny, this is Nick. He's going to help us look for Lois."

Nick gave Jenny a quick glance as he set his bag down and helped Jeff sit on the bench by the door. "I'll do what I can."

Breathing hard, Jenny stepped forward. Her face was horrified but expectant, like she was hanging from the edge of a cliff and only Nick could save her. "Do you think you can find her?"

Ignoring her, Nick turned to Lilian. "What kind of car was he driving?"

"A sedan."

"Did you check the plates?"

"No." Lilian scrunched her nose. Check the plates? That hadn't occurred to her.

Nick scraped his muddy boots on the floor, leaving dark smudges. "How did you find out about him? How do you know he was looking for me?"

"He told me right before he left."

"Everybody else is outside looking for the girl?" Catching his breath, he wiped the rain from his face.

"Yeah." Violet stared at Jeff. "Are you okay? What happened?"

"He was shot. Clara's outside?" he asked Lilian.

"Yes."

"Help me round everybody up. We have to leave as soon as we can. My truck got stuck, but Devan's should be fine getting us down."

"Leave?" Jenny moved closer to them. Erin hid behind her legs. "What's going on?"

Lilian ignored her and looked out the screen door. "We'll never make it down the mountain."

"And what about Lois?" Violet gave her father an angry look.

"The girl?"

"Yeah, we can't leave without finding her."

"I'll get you all to safety and come back up to search."

Crossing her arms against a sudden chill, Lilian leaned forward. "We'll get stuck or slide off the road. It's not safe to leave."

"Kyle's not getting up the road anytime soon," Jeff said, staring at his muddy shoes. "We barely made it up, and now it's raining harder."

Nick gave all of them a steely stare. "I know we can't get down the mountain right this second, but we can all get ready for when the rain clears. For now, I need everybody in one place."

"Tell me what's going on," Jenny said loudly. She stood stiff and straight, her shoulders thrust forward. "Why do we need to leave?"

"You explain," Nick ordered Violet, and picked up his bag. He slung it over his shoulder and took Lilian's hand, pulling her out the door and down the porch steps into the rain.

"Nick!" Lilian tried to tug away, but he gripped her tighter and led her into the grassy clearing where her feet sank an inch into the drenched ground. Facing her, Nick took her by the shoulders. Fear filled his eyes, but he seemed to be keeping it in check.

"I don't know how this is going to end," he said, "but I'm going to do everything I can to keep you safe."

Lilian looked at the bruises on his cheeks, harsh from the porch lights. Those hadn't been there when he'd left. Neither had the pressure in his hands, the urgency in his voice. Something had happened, and Lilian wondered if it even had to do with Kyle.

"I know you'll keep me safe," she choked.

Nick pulled her into a tight embrace, burying his face in her hair. Rain slid between them, surprisingly warm. Lilian closed her eyes, hoping to feel some peace, but all she could see in her mind was black and yellow caterpillars.

Chapter 27

As soon as Devan spotted Nick, he ran up the bank toward him. Clara kept close at his side, slipping and sliding, but always catching herself on his arm.

"Do you think he brought Jeff?" she asked between heavy breaths.

"I don't know. Is that what you want?"

Stopping, Clara blinked through the rain. For the first time, her eyes didn't look blue. The darkness, tinged yellow from the flashlights, made them gray. Forlorn. He thought he caught a glimpse of excitement, maybe fear. She opened her mouth and then shut it again.

"Do you want to be with him?" Devan asked. He needed a straight answer from her. Facts, not actions. He had enjoyed the closeness between them, but a dark fear that had nothing to do with the missing girl or Robert settled around his heart.

Clara opened her mouth again, this time with a glance at her dad and his mom jogging toward them. Clara's words came out muffled, almost unrecognizable. "I need to see him again. For the first time in my life I feel like I can face him and ask him things I've never dared ask before. I need to know."

"Know what?"

Nick called out Clara's name. They would catch up any second.

"I need to know if he loves me."

Turning, Clara jogged to her dad's embrace. She smiled when he told her Jeff was at the inn. Devan stopped in front of his mom, staring at her flat, wet hair and dripping eyelashes.

"Did you find her?"

"No. Nick wants us all to leave. We found Jason and Rachel. They're back at the inn with the others."

"But what about Lois?"

"I'll find her." Nick pulled away from Clara and motioned for everybody to follow him back up the shore. He walked briskly, not even bending his head from the rain.

"Why do we have to leave?" Devan asked. "Does this have to do with Robert?"

"His name's Kyle," Nick said without looking back.

"Kyle." The name came out of Clara's mouth like a breath of wind. "That's his name. He's the one I remember."

Nick stopped to face her. "Honey, I asked you before if you knew him. You said you didn't."

"I'm sorry, I didn't remember him then. I should have done something. I should have—"

"Shhh." Nick took her hand and continued on. "Don't ever say you're sorry. This is all my doing. My fault. Honey, there's something you need to know about Jeffrey."

Clara's shoulders stiffened as she walked beside him, her hand still curled in his. Devan watched them walk faster.

"He was hurt in Brazil," Nick explained. "Shot in the leg. He's fine, but there are other things he's going to tell you as soon as he can. I know you're strong, but you're not going to like what he has to say." His voice grew softer as he and Clara quickened their pace. Eventually Devan couldn't hear him at all.

His mom lowered her flashlight. "I'm not mad at you," she said, watching their feet splash through the mud.

"You're not?" Devan rubbed his thumb as he remembered cracking his door open to see her concerned face and accusing eyes. He'd been mortified, almost wishing she had knocked twenty minutes earlier when Clara had first kissed him. It was too late by the time she did knock, and he'd shut the door and turned around to see Clara clutching his bed sheets to her naked chest, breathing heavily after what they'd just done.

His mom looked him directly in the eyes. "Are you going to stay together?"

"No."

The answer came out fast, and Devan clamped his lips shut. He sensed that she knew what had happened, that she understood he was regretting it more every second. The only thing he didn't understand was why she wasn't lecturing him about being just like his dad.

"We make mistakes," she said slowly, and clicked off her flashlight. "I've made them too, Devan."

"Huh?" She couldn't mean cheating.

"I drove your father away. It wasn't just him. These things go both ways."

In the dim light, Devan tried to study her expression. Her voice was fragile, as if it might shatter with a few more words.

"Dad mentioned something like that," he said quietly as they continued their brisk steps. "He told me it was your fault, but I didn't want to believe him. You didn't cheat on him. You didn't lie."

"No, I didn't."

Lightning cracked over a line of trees in the distance, outlining the shape of the heavy clouds sitting low in the sky. The thunder came next, a long growling roll.

Devan looked at his mom. Her lips were moving, but he couldn't hear her. "What did you say?"

She shook her head as the thunder died down. "Nothing."

"I don't believe that. Tell me."

They crested the hill and crossed the clearing. Nick and Clara were on the porch, outlined in yellow.

"I just said some things are worse than cheating."

Reaching the stairs, Devan stepped up the first two so he was sheltered from the rain. His mom did the same, and kept her eyes on him even though Nick and Clara were urging them inside. Clara slipped past the screen door and rushed into the entryway where a lean, good-looking man stood up from the bench and embraced her. He had to be Jeff.

"Some things are worse," his mom repeated. "Like letting your father slip away. I let him believe I no longer loved him, and maybe I didn't, in a way. We never talked about it. We never did anything until everything was already falling apart." Nick reached for her.

"Everything all right?"

"For now." She put her hand into his and they went inside.

Still standing on the porch, Devan stared at their backs as they stopped in front of Jeff and Clara, who were kissing.

Devan couldn't watch. It was too much. What if she told Jeff about what had happened? He looked like a strong guy, injured or not. Devan didn't want to run away, but he didn't want to face them, either. He could search a few more minutes for the girl. Maybe when he came back, Clara would at least be a foot away from Jeff, but he knew she was happy to see him. His mother's last words pounded through his head and something stabbed him deep in his gut.

"I'll be right back," he called out, and ran into the rain. He had to focus on something else.

Where would a ten-year-old hide? He doubted Kyle had taken her. He didn't seem like the type to kidnap a little girl, but then again, he'd had a picture of that boy in his book.

Another flash of lightning lit up the sky. Everything turned a bright eerie blue. The lake, the inn, the trees, the boathouse.

The boathouse.

How could they have missed it?

Devan ran to the whitewashed shed, his heart thudding. They kept the door secured with a small metal padlock. It had been smashed open with a rock or something; Devan saw it lying on the steps, and pushed the door open. He aimed his flashlight inside. "Lois?"

"Go away!"

"Lois!"

He rushed to the back of the shed, past the canoes hung along the wall, the gardening tools, the mower, the paddle boats. She was sitting in one, her knees up to her chin, a dirty jacket pulled around her shoulders.

"Go away, go away, go away!" She hugged her knees tighter to her chest and moaned something unintelligible.

"Lois, it's just me. Devan. You remember me, right? I rowed you around the lake."

She lifted her head. In the yellow light her face looked brittle. "You don't have to talk to me like I'm five."

Devan lowered the flashlight when she put a hand to her eyes. "Sorry. You seem upset, and your parents are worried sick. We've been looking for you."

"I know. I heard people talking outside."

"Then why are you still in here? You don't have to hide."

Careful to keep his movements slow, he approached her and squatted down to look her in the eyes. He set his flashlight face-up on the floor so the beam bounced off the ceiling and filled the room. The air smelled musty. A green smell, like the wet forest.

Lois looked away. "I wanted to go with him," she said softly, and rested her cheek on her knee. "But he said I had to stay here. He didn't want me with him. He didn't want me, just like Dad doesn't want me."

"What?" Devan touched her shoulder. She was cold, a block of ice, and just as stiff. He lifted his hand and pushed back her hair. "Your dad is scared to death he'll never see you again. Lois?"

She lifted her head.

"He loves you."

"No he doesn't. How do you know that?"

He opened his mouth, but he didn't know what to say. He didn't know how he knew. "Because he was out in the rain looking for you in the mud and the dark. He was nice enough to bring you here for a vacation. He knows you love butterflies and wanted you to see them. Right?"

Sniffing, Lois wiped her nose. "I guess so."

"See?" He leaned close to her face and smiled. "He loves you. Why would you want to leave with Robert when you have your dad? And your mom and sister, too. They're inside crying."

"They are?"

"Yeah."

A fat tear rolled down Lois' cheek. "I didn't want him to leave. Why did he leave? He didn't even say goodbye. He told me to stay in the hall."

More tears dripped down her face. She sniffed again, whimpering until Devan pulled her into a hug. Her thin arms wrapped around him and squeezed.

"I really liked him," she said through shaky breaths. "I really, really liked him."

"I know you did." Devan squeezed his eyes shut, seeing Clara as she looked into Jeff's face and smiled, love playing on her lips, love in the way she held him, love in the words she would say when she confessed her mistakes. But Jeff had made mistakes, too. Now they could be even.

"Lois?"

Devan looked up to see Jason standing in the doorway.

"Lois!"

He ran past the boats as Devan let Lois go. Jason gathered her into a tight embrace, smothering her hair with kisses.

"Oh, honey, why? Why were you hiding?"

Lois whimpered into his shoulder. "I don't know. You're always mad at me or ignoring me." Her breaths shuddered into silence, and Jason squeezed her tighter. He gave Devan a thankful smile.

"I'm sorry, Lois. I've been a terrible dad for you lately. Work has been extra stressful and this vacation was supposed to be a way for me to unwind." He looked her in the face. "I've gone about it all wrong. Can you forgive me?"

Lois sniffed. "I guess so."

Devan stood up and left the boathouse. The rain hit his head harder than before. The drops were tiny fists beating him to a pulp. He headed back to the inn, walking as slowly as he could. One foot in front of the other. One more minute and he'd have to see Clara again. See her again in Jeff's arms. One more minute and he would tear himself to pieces over his stupidity. The worst part was that he knew he didn't love her. It was nothing but an illusion.

He saw Clara in the monarch grove, her eyes closed as she spread her arms wide to feel the morning sun. She was just as untouchable now as she was at that moment, so beautiful he was afraid to speak. He saw his mom's hand closing around Nick's, Lois' arms wrapped around her father's neck, Clara's relieved smile as Jeff held her close.

Chapter 28

Nick wanted weapons. Since the rain was coming down heavier than before, he didn't expect Kyle or anybody else to show up soon, but the fear in his heart grew more intense with every thunder clap and every raindrop slamming onto the roof.

He had gathered everybody into the library as soon as he followed Jason and Devan back inside with the little girl. Thin and gangly. Ten. Nick remembered Clara and Violet at that age, innocent and sweet. They didn't fight then like they did now.

Lois ran to her mother and sister, tears streaming down her face.

"Don't you ever do that again," Jenny scolded as she kissed Lois' head and cheeks and squeezed her close.

"Okay, we've found Lois," Jason said, sounding flustered as he approached Nick. "Why the hell do we need to leave?"

Jason's expression told it all. He didn't trust Nick, probably because he had no idea who he was. That was fine. Nick added sympathy to his voice, softened his eyes, leaned back just bit so he wasn't threatening. Although he always tried to keep his connection to the CIA a secret, right now it didn't seem to matter. "Please trust me, Jason. I'm with the government ... the CIA. I'm here to protect you."

Jason's hardened expression twisted into surprise. "Oh," he said, glancing at his family. "How much danger are we really in? And why are your daughters here? That doesn't make any sense."

Nick warmed his expression even more. He'd keep it vague and confusing and see if that worked. "Robert isn't who he said he was, that's all I know."

Jason glanced at his wife and daughters. "So we can leave when the rain lets up?"

Good. No more explaining. "Yes. Take a minute with your family."

Jason sat with them and Nick studied everyone in the room. Clara and Jeffrey sat in one corner, talking quietly. Nick squeezed his eyes shut. His skin was cold from the rain. He listened to the soft chattering, the sniffles, some heavy, nervous breaths, and sensed the right amount of caution—except within himself. He felt like he might explode.

"Nick?"

He opened his eyes to see Lilian leaning forward. There were dark circles under her eyes.

"Are you all right?" she asked. "What do you want us to do?"

Everyone was looking at him now. He had taken charge easily, but his concern might be unnecessary. Had Kyle given up? It didn't make sense for him to put so much effort into finding and trapping him. It was obvious he wanted leverage. But for what? If he wanted Nick dead, he would have gone about it in a much simpler way.

Nick walked to where Lilian sat on the couch and leaned down. "You said he liked the little girls?" he asked in a lowered voice. Jason's family didn't seem to hear.

"Yes."

"He liked kids," Devan interrupted, leaning forward. "I was searching his bags and found a picture of a boy in one of his books."

"You searched his room?" Lilian's eyes went wide. "So did I."

"Did you find the picture?"

Lilian shook her head. "I didn't look in his bags."

"Wait a second." Nick kneeled. "What boy? What did he look like?"

Rachel twisted her expression and leaned toward Nick. "You think he came up here for the girls?"

"No." Nick looked down at his knees sitting in a puddle of rainwater. He didn't feel cold anymore. "What did the boy look like, Devan?"

"Young, maybe twelve or thirteen. Black hair. Green eyes."

"Alex."

"Who?"

Nick stood up. "Alex. Damn it, I should have known. He wants Alex. That's what this is all about."

It had to be. Pieces came together, connecting perfectly. From what Nick knew, Kyle had no family other than his son that he'd mentioned in the jungle. Kyle had always seemed lonely to Nick. Never anything overt, just an undertone. Now it was clear what he wanted. Not money. Not power. Neither of those could have put the smile on Kyle's face whenever he came back from an "assignment" for Ferreira.

Nick looked around the room, noticing the cold glances between his daughters. He had always taken his girls for granted, even their anger with each other. He turned to Jason's family, and his chest burned with an ache he hadn't felt in a long time.

It's not what you think, Catarina had said.

And it wasn't. Treason? Maybe. She might ask that of him. He saw her standing on the airstrip, her arm wrapped around Alex before he walked away from her, the tears in her eyes as the plane taxied away. Nick tried to piece more of the puzzle together, but the facts were still hazy. He felt more uneasy now than he had all evening, and clenched his fists. He needed weapons. Now.

"Everybody get your things and meet back here in ten minutes," he said sternly, and reached down to help Lilian stand. "Come with me."

He led her to her room where she opened the safe in her closet. He'd left his weapons there when he'd gone to get Clara. He snatched his rifle and loaded it.

"Nick?"

There was fear in her voice. He'd felt it in her hand as they'd walked to her room. She was cold and wet and scared to death. She had every right to be. He tried to keep his voice calm. "What?"

"What's going to happen? Are you staying here or coming with the rest of us?"

"I'm leaving, too, now that we found the girl."

"Where are we going?"

"Jason's family can go wherever they want. But you and Devan and my girls are coming with me to Langley. There's something I have to deliver, and you'll be safe there."

"Langley? The CIA?"

"Yes."

"So that's what you do? You're an agent?"

"Technically, I'm an officer." People never got that right.

"Oh." She seemed to hesitate, her breath hanging on one word Nick knew she wanted to say, but wouldn't.

"I thought you might have figured out a long time ago what I do," he said gently. He knew the word "spy" was doing cartwheels through her head.

"I did. Kind of." She looked down at her hands. "What are you going to deliver?"

"Names. Catarina gave them to me. They'll help me get out of this mess." He thought of the briefcase he'd left in his bag. It was still in the library. Shit. He hadn't let it leave his side since Catarina gave it to him.

"What names? Who is Catarina?"

"You don't need to know." He propped the rifle against the wall and grabbed his pistol. "Get your bag ready. Clothes, anything you'll need for a few days."

Lilian leaned past him and grabbed a bag from the top of the closet. She took it to the dresser and opened a drawer. Her movements were quick, shaky. "But if you're going to the CIA, will they arrest you? You said they were after you."

"Yes, they might arrest me."

"Will they let you go when you give them the names?"

"I don't know. Maybe."

"But Nick ..." Her voice trailed off, and she turned to face him. Chewing on her bottom lip, she looked at him like he might disappear any second.

"This is the best way," he said stiffly, thinking of Catarina. She had let him go, given him the names—a shot at freedom. But for what? What did she really want?

"Did you come back here for me or for your girls?"

Nick froze when he heard the question. "Is that what you think?" He slid an extra clip of bullets into his back pocket. He'd have to get rid of the weapons as soon as he got close to Langley, but for now something felt wrong, and it wasn't Lilian's question. He was sure to make his voice steady and convincing. "I came back for you and my girls."

And that was the truth. Even after Catarina, after feeling that he might never change, he had still come back, hoping things would work out with Lilian. Somehow.

Lilian's hands hovered over the drawer, where she had fished out most of the shirts and put them in her bag. Nick doubted she needed that many. "I've been worried sick the whole time you've been gone," she said. A tear rolled down her cheek, and as quickly as it had fallen, she wiped it away and started grabbing more shirts. "I've been hoping things would get easier for me when I saw you again, but I've always blamed Chris for everything, and I shouldn't have."

Nick watched another tear roll down her cheek. This time she let it stay. It curled around her chin, wavering for a moment before it dripped into her bag. Nick was torn between wanting to grab his guns and yank her out of the room, bag or no bag, or pulling her into his arms to comfort her.

"Lilian," he said as gently as he could. "I have to get everybody out of here. I might be wrong, but Kyle's not going to disappear easily. I think the storm's the only reason we're going to leave here alive."

"I-I'm sorry." Lilian zipped up her bag and slung it over her shoulder. "We can go whenever you want."

The gun in Nick's hand felt like a ten-ton brick. He held onto it tightly as Lilian approached him. He wanted her to trust him—more than he'd ever wanted anybody to trust him. He didn't know why. He just knew he didn't want to leave her, the way she laughed, dainty but loud, like a bell. He would miss the way she kissed, eager and fast, how much he could see she wanted to be with him, too. It was all over her face, and although he felt like he had barely begun to get to know her, he wanted to peel back every layer she had to offer, hold each one close to him, like a second skin. He wanted to fall in love with her—maybe he already had.

He almost dropped the gun in his hand, but caught it at the last second. With a thousand words catching in his throat, he reached out to pull Lilian close. Everything faded around him as he leaned down to kiss her. He remembered Catarina's lips, soft and full. He remembered the tears and the blood and the feel of her skin. Catarina was nothing to Lilian. No woman was, not even Annabelle. He finally knew it, and like a burst of light exploding around him, he wanted to change. Really change. For Lilian. For himself.

He pulled away, the world spinning. He was wasting time. He was sloppy. Slow. Fear swelled inside his chest. He looked around the room, and his breath stopped.

They weren't alone.

Chapter 29

"How sweet," Kyle laughed.

Lilian spun around, a scream catching in her throat as a strong arm, not Kyle's, grabbed her waist and pulled her away from Nick. Her fingers slipped away from his, and she stared wide-eyed at the scene before her: Nick raising his loaded pistol to take a shot at Kyle. Or another man. There was more than one. Two. Three.

Nick didn't have a chance. By the time Lilian saw the surprise on his face, it was too late. The men had burst in through the door from the hallway, but Kyle had been there before that moment, a silent shadow looming in the kitchen. He must have come in from the back door.

A rough voice scraped across Lilian's ear. A foreign language. Spanish or Portuguese. Lilian craned her neck to catch a glimpse of a dark face above her. He didn't look or sound like Kyle. He spoke to her again, squeezing her ribs, crushing her lungs. She had no idea what he was ordering her to do. It was an order of some sort. Her breaths cracked into gasps, and she heard Nick growl as the sound of a body slammed into the wall. No gunshots. Yet.

She saw Nick one more time. He was the one who had been thrown. The pistol dropped from his hands and clattered across the wood floor. Instinct thrust Lilian forward. Stretching her fingers toward the weapon, she remembered the rifle Nick had propped against the wall, and twisted her body for it. Closer. The arm around her waist squeezed harder, yanked her backwards, threw her against the bedpost. A short scream erupted from her throat, and a hand slapped her face.

"Keep her back!" Kyle ordered.

Looking up, Lilian saw him fighting Nick. Her heart plummeted. Nick was losing. Kyle blocked the fists flying at him, every blow and kick, until he slammed Nick into the dresser. A vase fell to the floor with a deafening crash, and Nick cried out as the third man in the room kicked his knees and sent him to the floor.

Lilian tried to duck two hands coming at her, but she was too slow. They grabbed her shoulders and shoved her onto the bed. An elbow dug into her throat, and she stared up at her attacker as he leaned close. Silent laughter. A whimper from the other side of the room. Nick coughing.

Now she understood what Nick had meant when he'd first showed up and told her she might be in danger. She'd been naïve enough to think this amount of violence was impossible. She'd never felt like her life might end, the air in her lungs disappearing, her head lighter, lighter, and she'd never told Nick how she really felt—how much she'd missed him, how much she wanted to be with him.

"It's over, Nick," Kyle's voice said loudly. "Tell me where she is."

"Who?" Nick gasped.

More coughing. Lilian imagined blood dripping onto the wood floor. Nick's blood. Her stomach turned as she gasped for air. The man's elbow dug deeper. Her face felt numb.

Kyle growled. "Catarina, you idiot. Where the hell is she? Nobody can find her, and you were with her last. What are you two planning?"

"Nothing. I don't know where she—"

Nick's words cut off, a pained groan as Lilian imagined Kyle shoving his foot into Nick's ribs. She turned her head and saw Kyle bending down to look at Nick collapsed to his knees. "If you don't start talking, I'll kill her."

Nick looked up at the bed, his eyes watery. His jaw tightened. His forehead glistened with sweat.

"I'll kill her slowly while you watch," Kyle said with a laugh. "Then I'll move on to your daughters." He licked his lips. "One at a time."

Lilian locked her eyes with Nick's. She couldn't deny that doubt had crept into her heart. As much as she cared for Nick, it was obvious Kyle was stronger.

Nick swallowed as Kyle grabbed a handful of his hair and yanked him backwards. "Don't be stupid, Kyle. Why the hell would I be planning anything with her? What's she keeping you from? Alex?"

Kyle's face fell.

Nick continued, a smile playing on his lips, but it was jittery. "What do you need me for? If she's in your way, just kill her. Oh, wait, you tried that already. Got the wrong woman."

A swift blow to his jaw sent Nick onto his side. "You know why I want you," Kyle hissed through his teeth. He squatted down. "Ferreira wouldn't like it if I murdered his wife. But if I pin it on you, I have nothing to lose. If she's gone, she's not trying to take Alex away. Ferreira trusts me with him, and I've got big plans for that kid. We'll make a perfect team when he's older. He just needs the right direction." He leaned down and pushed Nick's head against the floor. "Only problem is finding Catarina."

"So it is about power," Nick spluttered against the wood. "I thought you wanted Alex to replace your own son."

"What do you think I am, some sentimental bastard? You thought wrong." But there was a tremor in his voice, a tone that sounded off.

Nick coughed. "I know you're not getting Catarina."

"You're wrong. I'll get what I need." Kyle stood up with a nod at his partner. The man leaned down and yanked Nick to his feet. "You'll lead me straight to her. I'd bet my life she trusts you."

Nick clamped his lips shut and shook his head, wincing when the man holding him shoved a knee into his stomach.

"You can stand there and watch, then," Kyle laughed, and turned to Lilian.

She looked away, sensing Nick's pain from across the room. She felt it in her attacker's angry grip around her shoulder, his elbow pushing the air from her body. Stars danced in front of her eyes. Nick's voice faded in and out. Squirming, she tried to gulp some air, and the elbow suddenly lifted. The man slid off the bed and a gentle hand closed around hers. Kyle's familiar scent drifted to her nose. It made her gag.

"Sit up," he ordered as he tugged on her hand.

There was no way she would do anything he said. Not here. Not with Nick six feet away, weak and limp, watching helplessly. She shook her head, tears springing to her eyes. Kyle's presence dug deep into her fear, stronger than anything physical she'd ever known. Why was he speaking with kindness in his voice? Why was his hand tender around hers?

He tugged again, and she gave in, sitting up to look him in the face. He had a knife in his hand. A long, wide blade with a feathered design etched into the metal. It was strangely beautiful as he waved it in front of her face, his lips breaking into a smile.

"I like them light," he said, letting go of her hand to touch her hair, still wet with rain. He moved his finger to her jaw, then her lips. "And fragile. But you know that already, don't you?"

Goosebumps broke out along the back of her neck. "Don't," she whispered. "Please don't." She glanced at Nick staring at the floor. Why wasn't he doing anything? She was sure he was in pain, but every inch of her wanted him to do something.

Tears in her eyes spilled over, hot down her cheeks, salt seeping between her lips as Kyle moved his hand to the fitted T-shirt stuck to her skin from the rain. He pulled the collar from her chest, and in one swift movement, slid his knife through the material. She shuddered as the cold metal brushed her skin.

Kyle ripped away the two shirt pieces from her arms. He eyed her hungrily.

"She's a beauty," he said, glancing at Nick, who was still staring downward. His hands were pinned behind his back by the Brazilian who'd yanked him off the floor. Lilian wondered where the third man was. He had disappeared. If she managed to escape, how fast could she run? Would somebody catch her in the hall?

Kyle gripped her bra strap and cut through it with a flick of his wrist. Then the other one. He was teasing, taking his time. He licked his lips and sliced through the back strap. The bra fell from her body, and she grabbed his arm. He laughed.

"Stop," she said in a shaky voice. Fear made her vision spin. "He'll tell you what you want. Won't you, Nick?"

Catching her breath, she glared in Nick's direction. His shoulders dropped as he looked up. Dry, cold eyes. "He won't hurt you," he said softly. "I promise."

Kyle's laughter filled the room. He pushed Lilian's hand off his arm. "You wanna bet? Talk, Nick, or I'll start cutting."

Nick's eyes narrowed. "I don't know where Catarina is, and I don't know how to contact her. I last saw her in Brazil." His voice was eerily calm.

"I know she was in Brazil. My men found her house a few hours ago, but she wasn't there. What's she planning, Nick? Something's going on, and you know what it is."

Tightening his jaw, Nick leaned away from his captor, his entire body straining. "She's not planning anything. She wants her son, and that's it."

"Bullshit." Kyle turned back to Lilian and grabbed a handful of her hair. She gasped. Stretching skin, muscle. Her eyes stung.

Kyle yanked her neck back and lightly traced the edge of his knife along her collarbone. "It's a shame to ruin something so lovely, kind of like those damn butterflies. How fitting that one of Ferreira's businesses is gonna kill 'em off, isn't it?" He dug the knife under Lilian's collarbone. "Tell me, Nick, or she'll bleed. Ferreira suspects Catarina's got something up her sleeve. If I didn't find you tonight, he would have tracked you down to find her. He's not as nice as me."

Nick grunted, and Lilian focused on as many things as she could—the blade pushing into her skin, Kyle's sweet scent surrounding her, the fan spinning on the ceiling. It would keep spinning no matter what happened.

Nick's breaths were suddenly loud. Lilian shut her eyes to block out the fan, and held her breath to try and forget Kyle. It didn't do any good. Pain seared across her chest, and her body jerked. Was she bleeding? She cried out Nick's name, but the room fell silent. Her face was numb. The air smelled even sweeter.

Nick, do something, she yelled inside her head. *Do something!*

His eyes came back to her thoughts. Gray. Sad, but strong. Strong. Devan was strong, too. Even Chris was strong. They all seemed to lift her up in their unique ways. Every part of her life—past, present, and future—needed them.

But in that moment, as Kyle's hand let go of her hair and pushed her into the mattress, she had no one.

Chapter 30

Devan dropped his toothbrush when a scream echoed through the inn. A high-pitched shriek. Young. Probably Lois.

The toothbrush clattered across the bathroom tile. Devan's heart thudded as his thoughts broke into a million directions. Should he grab his toothbrush? His bag? Run to find Lois? His mom? Nick?

Everybody was scattered around the inn packing their bags as fast as they could. Like an electric shock, Nick's orders had sent panic through the group. Devan had seen it in all their faces, especially Clara's. She, most of all, seemed to understand Nick's concern about Kyle. But she had Jeff now, and he apparently needed her, too, leaning on her for support as they'd left the library to go pack Clara's things.

Devan left the toothbrush on the floor and rushed out of his room. The brightly lit hallway was empty, the air silent except for the rain still coming down hard. Had he imagined the scream? His nerves were on edge. Maybe he had.

He rounded a corner. A body slammed into him. Pain shot through his shin.

"Devan!"

Rachel's arms wrapped around him to keep herself from falling. Her knee had hit his leg, and the ache made him grit his teeth. He steadied her by the shoulders and pulled away to look her in the face. It was pale, shocked.

"There are men here," she whispered between gasps. "They've got guns. They've got guns. They were talking in Spanish. They've got Lois. I hid behind my door. Devan, they've got g—"

He clapped a hand around her mouth, squeezed her to his side, and dragged her down the hall. Looking back and forth, he prayed they could make it to Violet's room before anybody saw them.

Most people forgot about the room where Violet was staying. It was the only room at the end of a short hallway, quiet and out of the way. Devan led Rachel there and turned the handle, half expecting it to be locked. It turned easily and the door swung open.

"Violet?"

No answer. Devan closed the door as quietly as he could, and locked it. He turned around to see twenty or thirty Mason jars set throughout the room. They glittered in the blue light from a digital clock on the dresser, some of them appearing to move as their tiny prisoners scrambled or crawled against the glass.

"Where did she get all the jars?" he asked nobody in particular. His mind reeled faster than he'd ever felt in his life. Guns. Kyle was at the inn, he was sure of it. Even after Nick had confirmed Kyle was bad, Devan didn't truly believe it until that moment, staring at Violet's bugs, wondering how the hell she could sleep at night, wondering what a bullet would feel like if it pierced his body.

Rachel stepped forward, looking as confused as Devan. "I had extra jars in the kitchen I gave to her. Where is she?"

Devan opened his mouth and shut it again. He didn't want Rachel hurt. He felt her next to him and thought about her hand on his arm as they had watched the newlyweds walk down to the lake.

"I don't know," his voiced cracked as he turned to her. "Rachel, you've got to get out of here."

A soft rustle came from the bathroom. Rachel rushed past him, and he followed to see Violet stepping out of her hiding place in the bathtub. Her face was calm, but her movements were jerky and uncertain.

"Are they gone?"

Devan turned to Rachel. "Call the police." She could use the landline phone sitting on Violet's night stand.

Rachel rushed out of the bathroom and came back a second later, her face even whiter than before. "The line's dead."

"What about your cell phone?"

"Lil still has it."

"Mine doesn't get reception here," Violet said. "Don't you have one?"

Devan shook his head. "Mine broke a month ago and I just didn't bother getting a new one yet." He wouldn't get upset with himself since there was nothing he could do about it now. He switched gears. "Did the men come in here?" He was getting more confused by the second. Why hadn't they taken her?

"They left a minute ago. You didn't see them in the hall?"

Devan narrowed his eyes. "No. They didn't see you?"

Violet nodded to the tub where she'd thrown her bag, its contents spilled across the porcelain. "I was packing. I heard voices in Spanish. Someone started opening the door, and I ran and hid."

"They didn't look in here?"

"They might've, but they didn't look behind the shower curtain. I'm glad I left the lights off. That's probably why they didn't look too hard."

"How many?"

"Two, I think. They didn't like my insects."

Devan scrunched his nose. "What? How would you know?"

"I understood enough to know they were grossed out. They left fast." Violet's voice got higher, more irritated, more urgent. "I've got to find my dad. You've got to help me."

Devan glanced at the bedroom window. "I want both of you out of here. You can sneak out the window to my truck. You can make it down the mountain, right? You're a good driver, Rachel."

"In this rain?" Rachel backed herself against the wall and squeezed her eyes shut. "They're huge. They have rifles. Devan, there's no way we're getting out of here."

"You're leaving." He grabbed her arm and pulled her out of the bathroom. "I'll kick the screen out. Here are my keys." He dug into his pocket and shoved his keys into her hand. "Take Violet with you."

"I'm not going anywhere."

Devan made his face as angry as possible. He should have known she'd be difficult. "Yes you are. This is what your dad would want. I don't have a gun. Do you?"

"No, but—"

"Then I've got to get you out of here! We're no match for this." He let go of Rachel and yanked open the window. With one swift kick he knocked out the screen. Rain splattered against the sill, and as he lowered his foot, it sent a jar to the floor. The crash made them all cringe.

"Nice," Violet growled, and bent down to pick up a praying mantis scrambling across dirt and broken glass.

"What are you doing?" Devan stared, wide-eyed, as she cradled the mantis in her hands. A cold wind swept through the room. The curtains billowed.

"I have an idea," she said softly, and stared at the bug caged in her hands.

Devan shook his head. "No. No crazy ideas."

Violet looked up, eyes cold, her face twisting into a livid glare. She looked like Nick—tall, sure, and menacing. For the first time in his life, Devan felt intimidated by a woman. He leaned away from her as she spoke. "I'm not sneaking out a window like some coward so you can go play hero and get yourself shot."

"That's not what I said." He squared his shoulders. "If I remember right, you're the one who can't keep people alive."

He snapped his mouth closed the moment the words came out. It was something Clara might have said.

"I'm done," Violet sighed and rolled her eyes. "I'm done with all of you. Clara, my dad, even you. And I hardly know you!" She turned on her heel and snatched a jar from the desk on her way to the bathroom.

"What are you doing?"

"I think I know," Rachel said softly.

Devan had almost forgotten she was standing next to him. He looked out the window at the rain. How had Kyle traveled back up the road? There was already a lake pooling across the grass. The road would be impossible. He looked at Rachel, avoiding her eyes. Something was changing inside of him, and it hurt.

"Please," he said, touching her hand. "Please, Rachel. If they're here to kill people, I don't think I can handle seeing you ... I don't think I ..."

She closed her hand around his. Her brown eyes looked deeper than he'd ever seen them. "We'll get through this," she said. Even though the light was low and tinged with blue, he could see color returning to her face. She smiled. "You want to be in the military, remember? You can do this."

"But I've never been trained. I'm trying to get you safe."

Squeezing his hand, she smiled even wider. "I am safe, Devan. I've never seen you like this before."

"I don't want you shot. At least stay in here and hide." He nudged her away from the window.

"Maybe." She let go of his hand and moved her attention to the bathroom. Violet was busy unscrewing jars. She had grabbed more, and was reaching into each one.

"What are you doing?" Devan hissed at her back. She was intent on some idea, something he was sure would get them killed.

Violet shrugged. "Get me some more jars." She looked over her shoulder and laughed. "You're not afraid of bugs, are you?"

Chapter 31

The moment Kyle pierced Lilian's skin along her ribs, Nick broke free from his captor. It didn't take much. He'd given the man enough time to grow lazy, relaxed. He spun around, knocked him to the ground with one blow to his head, and headed straight for Kyle, who looked up, wide-eyed. He aimed his knife and jumped off the bed.

Heat sliced across Nick's face. He fought past the pain exploding through his body. He felt the bruises from earlier, the aches in his back, smelled his own blood dripping down his cheek.

Kyle was bigger, stronger, better trained. He fought Nick with clean precision, bringing him to the floor in less than three moves. Nick smelled mud on the floor when his face hit the wood. Rain. A burst of darkness.

A scream rang through the air. Not Lilian's. It was too high, too far away.

"They're rounding everybody up," Kyle said with a chuckle as he dug his knife into the back of Nick's neck. The metal felt wet, probably from Lilian's blood and his own. "I'm sure you'll talk when I get my hands on your daughters, especially the blonde one."

"I'll help you find Catarina. Just leave them alone." A groan escaped his lips, filled with shame.

"I knew this was a good idea," Kyle said, laughing. "The second he told me someone bought a phone in Charleston, I had to look into it."

Nick's heart sped up. "He?"

"Larry, remember? You sent Devan in to get you a phone. You must've thought you were being smart. Didn't even notice the surveillance camera, did you? The truck's license plates led me right here."

Nick closed his eyes. He should have known it would be something so small.

"You're weak," Kyle said with a laugh. "All I had to do was get you close to them. You'd maybe sacrifice one, but not all three. Better yet, there's an innocent little family you'll want to protect. Pathetic." The blade dug deeper. "You'll take me to her?"

Nick opened his mouth to answer, but a thump and a sudden jerk made him look up from the floor. Kyle had dropped the knife. Lilian was off the bed, still half-naked, blood dripping down her ribs, a livid glare on her face as she raised the lamp in her hand to hit Kyle one more time. Nick guessed she'd managed to hit his shoulders the first time. Now she aimed for his head, but he was quicker and sent her crashing to the floor with a punch to her legs.

Nick scrambled to his feet. It was now or never. He looked around for his guns, but they were gone, and turned in time to see Kyle raise his arm high, the butt of his knife aimed for the base of Lilian's skull. She collapsed when Kyle's arm came down.

Nick started forward, gasping when a pair of arms pinned him into a chokehold. Damn. Kyle's partner should have stayed unconscious longer than that! The barrel of a gun rammed into his ribs.

"It's time to get serious," Kyle said, standing up. He narrowed his eyes at Nick. "Start walking."

Nick took a last look at Lilian's body on the floor. Her hair covered her face. Her arms were bent at a strange angle.

Kyle's partner led him down the hall, and he considered what might happen if he helped Kyle find Catarina. More than likely, Kyle would kill everybody in the inn anyway. He knew better than to stay up here too long. Whatever his plans were, Nick had never seen him so gleefully violent, even in the bunker with Catarina.

Nick stepped into the library and followed Kyle's orders to sit on the rug in front of some bookshelves. Jason and Jenny were on the opposite end, huddled with their children as a man with an AK-47 guarded them. Fantastic. If the man fired, they'd be obliterated. Backing up, the man kept his attention on Nick, too.

"Mr. Allen!" With a jerk, Lois pulled away from her mother's arms and stood up, her teary eyes fastened on

Kyle. She rushed past the guard and threw her arms around Kyle's waist. "I knew you'd come back." She looked up. "They keep telling me you're going to hurt us."

"Lois, get back here!" Jenny hissed. Her voice was high-pitched, her cheeks red and splotchy. She tried to stand, but her husband pulled her back.

Kyle stared down at Lois, his face a mixture of pain and anger. His fingers tightened around the pistol at his side. He trembled. Shifting his feet, he touched Lois' shoulder with his free hand. "Go sit down," he said gently. "Now."

"But Mr. Allen, I—"

"Now." He jerked his knee to shake her off, and she stumbled backwards.

"But I—"

"Tony," Kyle growled, nodding at the man with the rifle.

Tony grabbed Lois' arm and yanked her back to her parents. She stood stone-still, her tears gone, her mouth hanging open. Her knees shook, and she lowered herself down with a short whimper.

"Stay quiet," Jason whispered, and pulled her into his arms. He stroked her hair as Nick swallowed a bitter taste in his mouth.

Kyle ordered the man with the pistol to get Lilian from the bedroom just as Jeffrey and Clara came into the room, led by an armed man bigger than the others. Clara straightened her shoulders and gave Nick a resolved smile, one that seemed to say, *I know you can fix this.*

Nick's heart warmed at the sight of her. Fear was in her eyes, the same as when he'd found her in the closet, but this time she was controlling it. Violet, on the other hand, had him worried all of a sudden. Where was she? And Devan? Rachel? The inn wasn't that big.

"Where do you want her?" Kyle's man asked, entering the library with Lilian in his arms. A blanket was thrown across her body. It brushed the floor in front of the man's boots.

Nick's breath stopped in his throat. In the brighter light, he saw a bruise across her face.

"Put her on the couch," Kyle grumbled as he motioned Jeffrey and Clara to sit next to the family. "She's not waking up anytime soon." He turned to Nick. "Where are the others?"

"I don't know." Nick shrugged and studied the men in their camouflage clothing. They were dirty, their faces, their boots, their hands, stained with black soil. Even the rain hadn't washed it away. Nick guessed they had been camping in the woods since Kyle had shown up a week ago.

"Did you check all the rooms?" Kyle asked the biggest man as the other one dropped Lilian onto a couch near Nick.

"Yeah, we checked 'em all. You want us to check again?"

"In a minute. They're here somewhere. Three, like I told you. Two girls and a boy, in their twenties."

"We can check that back room again."

Nick studied their accents. Two Brazilians and an American. He guessed this was all of Kyle's gang: the short one who'd brought him into the library, Tony with the AK-47, the big one with a chest like a barrel, and Kyle. Tony and Barrel-Chest looked Brazilian, but the short one was white with long, stringy brown hair and poor Portuguese. Were there only four? Four might be doable with Jeffrey's help. Except that Jeffrey could hardly walk. Turning to him, Nick caught a glimmer of hope in his eyes.

They could do this.

Maybe.

Jeffrey nodded and discreetly held up one finger—Let's wait a minute.

Kyle motioned to the stringy-haired man. "Jairo, let's look." He nodded at Barrel-Chest and Tony. "You two keep a close eye on Nick and Jeff. Don't let 'em talk or move. Not that Jeff can do much, anyway." He glared at Jeffrey as he left the room.

Nick breathed a sigh of relief. Two. He and Jeffrey could handle two.

Lois started whimpering again. "Are they going to kill us?"

"Shut up." Tony waved his rifle at Nick. "Get back there." Nick inched closer to the bookshelf, tensing his muscles.

What he needed was a diversion.

Chapter 32

Devan was in the middle of convincing Rachel to go through the open window when the door flew open. He spun around–Kyle and another man rushed inside, two pistols aimed. Devan grabbed Rachel's hand and squeezed. The plan had been to get her out of the room.

"Where's the blonde?" Kyle growled. His partner rushed into the bathroom.

"She just went out," Devan lied through heavy breaths. He jerked his head toward the window. The room was cool and the air felt wet.

"Shit. Jairo, get outside!"

Jairo came out of the bathroom, wide-eyed. "Out the window?"

"Yes. Find her. Now!" Kyle leaned forward and grabbed Devan's arm. "Come on."

"What do you want?" Devan asked, struggling to keep calm and not fight back. He wasn't stupid enough to fight Kyle. Not against those muscles. Or the gun.

"None of your damn business. Move it." He shoved Devan into the hall ahead of him. Rachel followed, her hand still inside Devan's. She seemed calm.

But it was more than that.

An emotion hit Devan with a force that almost made him stop in his tracks. He remembered the gun pointed at his back, and kept moving. The emotion grew heavier inside him. It felt foreign, and he tightened his hold on Rachel's hand, hoping that might cement him somewhere. It did nothing.

Kyle pushed them into the library, and Devan's heart skipped a beat. They had Nick, Lois' family, even Jeff and Clara.

And his mom.

He let go of Rachel and ran to the couch. Falling to his knees, he swept her hair away from her closed eyes. A purple bruise covered one cheek. He winced and looked down at the thin blanket covering her body. What had they done? He pulled back the blanket to her bare shoulders. Naked? Blood? There was blood seeping through the blanket.

Devan's mouth fell open. He touched the wet material, a cry catching in his throat. She couldn't be dead. He was supposed to protect her. He had always protected her. She couldn't be—

"She's okay," Nick said.

Devan looked up, tears filling his eyes. "What did they do to her?"

"Nothing. She's fine. Get over here."

"Stand up," Kyle hissed, and yanked Devan to his feet by the elbow. He shoved him forward to Rachel. Was this really happening? He hadn't expected the emotions surging through him. Fear. Sickness. His stomach felt like it might cave any second.

"I'm scared," Rachel whispered as he pulled her into his arms. "They're going to kill us."

"Just do what they say."

"Get away from each other," Kyle said, kicking Devan's leg. Devan pulled away. Warmth drained from his face when Kyle pointed his pistol at Clara's head and looked at Nick, his eyes bulging with anger. "Last chance. What's Catarina planning?"

Sweat rolled down Nick's face. He looked between Kyle and Clara. Jeff wrapped his arms around her and pulled her so close the veins in his hands swelled blue beneath his skin.

Devan thought of jumping to his feet. He didn't care about the dark man with the rifle or the other two with pistols. It didn't matter. He couldn't sit here and watch Kyle shoot Clara in the head. Why wasn't Nick doing anything?

Time stretched into silence until Nick spoke "Killing her won't get you anywhere." He lifted a hand as if to calm Kyle down. "I know why you've pulled us all in here. You don't trust me, and this is the only way you think I'll give you what you want."

"Glad you figured that out," Kyle said, a rumble vibrating in his throat. "But don't be blind. There's no trust in this room at all. Not with her." He waved his gun at Clara and then Devan. "Or him."

Devan froze as Jeff stared at him.

"Or your traitor of a son-in-law." Kyle laughed, then turned to Jason and scowled. "Even your little family has its issues, doesn't it? Bring your kids up here and ignore 'em."

Jason narrowed his eyes and swallowed, but kept his mouth shut. He squeezed Lois tighter. Glancing at Nick, Kyle snapped his pistol to Lois' head. "Maybe I should kill the little girls first."

Jason sat up rigid, his face filling with agony. "Don't, don't, please—"

"You wouldn't kill her," Devan heard himself say. He knew Kyle had feelings for Lois and her sister; he'd seen it in his eyes every time he played with them. He clamped his lips closed when Kyle glared at him.

"Watch me." He looked at Nick again. "It's up to you."

Nick lowered his hand. "You've lied about Alex. Admit it. He's more to you than a ticket to power."

Alex. The picture Devan had seen in Kyle's book. No matter how much of a badass Kyle tried to seem, he cared about something. That meant weakness. Devan saw it in his eyes as they stared at Lois; he was softening behind his angry shell. It only lasted for a split second, and Devan thought Kyle might pull the trigger and kill Lois just to spite Nick. Instead, he whipped his aim back to Clara. "Decide, Nick."

Nick lifted his hand again, filling his expression with a stillness that surprised Devan. "Just put your gun down. I'll give you what you want. We can go into another room. Talk things out. We can—"

The gunshot exploded. Devan jerked as if the bullet had pierced his own body. His eyes slammed shut. Darkness. For a minute everything dropped into silence. The air felt white-hot. Lois screamed.

Then another scream. Rachel.

Devan opened his eyes. Clara was on the floor, Jeff huddled over her. Soft moans filled the room. Devan couldn't tell who it was coming from, probably the little girls.

Kyle had done it. He had shot her. Words came to Devan's throat, but that's as far as they got. Rachel dug her fingernails into his arm. He barely felt it.

"I'm serious, Nick!" Kyle's voice sliced the air. "The next bullet will be through her head. Is that what you want?"

Nick was standing now, his hands balled into fists, his face red with panic. Turning back to Clara, Devan saw that Jeff had rolled her over. She was alive. Kyle had shot her in the shoulder. Blood pulsed from the wound, already soaking her shirt. It was darker than any blood

Devan had seen, almost black. Bile rose in his throat, but he pushed it back down. He could handle this. He could.

Tears poured down Clara's face. She breathed hard, her eyes trained on Jeff. Devan couldn't miss the connection between them—something beyond the physical connection he'd experienced with her. A pent-up scream left her throat, and she writhed in Jeff's lap, grabbing at her shoulder. Jeff pulled her arm away and pinned it to her side. In a gentle voice, he repeated, "Calm down, Claire, calm down," and stroked her forehead until she slowed her breaths.

Jeff had called her Claire. It seemed so intimate, something foreign to Devan's ears. For the first time, like a breath of cold air, he knew she had never been his, no matter how close he'd been with her. He knew he shouldn't care, but he did. He shouldn't feel this much torment seeing her in pain and not be the one to hold and comfort her.

"I'm sorry," she whimpered. "I didn't tell you, I didn't tell you I, me and Dev—I didn't tell you, I'm sorry."

"Shhh." Jeff put a finger to her lips and glared up at Kyle. "How could you? I didn't think you could do this. What is so important you'd go to all this trouble?"

"I'm not finished yet," Kyle hissed through his teeth and turned back to Nick. "Sit down."

Nick dropped to a loose runner's stance, and Kyle glanced at his watch. "Your blonde one's next, whenever Jairo finds her. And I'll do a hell of a lot more to her before I kill her. You have exactly five seconds to start talking before I put a bullet through that one's head." He jerked his chin at Clara, who had gone limp in Jeff's lap.

Devan watched her pass out. He wanted to scream. He wanted to hold her and make all of this go away. He looked down at Rachel's hands gripping his arm. She was steady, but stiff as a board.

"In the bag," Nick said with a heavy sigh. He pointed to a dark green bag sitting next to a couch on the other side of the room. It was soaking wet, a puddle gathered around the heavy canvas bottom. "There's a briefcase in there. That's what you want."

Kyle grunted and motioned the man next to him to get the bag. "Now we're getting somewhere."

"You're full of shit, Kyle," Nick said in a low voice. "You're going to kill us all anyway. Just do it."

Don't egg him on! Devan screamed inside his head. But from what he had gathered, Nick probably knew Kyle better than anybody in the room. Devan had to trust him, even past Clara's blood and Jeff's trembling hand as he pushed his palms into her wound to try and stop the bleeding. It looked like it would never stop.

Chapter 33

Kyle knelt down to unzip Nick's bag. He pulled out a the briefcase and looked up at Nick. "The combination. Now."

"Two-eight-four-three." The numbers came so fast to Nick's tongue he couldn't stop them. He would do anything now, anything for his Clara, now bleeding in Jeffrey's arms. He stared up at Barrel-Chest guarding him with a pistol. The man was a brick wall. Nick wasn't sure he'd be able to bring him down on his own.

Kyle spun the numbers and clicked the case open, his face twisting into confusion. "What the hell is this?" He lifted a manila folder, one of many inside the case. Flipping it open, he thumbed through the papers, then snapped his attention to Nick. "Who gave you these?"

"Catarina. You said you wanted to know what she was up to. I was going to take those to Langley."

"It's good you didn't. I should put a bullet through your head right now." Kyle aimed his gun at Nick's face. Nick didn't even flinch. "You had to know someone would find you in the end. She's used you, Nick. You're a damn fool."

Fighting the urge to swallow, Nick wondered if Kyle was right. He opened his mouth to defend himself, but movement caught his eye. He looked up to see Violet.

She swept through the doorway, her shoulders thrust back. Her eyes blazed with a strangely wicked fire. Tony spun around to face her, and she stared down the barrel of his AK-47, walking straight at it with a smile.

Nick was shocked—not at her courage or resolve—but at his own faith in her, at how easily he believed she would succeed. She raised a jar of insects to thrust its writhing contents into Tony's face, and Barrel-Chest took the bait like a fish, twisting away from Nick to look.

Nick leapt to his feet and ripped Barrel-Chest's pistol from his fingers, snapping the man's arm like brittle clay. Easier than he'd thought. He kicked the man to the floor and turned to see Jason lunging past Devan, who was heading for Violet.

Devan?

Nick turned to aim his gun at Kyle, but was too late. Jason had decided to try to bring down Kyle on his own. Weaponless. Stupid. A shot split the air. Jason crumpled.

A single memory pounded through Nick's mind—Kyle's blade. Kyle had used it to cut Catarina. Now Lilian. Nick recalled its wing-designed blade stained with their blood and he leveled his gun and pulled the trigger. Two bullets went straight into Kyle's back. He collapsed on top of Jason's legs.

Nick looked up to see insects covering Tony—a huge spider clawed at his hair, a praying mantis clung to his thumb. Batting beetles from his face, he aimed his gun at Violet.

Nick shot the backs of both his knees. He dropped instantly. Nick lowered his pistol as Devan spun around in his direction. His eyes were big and round, bright moons in a pale face, and they got wider when he looked down at Jason by his feet, groaning as blood gushed from his abdomen.

"He was, he tried, he ..." Devan's voice dropped to a whimper, and he gasped as the two little girls screamed, "Daddy!" and ran past him to Jason.

Nick gathered his wits. He knew Jairo, the last man, would come running if he'd heard the gunshots. Not much time left. He checked to make sure Violet was okay. She stood stone-still over Tony, still covered with bugs. The injured man gaped at the blood spilling from his legs into a crimson pool. A white cabbage butterfly twisted itself in a pained effort to fly, but it was already half-drowned in the sticky mess.

Nick looked past Kyle, limp, nearly dead since the bullets had pierced him in the lungs. Maybe another minute and his heart would stop beating. Another minute and Nick could add one more death to his list. Until now, each one had felt like a stone inside him. Now the heaviness lifted. He looked at Kyle, collapsed over Jason's legs, his bullet wounds clean and precise. No wings. That was in the past.

"Get up," Nick ordered Barrel-Chest. He reached down and pulled him up by his good arm. Dragging him across the room, Nick kept his eyes on Devan.

"Get Kyle off Jason and call 911. Tell them everything." He threw Barrel-Chest, groaning in pain, onto the floor at Tony's feet. Tony grasped for his rifle an inch from his fingers.

"Don't even think about it," Nick spit into his face. He snatched the AK-47 and aimed it at Tony's forehead, then glanced at Violet. She muttered something unintelligible and stared straight ahead.

"Violet," Nick said loudly.

She blinked.

"Violet!"

Nick touched her shoulder. "You need to guard these two."

She blinked again and turned her attention to Devan and Rachel, who were rolling Kyle off of Jason. Kyle's arms hit the floor with two thumps, his chest soaked with blood. His eyes fell open, staring at nothing.

A stab of pain wrenched Nick's heart. Seeing Kyle's lifeless eyes hurt him more than he'd thought possible. He didn't know why. The man deserved to die, but something about him losing his son to drugs, his desperate attempt to try and replace him with Alex—it was so pathetic. He looked away and shoved the pistol into Violet's hand. "It's loaded." He nodded to the two guards at her feet. "Watch them."

Her face softened, and she aimed the pistol at Tony's head. "Sorry, Dad. I thought I was going to die. I thought ..." She shook her head. "I can guard them."

Nick gave her a brief smile. She knew how to handle a gun. He raced for the doorway as footsteps echoed off the walls. Maybe only thirty seconds had passed since the gunshots. Jairo was coming. A second later he appeared, wet from the rain outside. Nick shoved the butt of the rifle into his temple, sending him back into the hallway. His body slammed against the wall and crumpled to the floor. Now all Nick needed was first aid supplies and rope.

He ordered Rachel to gather supplies from around the inn. As Devan tied up the injured guards, Nick put all his energy into saving Jason. He felt numb and tired. His ears buzzed as he tried to stop the bleeding.

But it was a lost cause.

The man would die soon, and Jenny was crying. Lois was screaming. Nick tried not to yell at her to be quiet, but annoyed hisses came out of his throat. He tried to calm himself. He tried to stop his hands from trembling. He looked into the man's terrified face, listening to his incoherent babbles as he slipped into unconsciousness.

"When will the police get here?" Jenny asked through her whimpers.

"Devan called 911," Nick muttered. "LifeFlight's on its way, but it might not get here in time."

"Is he going to die?" Jenny dropped to her knees. She touched Jason's face, her tears falling onto his eyes. They dripped down his temples, and Nick softened his voice.

"I'm sorry."

Jenny's wails grew louder, and Nick winced. He knew what death looked like, and Jason was gone. Nick looked away. He saw blood on his hands and asked Rachel for a rag. She handed it to him, trembling. "Lil's cut wasn't that deep. I bandaged it up already."

"Good."

Nick turned to Lilian. It felt like an eternity since he'd last noticed her. She was still unconscious, her chest rising and falling more calmly than anyone else's in the room. He was glad she didn't have to see this. He didn't want her to witness him fail at saving a life.

Wiping the blood from his skin, he saw Clara and Violet in the little girls faces. He remembered ten years earlier, his own beautiful daughters standing next to a coffin, roses in their hands, anger in their glances at each other. Now Violet was huddled over Clara, pushing her hands on top of Jeffrey's over the bullet wound. Violet's face was wet with tears. Nick hadn't seen her cry since she was a child. He stood up and walked to her.

Kneeling down, he pried her stiff fingers away and asked Jeffrey to let go. He studied the wound. Kyle had aimed high, possibly shattering her bone, but the bleeding had already slowed from the pressure Jeffrey and Violet had applied. She would live.

"Get some clean gauze from Rachel and keep pressure on it," he said to Jeffrey and looked at Clara.

She was pale, her features calm. She was breathing. He touched her lips, shaped so much like Annabelle's. Clara was his favorite. She had always been his favorite, and Violet knew it. No wonder they hated each other. Annabelle's death was an excuse. He turned to Violet and pulled her into his arms.

"I'm so sorry." He squeezed her as tightly as he could, Annabelle's face flashing across his memory, the anger, the blame, everything ugly he'd ever felt for Violet building up like a whirlwind inside his heart. He let out a long sigh, releasing it from himself as much as he could. "I love you," he whispered. "I love your mother. I love Clara, and I love you—just as much."

"I know, Dad." Her breath came out shallow, but warm on his neck. "I know you think you weren't ever there for us, but you were. You took us camping, you loved Mom, you taught us things normal dads never could. I can outshoot you any day." She laughed softly and squeezed him closer. "You weren't the traditional dad. So what?"

"I'm glad you feel that way, Violet, but you know I've blamed you for your mom's death, and I'm sorry. You didn't kill her. It was an accident, and I don't blame you now. I love you."

She let out a heavy sigh. "I love you, too, Dad. I made a mistake. I thought you understood."

"I tried to," he said softly. "I tried to, but I was too stubborn and blind to see the truth of my own actions and mistakes mixed with everything else. She made her own choices, just as we all do." He closed his eyes. The rain had slowed. In the distance the thump, thump, thump of a helicopter's spinning blades grew louder.

Nothing ever lasted, even this moment with the one person who had loved him through every wrong decision he'd ever made. Violet was stronger than he'd imagined. He looked at Lilian on the couch, wondering if she had the same strength as Violet. Maybe he had overlooked it.

Tightening his hold on Violet, he wanted to believe Lilian could love him despite everything he had done wrong. But the helicopter grew louder, reminding him the police would arrive soon, possibly even the FBI by the time all of this was over.

"They're going to arrest you," Violet whispered. "Aren't they?"

"Yes."

"Then what?"

He shook his head and held her tighter. "I don't know."

A loud groan from a corner of the room made him pull away. Tony writhed in pain on the floor, fighting against the nylon rope Devan had used to tie his hands behind his back.

Nick stood and surveyed the room. Wounded guards in one corner, Jason's family mourning his death in the middle of the room, Devan standing a few feet away with his arms folded tightly to his chest. Kyle lay dead at his feet, his eyes still open.

Nick grabbed a blanket and spread it over Kyle. "Are you okay?" he asked Devan.

"Not really."

Jenny's sobs had quieted, but the room felt fragile with her grief. Devan sniffed and wiped away a tear. "He jumped between me and Kyle. He saved me."

"Yes, he did." The thought hadn't crossed Nick's mind, but when he replayed the events in his mind he saw Devan flying to his feet to help Violet, Kyle turning in response, Jason heading for Kyle. One shot, close range, into Jason's stomach. It felt slow now, but Nick knew he was missing details. He didn't want to know them, anyway. He'd have to retell the story a hundred times over, document it in a tiny dark room with men watching.

"He saved me," Devan repeated. "He's dead because of me."

"He's dead because Kyle shot him. It has nothing to do with you." Nick looked down at his hands still stained and stiff with blood. "He was brave. His family will always know he was brave."

Devan chewed on his bottom lip, still watching Jenny and her daughters. Finally, with a heavy sigh, he looked at Nick. "Is that why you do this?"

"What?"

"This." Devan motioned to Jenny. "Protect them. That's your job."

"It's not like that."

It wasn't. At all. Nick rarely saw results of his work, good or bad. He passed on information, bribed people, stole, lied, and cheated for reasons he sometimes couldn't fathom. Tonight, though, as he looked down at Jason, he wondered if he was that brave. Annabelle had never admitted seeing it in him, and he couldn't either.

Chapter 34

The monarchs were everywhere. As Lilian walked the trails, she saw orange wings caught in the flattened grass, stuck in the muddy edges of the trail, floating like fallen leaves across the smooth lake.

The rainstorm had come at a bad time, right at the beginning of the migration, and Lilian doubted any more would fly through now. The storm had been widespread, blowing in cold air with the early smells of autumn—green leaves rustling around her, threatening to change color before her eyes. She smelled wet wood. Her feet splashed through stagnant pools of muddy water. It was too late for the butterflies now. Too cold.

Folding her arms, Lilian headed farther up the trail, breathing in the cool air, ignoring the ache along her ribs where Kyle had cut her. He was dead now. Everything was dead. The monarchs. Jason. Her hope of ever seeing Nick again.

The last she'd heard, he would be charged with Catarina's murder and a handful of other accusations that meant only one thing to her—never seeing him again. Trials were set. That meant years of waiting. If she was lucky she would see him through thick glass.

She stopped and turned to the lake. The silvery surface reflected a string of clouds drifting across the sky. The inn, no longer as white or majestic as she wanted it to be, made her remember the day she'd found it. That hike had been solemn, like this one, the same time of year and abnormally cold as she had cried over Chris. Three years later, and she was still frustrated. Part of her still loved him. Their marriage had sealed it, and she couldn't let it go no matter how much he had hurt her. It was different from what she felt for Nick, more final. At least, she wanted it to be. Nick could make her happy, she knew, but she couldn't get Catarina's name out of her head.

"I slept with her," Nick had told her right before he was arrested. "I lied to you. I lied to myself."

Lilian had seen the hurt in his eyes, the absolute shame, and she was surprised at how quickly she wanted to forget what he'd said and move on. She knew how much time could be wasted on jealousy.

"Ms. Love!"

Lilian turned to see a pot-bellied man with white hair and a bushy beard jogging up the trail. Thomas, one of the scientists who came every year. Lilian smiled and walked down the trail to him.

"We've got some late bloomers," he said when she reached him. "Some are emerging right now if you want to see."

"You ran all the way up here to tell me that?" She smirked at his anxious breaths and sweat rolling down his forehead. He was always excited about something, despite the latest reports that the logging hadn't slowed in Mexico, and that so far, this year's migration was anticipated to be the worst recorded in history.

"Your son said he'd come, but I thought the exercise might do me some good." He patted his belly and spun on his heel to head back down the trail. Lilian followed him. He was short, and she could see the top of his head where he'd combed his hair over a perfect circle of pink skin.

"Aren't you worried about the forests in Mexico?" she asked as they walked briskly down the trail.

"The logging? No, not really."

Lilian almost stopped in her tracks. "Why not? Everything I've read said it keeps getting worse. Nobody can stop them."

"Yes, I know." Thomas stopped and turned to face her. "I know all about it. They go at night. It's their livelihood, how they feed their families. But I'm guessing they're funded by an outside source since they seem to have tripled their forces in the past few years. They've cut back more than half the forest now."

Lilian looked away, and Thomas clasped his hands behind his back and started walking again. "There's not a lot anyone can do on a large scale. But you can keep helping the butterflies right here. I've been down to Mexico. I've seen what's going on, but—"

He slowed his pace and looked around at the trees. Lilian watched him out of the corner of her eye, confused by his smile. "They'll find a way," he said. "More and more people are becoming aware of the problem. Change will happen slowly. I think there's hope."

Hope.

Lilian cradled the word in her heart. She'd felt her hope slipping for so long, and not just for the butterflies.

They walked in silence the rest of the way, quickening their pace as they neared the inn. When they reached the steps, Devan was standing on a table, pinning pieces of paper to the porch roof. Each piece contained a clear chrysalis showing black and orange wings folded inside.

"The ones over there are hatching already," Devan said, glancing over his shoulder. "Fifteen."

Lilian walked a few feet and looked up. Sure enough, they were emerging. It was always a slow process. Three had broken through their chrysalises, probably hours ago, and unfolded their crinkled wings, mostly dry now. Thomas put on his glasses and peered up. "Always amazes me," he said with a smile and handed Lilian a card filled with small round stickers. "Would you like to tag them?"

"Sure."

Lilian slid a chair over and stood on it to retrieve the three monarchs. She made sure they were dry enough and slowly tagged each one. She set them on a pair of twigs Thomas had put on the porch railing then sat down in a chair to watch. Devan sat next to her.

The three monarchs teetered along the twig, their wings still closed. The sun broke through the string of clouds, and in unison, the three monarchs opened their wings. They flashed bright orange, and Lilian held her breath.

"Mom?" Devan touched her hand and she jumped. "Are you doing okay?"

"Yes, I'm fine."

"You've been spending a lot of time on the trails."

Lilian leaned forward and rested her elbows in her lap. "I'm fine." The monarchs opened and closed their wings, testing them, preparing.

"You're not fine. Nick's gone. You're lonely. You're worried."

"Aren't you?"

Devan cleared his throat and sat back in his chair. A patch of sun fell on his knee, and he rubbed his thumb over it. "I'm worried Nick won't get out of whatever trouble he's in, and that you can't be with him. I'm worried about Clara, too."

"The doctors said she'll be okay."

"Not her shoulder. Jeff."

"Oh?" Lilian looked up. She had been observant enough the past few days to notice Devan's sudden attachment to Rachel. It made her happy to see his affections moved on from Clara, but it annoyed her at the same time. She was sure he wanted to be faithful, but it seemed deep down he was fickle, like Chris.

"I thought all of this business with Clara was over," she said, careful to keep her expression neutral.

"It is, but I still care about her. Jeff's in a lot of trouble, like Nick. I don't want to see her alone, too." He shrugged and watched the butterflies. "Seems everybody's alone now."

"You and Rachel have been pretty close."

A faint smile spread across Devan's lips. "Yeah. It's weird."

"No it's not." Looking across the lake, Lilian pushed back images of Devan breaking Rachel's heart—or the other way around. She couldn't handle more drama, more loneliness, even if it wasn't her own. Instead, she thought of Devan's happiness. She looked at the smile on his lips, the glow in his expression, and her heart softened. For the first time in days, she felt a spark of intense joy. "You two have always been close," she said softly. "It just took something big to make you realize what that means."

"I guess so."

"I hope it works out, Devan. Really."

"You do?" His smile faded.

"Of course I do. I've worried about you a lot this past year." She studied the dirt smudges on her knees. She hadn't done laundry in days. She hadn't done much of anything except walk the trails, feeling sorry for herself. "I worried you'd decide to go live with your father," she said with a jittery laugh. "I worried he'd talk you into joining the Air Force earlier than you were ready."

"Really?" He laughed. "I wouldn't do that, Mom. I wouldn't leave you."

"I know." Her heart sank all the way to her toes. She shifted in her chair and watched the butterflies. Her mouth felt dry. The butterflies kept opening their wings. Open. Close. Open. Close. Orange patches, black bars, white spots.

"I'll be fine here without you." The words came out—to her ears, silvery and sweet. Lilian straightened her shoulders and sat up. Devan turned to look at her, his eyes widening.

"You will?"

"Yes."

Silence surrounded them. Lilian knew she didn't have to say anything else. All Devan needed was reassurance. "I'm sorry," she tried to whisper, but nothing came from her lips. Instead, she took Devan's hand and held it tight as the butterflies spread their wings and flew away.

Chapter 35

The hospital room smelled clean. It reminded Devan of the Air Force recruitment office he'd just visited. Stiff. Precise.

Clara looked up when he entered, her lips spreading into a grin. "You finally came to see me, huh?"

He shrugged and laughed. "Don't make it sound like I was trying to avoid you. You haven't been here that long."

"Jeff's only been able to come once." She glanced at her shoulder. It was bulky beneath her hospital gown. "They're doing all sorts of crap to him. Questioning. Drug tests. I don't know what else."

"How much trouble, exactly? Prison?"

Clara swallowed hard and stared down at her hands. "Maybe, for awhile."

Sitting on the edge of her bed, Devan wanted to be close to her again, to gauge his feelings against what he felt for Rachel. He was confused, off-kilter. He touched her hand, and she pulled it away.

"I'm sorry," she muttered, avoiding his eyes. "It was a mistake. My mistake. I'm sorry."

Devan smirked. "It takes two, you know."

"Yeah." She kept her eyes on the sheet covering most of her body. "I get to leave here tomorrow. I'm going back to San Diego."

"What about Jeff?"

"They're transferring him there so that's where I'm going. I want to be close to him." She looked up. "I love him, Devan. I made a mistake with you, I'm sorry."

Devan folded his arms and gave her a stern look. "Stop saying you're sorry. I'm sorry, too. It's over now. Does Jeff know?"

"I told him. He was angry for two seconds until I reminded him of everything bad he's done. I probably shouldn't have done that."

"Well, it's the truth. What about your dad?"

"He knows, too. I got to see him before they took him away."

Devan had seen enough of her tears to know she was about to cry. Her cheeks turned red, and she squeezed her eyes shut and bit her bottom lip. No tears came. Devan leaned down and hugged her.

He didn't like to think about her being alone. She seemed to have always been alone, and it hurt him to feel it in her touch, hear it in the soft tremor of her voice. She had Violet, at least. He had seen her in the hallway on his way into the room, but even though the anger was gone, their relationship still seemed fragile.

Clara buried her face in his shoulder. "This sucks," she whispered. "My dad. Jeff."

Devan breathed in the smell of her hair, still the same as he remembered, sweet and earthy, but it didn't make him feel anything now. It was just a smell. His heart didn't pound because of it.

Thinking about the moments he'd spent with her in his bedroom, wrapped in her arms, Devan wondered what it said about him that he didn't want her anymore. He thought of her racing across the log and realized everything came back to that moment when he'd seen she was stronger than he thought. So was his mom. And Rachel.

He squeezed Clara gently and let go. She took his hand and watched him straighten. "Are you okay?" she asked.

He nodded and slipped his hand away. He hated the word "Okay." It didn't mean good or great or fantastic. He was sure he wouldn't feel any of those things for a long time. Seeing Jason dead in his wife's arms still haunted him every five minutes.

"Devan?"

"I'm fine," he said softly. "It's only been a few days, that's all. They keep sending a counselor up to talk to me and Mom, but it hasn't helped."

"Time will help." Clara smiled, and it warmed him for a moment. "I promise. I know Jeff and I are going to get through this. Everything will work out."

"It will." Devan leaned down and kissed her on the cheek, one last gesture to say goodbye. "As long as you can swim again." He said it with a chuckle and a wink.

"The doctors said it'll take a lot of therapy and some more surgery, but I should be able to."

"Good. You can come up to the lake again, okay?"

"Sure."

She smiled as he left the room. He felt surprisingly calm. Rachel was right. This was exactly what he had needed. When he reached his truck, he saw her in the front seat, her eyes lowered to a book in her hands. He opened the door and climbed behind the wheel. "Thanks, I needed that, like you said."

Rachel closed her book and smiled. "I knew it would help." She stretched across the seat, sliding herself closer until they could kiss.

They had kissed a lot lately. Devan liked how it felt. No urgency, no expectations. Everything about her made him feel comfortable. To him, she always smelled like the kitchen, like rising bread and apple pie. It didn't make his heart pound. It made him want to lay back and hold her forever.

"You ready to go?" he asked when she pulled away, grinning.

"As soon as you are."

He kissed her again, this time remembering the recruitment office and the papers he had filled out only an hour earlier. Airplanes. Uniforms. Training. Alone. He wouldn't have his mom or Rachel, or even his dad.

Rachel leaned away and looked him in the eyes. "What's the matter?"

"Nothing. I'm just wondering if I've made the right decision."

"About the Air Force?"

He nodded, and she touched his jaw, rubbing the stubble he'd been too lazy to shave that morning. He wondered what it might be like to wake up next to her every morning, and what it might be like to leave her for months at a time, possibly never returning. He thought of Nick and his family, the sacrifices he'd made to do something he must have regretted a thousand times.

"How do we ever know what the right decision is?" Rachel asked, still touching his face. She tilted her head and smiled. "You have to make the best decision you can and go with it. Waiting for the 'right moment' wastes time." She kissed his nose and giggled. "I've wanted to tell you that for so long. I'll stand behind any choice you make."

Looking into her eyes, Devan saw a future spread before him. It wasn't two paths as he expected. It wasn't a log stretched over a fast-moving river. It wasn't the inn, his mom, or anybody he loved. It was unmarked, a clear sky, a new start only he could begin.

Chapter 36

The cemetery trees were starting to turn color. Red always came first, and today it looked especially bright against the taller evergreens and the crisp blue sky.

Nick kept his eyes on the dewy grass as he thought of the CIA director's firm grip on his shoulder when he'd shown up with the briefcase. His director had sounded frustrated when he explained that Nick's future didn't look bright unless someone could prove Catarina was alive. There was too much publicity so far, too much evidence against him with the real killer dead and the murdered mistress identified only as Catarina. Investigations. Trials. Nick had seen it all stacking against him. At least the CIA had kept his name under wraps.

A stiff wind rustled through the trees. Nick looked up, wanting to smile at the dancing leaves, but his mouth stayed frozen in a straight line.

The cemetery was peaceful, like the look on Catarina's face when she'd shown up to speak for him, shocking everyone, including himself. She had said she wasn't sacrificing anything, that the U.S. couldn't pin anything on her, but Nick knew she was walking a fine line and was grateful to her for that. He was mostly free now except for a few trial dates and daily check-ins.

He stopped and looked at the graves surrounding him. So many lives. How many had died needlessly? He saw Jenny holding her husband tight. He felt the blood on his hands as the two girls wiped tears from their cheeks. His career was over. The CIA couldn't keep him, even though he'd been so close to retirement. He thought of every death connected to him, so many written off as necessary to protect his country.

He stared across the cemetery and stopped in his tracks. Leaves twirled around him, gathering on the bright green grass. It glistened in the sun. He couldn't see Annabelle's grave from here, and he forced himself to turn away before he got too close. Outside of her smiles and laughter, she had always been a negative force yanking him in another direction. Yet he had never seen that until now. He had loved her for Clara's and Violet's sakes. He still loved her in a strange distant way. He turned around and headed back to his truck. When he climbed in, a beep from his phone on the dash indicated he had a message.

They'd found Ferreira, finally. It didn't matter. None of it mattered anymore. He could have spent the rest of his days in a prison cell and it wouldn't matter.

He slid the phone back on the dash and rolled down the window as he drove away. He didn't know what he wanted. Lilian was an hour away, probably piecing things back together at the inn. Clara was heading back to San Diego, Violet back to England.

Glancing at his phone, Nick felt guilty for not calling any of them. They thought he was still being questioned. The truth was he needed time. He watched the traffic speed past him and noticed he was driving twenty miles under the speed limit. He pressed the gas pedal, his eyes glazing over as he stared ahead.

He could drive back home again, walk past the kitchen floor where he would remember the assassin, see Annabelle's picture on the mantle, lie in his bed and stare at the ceiling. The blankets would never get warm.

"I think she'll forgive me," he said aloud as he clenched the steering wheel and pushed on the gas again. "Just get the guts to find out."

He reached for his phone and then stopped.

He was being followed. A dark gray sedan six cars back. Probably the CIA keeping tabs on him. The sedan slowed down as soon as he did, moving two cars back as he kept a closer eye on it.

Was it Ferreira's men? It didn't matter. Since the CIA had found Ferreira, they would find the rest of his men. They'd gone to a lot of trouble to keep it anonymous who'd given them the names, but even if someone traced the names back to him, he doubted they'd bother finding him. Part of him didn't care; he didn't have the energy to watch his back much longer.

The sedan followed him to a gas station where he drove past the pumps and parked. The car pulled up next to him. Catarina.

She stepped out and stood by her door, arms folded.

"You okay to talk a minute?" she asked as he looked at her through his open windows.

"I thought we already talked in Langley."

She shook her head. "Those were formalities."

Nick stayed where he was. There was a soft glow to her skin he'd never noticed before. Her hair blew in the breeze, and Nick looked past her into the car. Alex.

"You got your son back."

A smile spread across her face. "Yeah, before they found Matheus."

Alex peered through the window at Nick, his eyes narrowed to slits. Nick gave him a short wave and a smile and he turned away.

"Is he upset about his father?"

"He's relieved he's not dead, and that's what I wanted." She gave Alex a quick look and walked around the truck. Nick opened the door, slammed it shut, and stood in front of her.

"He'll be okay," she said. "I needed to see you alone. I've given your government information for my freedom, but I can't stay here. I've only got a few minutes."

"I understand. They're giving you protection, aren't they?"

She nodded. "I don't have much say where I go from here."

"You won't have much say in a lot of things." Nick winced. He knew how these things worked, what she was giving up. A new identity, never tied down to anything except her son. Looking into her eyes, he knew that's what she wanted.

"I know," she said with a frown. "I shouldn't even be talking to you."

Nick kept his arms crossed in front of his chest. She had changed, either because Ferreira was out of her life now or something else. The fear in her eyes was gone.

"You don't owe me anything," she said, tilting her head. "I know that's what you're thinking."

"That's not what—"

"Yes, it is. I can see it in your face."

She stepped forward and touched his arm. Her fingers were warm and steady. He held his breath, knowing even if he had the chance to be with her, he wouldn't take it. She felt like the past to him, like empty beds and cold sheets.

"There's someone else, isn't there?" she asked.

Nick looked away, thinking of Lilian and the disappointment in her face when he'd told her about Catarina. He uncrossed his arms and took Catarina's hand in his. He imagined the wings on her back turned right side up, the scars smoothed flat.

"Lilian's waiting for me," he said, ignoring the fear in his heart. But, the worst was over now. He'd told Lilian about Catarina, at least. It was the long haul afterward that had him worried, the day-to-day commitment he'd never shared with any woman, even Annabelle.

Catarina squeezed his hand. "Then I won't keep you much longer. I just wanted to say thank you." She looked away. "It was a silly dream. Whoever Lilian is, she'd be a fool not to know what she has. I know where I'm supposed to be now, and you made that possible. Thank you." She squeezed his hand before walking back to her car. She glanced at Nick, the dimples in her cheeks deep and pronounced.

Nick's hand felt cold without hers inside it. He saw her in the jungle again, the morning the helicopter came to pick them up. She'd been so out of it, he'd had to carry her to one of her men from the helicopter. Another man held a rifle at Nick's head.

"Don't shoot him," Catarina had said as Nick handed her over. "But don't help him."

Nick's body went frigid as one of her men pulled the rifles from his back along with the packs and his canteen. "You're leaving me stranded?"

She frowned over her shoulder as her man helped her onto the chopper's ladder. "I'm sorry, Nick."

Even after he'd found Kyle's camp and hotwired a truck, he'd been furious as he bounced over the ruts in the dirt road leading out of the jungle. He had thought everyone was out to get him—when that wasn't it at all. He hadn't seen that until now.

He shivered. He was cold all over. Another breeze kicked up, rustling his hair as he climbed back into his truck. He stared at his phone. Maybe it was best if he didn't call her. Driving faster this time, he rolled up his windows and hummed a song, his voice completely out of tune. He had to drown out his fear.

The day was getting warmer, or he was. As he drove up the mountain, he made himself smile at the colorful leaves against the sky. He smiled even wider when he pulled up to the inn and saw Lilian on the porch. This smile felt real, joy in his heart swelling stronger than he'd felt in a long time. Seeing her again wasn't anything like he had imagined.

Her back was to him as she stood on a chair to pin something to the wood beams above her. Nick shut the truck's door as quietly as he could and started toward the porch.

She was alone, her hair down to her shoulders in soft golden waves, her humming barely a whisper in the cool air. Nick cleared his throat and she spun around. Her mouth dropped open. "You're here."

"I am." He swallowed hard, trying to read her expression. Was she upset with him now? Disappointed? He couldn't tell, only that her expression kept changing.

"Lilian, I'm sorry about Catarina, I—"

"Oh, that." Her eyes misty, she glanced up at the wood beams where she'd pinned papers with monarch chrysalises. "You know, these creatures are incredible. They don't know all the odds are against them. Storms, dwindling forests, the cold. They press on until the end. It might be too late, but I think if they fly today they'll have a chance." She stepped off the chair, moving slowly toward him.

He tried to think of Annabelle. He tried to see her in the forest surrounded by monarchs, but nothing came to his mind. There was only Lilian in front of him, her soft smile making everything delicate and weightless.

"They'll make it," he said, ascending the stairs to embrace her. "They always do."